HOMEFRONT
The Voice of Freedom

**Raymond Benson
& John Milius**

TITAN BOOKS

Homefront: The Voice of Freedom
ISBN: 9780857682789

Published by Titan Books
A division of Titan Publishing Group
144 Southwark Street
London
SE1 0UP

First edition February 2011
10 9 8 7 6 5 4 3 2 1

This edition published by arrangement with Del Rey, an imprint of The Random House Publishing Group, a division of Random House, Inc.

Visit our website www.titanbooks.com

Did you enjoy this book? We love to hear from our readers. Please email us at readerfeedback@titanemail.com or write to us at Reader Feedback at the above address.

To receive advance information, news, competitions, and exclusive Titan offers online, please register as a member by clicking the "sign up" button on our website: www.titanbooks.com

A CIP catalogue record for this title is available from the British Library.

Printed and bound in Great Britain by Clays Ltd., St Ives plc.

ACKNOWLEDGMENTS

The authors wish to thank Peter Miller and the folks at PMA Literary & Film Management, Inc., Tae Kim, Campfire NYC, THQ, Kaos Studios, and everyone at Del Rey for all the splendid help and guidance.

ONE

The repaired, jury-rigged walkie-talkie crackled with an unavoidable burst of strident static before the Vietnamese resistance fighter's voice came through loud and clear with his distinctive broken-English speech.

"Hurry, my friend! They coming! I see now! Three—no, *four* tanks! Large number troops. Hurry! Fast! Over!"

Ben Walker cursed silently as he struggled with the wiring beneath the mixing console. "Kelsie, throw me the wire cutters!" he called, but there was no answer. He bobbed his head out from under the counter and saw that she wasn't even in the control room. "Kelsie, where are you?" he shouted louder.

"On the roof with the antenna!" she yelled back. He could barely hear her through the hole they'd made in the studio's ceiling. "The wind is *not* co-operating!"

"Where are the goddamned wire cutters?"

"Aren't they by the generator?"

Walker scooted across the floor on his butt toward the hand-cart-mounted engine-generator, where Kelsie Wilcox had left the tool case. He rummaged through the various tools she'd dropped and finally found the cutters.

"Walker!" spat the walkie-talkie after another rupture of noise. "You almost done? Over!"

He grabbed the device and spoke. "Nguyen, how much time do we have?"

The two-way radio spurted again. "Five, ten minutes, tops! I see troops, maybe five mile away on Highway 50."

Oh, Jesus, we'll never make it.

Walker left the walkie-talkie on the counter and returned to the mess of wiring under the console. As he cut and restrung the cables according to Wilcox's instructions, Walker feared his struggles over the last sixteen months had been for naught. After the ordeal of trekking across the desert, nearly dying, recovering, and then surviving the Las Vegas blitz, it made no sense that he should give up the ghost *now*. Not when he had finally found his true calling, a purpose that actually meant something. His college journalism professor, Shulman, once told him, "Walker, your thinking is way too existential for your own good. You need to relax and take life with a grain of salt." Back in 2011, when he was a mere twenty-year-old smart aleck and cynic, that kind of advice went right over his head.

Now that he was thirty-five, he could only dream of taking life with a grain of salt. No one in America could do that in 2026. Not with the destruction of the country's electrical infrastructure, the food and water shortage, the breakdown of mass communication and transportation, and, worst of all, the Korean Occupation.

Korean Occupation. Just thinking those words sent shivers down Walker's spine. Never in a million years would he have thought the United States could be invaded by a foreign power during his lifetime.

No, Walker wasn't about to die now. He had to get the broadcast out before the bastards from the so-called Greater Korean Republic overran the small but strategically important city of Montrose, Colorado. Walker had to get the abandoned and decrepit old radio station working so he could rally the resistance fighters. It was his job and his destiny.

On top of the small building, Wilcox struggled with the Yagi-Uda antenna she had built from scratch. The radio station's old antenna was no longer functional, as pieces of it had been scavenged long ago for its scrap metal and electronic hardware.

For a thirty-one-year-old woman with a degree in electrical engineering, it was ironic that her skills hadn't been in demand until a year ago. Before the devastating EMP blast that wiped out nearly every electronic device with an integrated circuit all across the United States, Wilcox had floundered in the country's collapsed economy by working as a blackjack dealer in a depressed Las Vegas that was a shoddy shadow of what the city had been fifteen years earlier.

The strong wind was an unexpected obstacle in their plan to make a broadcast before the Korean People's Army stormed the town. Wilcox quickly drilled holes for an extra set of brackets to secure the antenna. Once she was done, she tried wiggling the damned thing. It was sturdy enough.

She looked across Rose Lane and saw several members of the resistance cell on Main Street, otherwise known as Highway 50. Nguyen Huu Giap, the unconventional leader of the original rebel group from Utah, was busy supervising the Ragtag outfit and ordering them to guerilla-warfare defensive positions. Wilcox knew Giap was related to a powerful Viet Cong general from the Vietnam War, which she found paradoxical.

Then there was Boone Karlson, the head of the Montrose resistance cell. Wilcox spotted him issuing orders to men who had never had military training; now they were faced with defending their homeland with their lives. It appeared the team was busy setting roadside IEDs. Wilcox looked eastward. The dark mass of troops moved closer by the minute. The army must have come from Denver or some other point east of Montrose.

The resistance members scattered, taking positions behind buildings, natural objects, and piles of sandbags that were placed in the road.

How many of them were there now? Thirty? Forty? How could they hope to defeat an oncoming army?

"Is that the best you've got, you dog-eaters?" shouted Connor Morgan from the road.

Wilcox had to smile. Morgan probably could have taken on the Korean army by himself.

She then looked back along the lane toward the

elementary school. As it was mid-afternoon, classes were finished and parents flocked around the building to pick up their children.

Damn! Didn't someone tell them the Koreans were coming?

An explosion rocked the ground.

Screams and confusion. Moms and dads who hadn't connected with their kids ran into the building. Others fled in terror.

"Kelsie, where the hell are you? Aren't you done yet?"

"Coming, Ben!"

She couldn't worry about the civilians. Wilcox scrambled down the ladder and rushed inside the building that back in the day was the site of a popular country-and-western AM radio station.

"We're ready," she said. "How's it coming down there?"

Walker slid out from under the console and took a seat. He carefully tapped the homemade transistor board they had plugged into the console. "I think we might be good to go. Tell me again—you sure our signal will be stronger through this station?"

"Ben, remember this is still LPAM. When we were using our kitchen sink transmitter, we were lucky to be heard across the state—maybe two or three. You're usually not going to get a strong signal with low-power broadcasting. But the equipment here has what it takes to get your signal out across the country in both directions. Given that the airwaves are awfully damned empty these days, I think the chances are pretty good. Trust me."

"If you say so, sweetheart," Walker said. He and Wilcox had built the portable transistor board out of spare parts and old-school equipment. Now it was live, its indicators glowing dimly. He tapped the microphone. "Testing, testing." The needles on the control board meters jumped with his voice. "Kelsie, you're a friggin' genius."

They knew pockets of Americans around the country had access to repaired AM/FM radios. Ever since Walker began transmitting music over the air in the various locations where they'd been, the response was surprising—and encouraging. Not everyone in the country had capitulated to the unwanted guests who were wreaking havoc across the nation. Walker believed that in every town, in every state—even if there was no communication between anyone—there were clusters of determined individuals who were prepared to resist the attackers.

Another explosion rocked the building. Wilcox lost her balance and fell against the console. Then they both heard gunfire from their colleagues' M4s and M16s. Shouts. And some screams.

"Oh my God, Ben," she whispered as she dropped to her knees. "The school just let out so there are civilians all over the fucking place. Hurry."

"Goliath'll stop the Koreans," Walker said.

"Not if it's outclassed in firepower, and it is. I saw them. They have tanks."

Outside, the unmanned ground combat vehicle known as "Goliath" stood in the middle of Highway 50, firing at the Korean opponents with its .50 caliber heavy machine gun and four-barrel rocket system. The thing was a cross between a six-wheeled miniature tank and a dune buggy, covered in a hull made from high-strength aluminum tubes and titanium nodes protected by a steel skid plate able to absorb shocks from impacts with rocks, tree stubs, and even other vehicles. Its unusual suspension enabled it to travel smoothly over extremely rough terrain and overcome obstacles like man-made barriers, ditches, and boulders. Goliath carried up to eight thousand pounds of payload and armor.

Hopper Lee, a Korean American in his early thirties, and a member of the resistance forces, acted as Goliath's keeper and handler. He sat safely behind the wall of sandbags with the remote control device he had rebuilt himself. With it, Lee could send Goliath GPS coordinates and the robot would travel autonomously to its destination—and run over or destroy anything in its path.

Crouched next to Lee was Wally Kopple, a crusty former National Guard sergeant in his fifties. He sported a QBZ-03 assault rifle, using it to cover the robot in the road.

Kopple coughed and spat a glob of brownish phlegm.

Lee said, "You should have that looked at, man."

"Oh, sure," Kopple said. "I'll call my doctor up right now and make an appointment. Maybe he'll give me a lollipop for being a good boy. You think my insurance will cover the visit?"

Lee shrugged. "Just sayin'."

Kopple coughed again. "You keep your eye on Goliath and make sure we don't lose him. When Nguyen gives the word, we're heading home. There's no way we're gonna stop that blitzkrieg coming our way."

The Koreans were now a hundred yards away. The infantry marched alongside what appeared to be four Bradley Fighting Vehicles, obviously confiscated from the American military. Through binoculars, Kopple saw the offensive flag the KPA draped on the front and sides of the armored vehicles. Its design depicted the American flag completely washed out in red and covered by the North Korean star and wreath from their own coat of arms. The Korean soldiers strode forward, ready to bravely face whatever puny fire-power the weakened Americans managed to dish out. They were armed with assault weapons, wore dark brown and olive uniforms, and had painted their faces with black stripes.

Kopple raised his QBZ-03 and fired bursts at the front line of infantry. It was a decent weapon, not great, although the damage it inflicted was slightly better than that of an M4.

"You're wasting your ammo," Lee said. "Wait until they get closer."

Kopple released the trigger, coughed, and said, "I hate it when you're right."

Then he saw the civilians. A swarm of parents and children poured out from Rose Lane and into the line of fire.

"What the fuck?" Kopple stood and shouted, "Get

out of here! Now!"

The people were already in panic mode, running in different directions. Savvy fathers spotted the oncoming juggernaut of troops and attempted to herd everyone back toward the school.

It was too late.

Boone Karlson, the African American who brought the Montrose cell together, crouched behind the stone wall of an abandoned gas station, surveying the on-coming menace through binoculars. With the Koreans' arrival to the town, he knew the ensuing weeks—maybe months—would end up being the most significant time of his life. Before the EMP, Karlson had often wondered if he would go through the stereotypical midlife crisis when he turned forty. Now, at thirty-nine, that wasn't a concern. The crisis wasn't personal—it was global.

The troops, swarming up the highway like ants, would be in range within a minute. As he waited, he glanced across the road to see if his men—and women—were ready.

A few more seconds and they would unleash hellfire . . .

He started to count down from five. When he got to three, the civilians showed up.

No!

Karlson stood to warn them, but he heard Kopple's shout. Unfortunately, the alarm made the situation worse—the adults and children panicked and ran in a dozen directions.

The Koreans were in range. If the resistance cell was going to strike, they had to do it now.

Karlson shouted the order to fire at will *over the civilians' heads*. The adults heard the order, grabbed their children, and threw themselves onto the pavement. The few dozen resistance fighters reacted immediately. Gunfire erupted from their hidden positions, mowing down the Koreans in the front lines. Hopper Lee heard the enemy's leader shouting commands to keep marching. The scene reminded Lee of old movies he'd seen of Revolutionary War-era battles with soldiers, carrying crude single-shot rifles with attached bayonets, simply marching straight at each other and shooting.

Then the tanks fired again. And again.

The shells struck a mass of the civilians, as well as obliterating a resistance bunker occupied by four men.

Screams of horror almost surpassed the din of gunfire.

Kopple cursed, stood, and fired the QBZ-03 at the oncoming soldiers. "Get off our property you sons of bitches!" he yelled, but a coughing spasm grabbed him like a vise. He fell to his knees and spat more dark phlegm over the sandbags in front of him. After he got his wind back, the sergeant just said, "Shit . . . "

More shells from the Korean tanks hit the street in front of the resistance fighters' positions. When another cluster of civilians were killed in a blazing fireball, one surviving father had the tenacity to urge the rest to run back to the school. The dozens of parents and children who were still alive bolted across the road, directly into the streaking lines of fire.

Oh my God! Karlson thought. He watched in repulsion as several adults and children were cut down; but the cluster kept running, and many of them made it to the cover of buildings along Rose Lane.

Lee's walkie-talkie erupted in static and then Nguyen Huu Giap's voice cut through the noise of gunfire. "Hopper, be ready evacuate, yes? Plan we discuss. Route to Home through old cemetery and golf course. Over."

Home was the Montrose cell's hideout southeast of downtown, on the edge of the abandoned suburbs. With the addition of Giap's cell, from Utah, the small den had become an overcrowded, yet cooperative community of like-minded individuals. There, they shared food and water and supplies, slept, trained, and made plans to attack the enemy. Like other cells around the country, they were the Koreans' number-one target. Every day held the risk of being exposed. They were safe only as long as the enemy never discovered Home's location.

Kopple picked up the radio. "This is Kopple, Chief. We read you. Just give us the word. What do you hear from our boy inside the station? Over."

"I gave him five minutes. Over."

"Better give him two. Out."

Then the Korean infantry raised their own automatic weapons and sprayed the road and buildings in front of them. The barrage was a storm of deadly strength, forcing the small band of Americans to hunker down and take cover.

Goliath, unthinking and unfeeling, continued to defend the road by deflecting the Koreans' gunfire and returning volleys of hell at the approaching fire ants.

The old radio station building, not quite a hundred yards away from the melee, rattled with every detonation. The elements and tubes on the transistor board in front of Walker glowed bright and then faded. He pounded his fist on the counter. "Damn! Kelsie, I need more power."

The woman leapt to the engine-generator, which had begun to sputter. "We filled it with gas, it can't be empty yet! Wait—I see, the voltage regulator is loose. Hold on."

The gasoline used to fuel the generator was precious. Walker and Kelsie kept their own supply of the sequestered commodity at Home and used it only when Walker wanted to make a broadcast. Gas had been a luxury item that a minority of citizens could afford prior to the EMP attack. Now people murdered for it. Service stations that still carried and sold the valuable resource were few and far between, and they were protected with heavy security systems and often gun-wielding officers. However, bootlegging operations were widespread—supplies of petrol were smuggled over the borders of Canada and Mexico, which lay mostly out of the EMP's range. The stuff sold on the black market for less than what one had to pay at the legitimate service stations, but it was still costly. In a different era it might well have been gold—or drugs.

The walkie-talkie blurted the new orders. "Walker! Two minutes! You copy, my friend? Over."

The journalist grabbed the radio and answered. "All right!"

"We blow horn, yes? You move! Out!"

One of the guys in the cell had a bugle. Every day he blasted everything from *Reveille* to *Mess Call* to *Taps*. Giap was referring to the standard *Retreat* call. When Walker and Kelsie heard it, they had little choice but to run.

Wilcox fiddled with protuberances on the generator before sitting back on the floor and using her heel to lightly kick the unit—then the motor revved up and sounded healthy once again.

"There, try it now."

Walker unfolded a scrap of paper upon which he had scribbled, tapped the microphone again, and froze. He had rehearsed his speech a dozen times and suddenly he couldn't open his mouth. It was too important to mess up.

"Ben?"

He didn't move.

"Ben! Snap out of it!"

Walker waved her off. "I'm okay."

Then he spoke into the mic.

WALKER'S JOURNAL

Here we go again.

As I start this year's journal, I'm reminded of Frank, the head of the journalism department at USC. He was a mentor to me. Professor Shulman. Franklin Shulman. Frank. He was a great guy. I wonder where he is now?

Frank instilled in me the habit of keeping a journal. He said it works better if you do it in longhand, pen on paper, in a small notebook. I started doing it when I was a junior, in 2012. I was still keeping a journal when I graduated with a bachelor's degree, in 2013. Ever since then, I've started a new one at the beginning of every year. So I have thirteen different little spiral notebooks on the shelf, each dated 2012, 2013, 2014 . . . and so on.

As you can see by the date, I hadn't yet started the journal for 2025. I don't know why. Usually I've tried to pen the first entry on New Year's Day. Maybe I was just abnormally lethargic this year.

Never mind, here's the first entry, halfway through the month. And I've got great news! I think I'm going to quit my job tomorrow! The economy is in the shithole, unemployment is 30-something %, I have no savings, no alternate plan . . . and I'm going to quit my job.

And you know what? It's going to feel damned good. I'm going to tell that asshole boss of mine where to stick it. It's something I've wanted to do for months. No more interviewing idiots who are famous for being famous, no more hunting for scandals, no more unscrupulous yellow journalism.

So what am I going to do instead?

I don't know! Isn't that great?

I can always try to be that serious investigative reporter I saw myself being when I got out of college. Or I can write that important American novel no one will read. Who knows? Maybe I'll just sit on the sofa, watch TV, and drink my last bottle of Jack Daniels.

Hey, sounds like a plan! For now, anyway.

But first I have to go do one more bullshit job for Celebrity Trash. *I've already committed to ride out to the LA Arena tonight to cover Saint Lorenzo's "concert," if you can call it that. What can I say? I keep my promises.*

Later, man.

TWO

JANUARY 14, 2025

Ben Walker checked the fuel level on his vintage 1967 BSA Spitfire 650 and figured he had enough to get to the LA Arena and back. Ever since the price of gasoline skyrocketed about ten years earlier, travel by personal vehicle had become a luxury few people could afford. Gas stations—the small number across the country that stayed open—received a supply once a month and it was gone in a day. State governments had instituted different levels of strict rationing, forcing families to make do with buying gas every *two* months. People lined up for blocks, hoping to buy three or four gallons, just so they could get to work—if they had jobs. Public transportation facilities were given something of a break. City bus companies received a state-allotted amount, but a one-way ride on the damned things cost around $10. Walker hadn't necessarily had the foresight of what was to come when he restored the motorcycle back when he was in college. It turned out to be one of the more fortuitous things he'd ever done. The Spitfire got fifty-sixty miles per gallon; with the bike's four-gallon capacity, a tank could last him a month. As long as he used the bike only for work.

Work. What a joke.

Walker called himself a journalist, but he didn't do the kind of writing he had envisioned back at USC. As a twenty-one-year-old, cocky but naïve college graduate, he had visions of accepting a Pulitzer one day for investigative reporting. Instead, with the collapsed economy, the extinction of newspapers and magazines, and the dumbing-down of America, the only "news" people wanted to hear was not the typically bad truths coming out of Washington and the rest of the globe, but ridiculous celebrity and pop culture garbage that had no relevance in the real world. Hence, the only work Walker could find was penning junk for an online site called, appropriately, *Celebrity Trash*.

As he had just written in his journal that morning, Walker was committed to covering the LA Arena performance by the new ten-year-old evangelist sensation, Saint Lorenzo. Professing to be a faith healer, little Lorenzo had captured the public's imagination because everyone just wanted something to believe in. Things had gotten so bad in America that a guy as crackpot as Saint Lorenzo was more newsworthy than anything the president of the United States had to say. While he was growing up, Walker had noticed how when things got really bad, nearly everyone became even more desperate in turning to religion as the answer to their problems. The government couldn't save them from unemployment, shortage of food and water, and of course, lack of their beloved gasoline, so why not little Saint Lorenzo?

As Walker rode down from his home in the Hollywood Hills into the stinking metropolis, he reminded himself there was at least one good thing about the energy crisis—there were fewer cars on the road. And yet, all around him were more sobering reminders of America's depressed condition. Strip malls had become parking lots for the homeless. Movie theaters were empty and the studios couldn't afford to make product. LA was no longer the entertainment capital of the world. The once elite Hollywood nightclubs had either closed or become even *more* choice locations for the very, very rich. Not that being wealthy did one much good these days. Anyone with serious money had become a pariah. The wealthy took their lives in their own hands if they ventured out in public. One of the few businesses that prospered in the last ten years was the security profession. The fancy homes in Beverly Hills had become fortresses. Bodyguards could easily find work. Too many fat cats had found themselves attacked and murdered on the streets for their Rolex watches or for what was in their wallets. Crime was at an all-time high.

Billboards along the Sunset Strip no longer advertised blockbuster movies or television shows; instead they were simply blank or covered with graffiti. The exception was a pristine display for controversial talk-show host and blogger, Horace Danziger. It was a gigantic photo of the celebrity, pointing a finger straight at the camera. A word bubble proclaimed: "Are you as pissed off as I am?" Danziger had become a media sensation by being one of the few outspoken critics of North Korea, as well as slamming the U.S. government for not doing anything about it. Nothing was sacred for Danziger—he attacked everyone. Walker both admired and was jealous of Danziger. That was the kind of journalism Walker wanted to do.

And then there was the Korean presence. Everywhere Walker looked, there were signs of Kim Jong-un's superiority in the global markets. Where once upon a time it was Japan that had exported much of what America consumed, now it was Korea. Just about every electronic component these days was made in Korea or its member states, the various countries that fell in line with the regime. American automobiles were a thing of the past. All new cars—for anyone foolish enough to buy one—came from the Far East, mostly Korea.

There was no doubt, though, that ever since the charismatic leader managed to reunite North and South Korea back in 2013, the "Greater Korean Republic" had become a world power—and an international threat. Kim Jong-un spent the last several years preaching cooperation and peace, but most everyone in America, including Walker, smelled a rat. The so-called "reunification" of North and South Korea was looked at by most Western countries as a "takeover." And then when the country declared war on Japan in 2018, it was obvious that Kim was up to no good. Unfortunately, America had lost its standing as the symbol of democracy and freedom in the world. With its collapsed economy and reduced military presence around the globe, the United States was the object of pity—and distress, considering how important the country's economy was to the world.

As Walker merged onto I-110, heading south toward the Arena, he reflected on how his and every other American's life had changed in a short thirteen years. In 2012, the country suffered a major economic downturn as a result of complex derivatives coming due. The government's credit with lenders finally dried up. Walker was still in college at the time, so he paid no attention to the major military policy changes. The armed forces and advisors pulled out of Iraq, Afghanistan, and other key strategic locations in the Middle East, Europe, and Asia. Even defense procurement aid to Israel began phasing out and quickly came to an end.

In 2013, the year Walker graduated with his bachelor's, the oil prices spiraled out of control, leading to a true breakdown of the economy within a six-month period. The U.S. was completely unprepared for the lack of oil and the country's modern way of life declined irrevocably. The American dollar dropped considerably in value, leading markets to crash around the world. The end result was protectionism, economic nationalism, and race and trade wars between old allies and foes alike. Needless to say, Walker found it difficult to find a job in journalism.

Words between nations got ugly in 2014. While Walker worked at a hamburger joint in Los Angeles, the U.S. and Japan accused each other of unacceptable imposition of duties on imports in order to protect respective domestic industries. The two countries couldn't find common ground in sharing the burden of their shaky military alliance; this chasm slowly led to a break in the U.S.-Japan coalition. By then, North and South Korea had reunited, so the American presence in South Korea was deemed unnecessary (and unwanted). The same thing happened in Japan. A combination of the decline of global economy and the emergence of modern asymmetric warfare led to a new kind of military—light, fast, and heavily automated. Drones and other unmanned vehicles were the key components. The large scale United States military of the past disappeared. In Walker's view, America was sent away with her tail between her legs.

Meanwhile, back home, General Motors declared bankruptcy for the last time. The federal government refused to step in again, and unemployment in Michigan reached 44 percent.

In 2015, the United States protested human rights violations in Korea and attempted to bring attention to Kim Jong-un's growing threat. There was no international support to act against the Asian nation. That same year, the USS *Theodore Roosevelt* and USS *John C. Stennis* aircraft carriers were decommissioned as a part of widespread reduction in high expenditure capital ships. Later in the year, other major ships were also removed from active duty as cheaper drones took a more prominent role.

Walker distinctly remembered these events because this was also the year America's total unemployment rate tipped 30 percent and the stock market plummeted. Gasoline hit a dreaded $12/gallon mark. The rationing laws began. Walker lost his job and spent three months bumming around Europe. He returned to the States just in time for the so-called "Wal-Mart Riots." Due to an economic crisis in China, certain medicines and other vital products were no longer available. Angry customers demanded what they had become accustomed to, and the fallout was disastrous. Ironically, many suburbs, not the inner cities, were the first to burn.

Miraculously, Walker fell into a job as a *real* reporter for a news website operating out of LA. One of his first stories, in 2016, concerned how Madison Square Garden, the United Center in Chicago, The Palace in Detroit, and other large indoor stadiums in the northern U.S. were turned into "Federal Heating Centers." Even with this action, the winter of 2016–2017 claimed over 178,000 American lives. Warmer states such as Texas, Florida, and California enacted strict new interstate immigration laws to curb the influx of homeless Northerners. Walker also covered an incident in which Texas state troopers opened fire on a bus of Chicago inner city youth who had commandeered a bus with stolen gasoline. Fourteen were killed. The president ordered the National Guard to restore order but many local troops refused to act against their own states' men. It was a mess.

Things went from bad to worse in 2017. As a result of the inability to finance its debts and the rapid decline of income tax revenues, federal and state governments were unable to maintain basic infrastructure and some essential services. The interstate highway system and national power grid fell apart. Riots and looting broke out across the country. A conglomerate of Silicon Valley businesses hired Xe Services (formerly known as Blackwater Worldwide) to bring order and control to a narrow slice of California real estate. Ironically, these companies continued to create high-tech components and sell them to Japan—all of which ended up in the hands of the Koreans.

The Great Arab War—named as such by Western media—between the likewise ignorantly designated "Arab Holy Alliance" (Saudi Arabia, Syria, Jordan, Egypt, and Turkey) and other Muslim nations (Iran, Afghanistan, and Iraq) had broken out in 2016, so by 2017 the price of petroleum shot up to its current rate of $20/gallon. The U.S. military was forced to close its Asian bases due to sharp cuts in military budgets, rising global anti-U.S. sentiments, and the failing economy. A spike of nationalism in Japan resulted in the U.S.-Japan military alliance finally expiring for good. The U.S. Navy's vastly diminished Pacific Fleet was consolidated to Pearl Harbor, the first time since World War II.

Walker often questioned the wisdom of getting married to his now ex-wife Rhonda just as all hell broke loose in Asia in 2018, when the Greater Korean Republic declared war on Japan. Large numbers of American citizens in Japan were taken hostage by Korea. The two governments came to an agreement to return the U.S. captives, but only in small numbers at a time due to the costs involved. With a population of hundreds of thousands of Americans in Japan and Korea, it was expected to take over ten years to return everyone.

Even in the face of likely Korean aggression, America's military spending was drastically reduced to a level that meant running the most essential overseas bases in Europe was too expensive. Throughout 2019, the United States once again attempted to garner international support against Korea, but with little success given its internal situations and global economic issues.

In the meantime, Walker and his bride struggled with the challenge of surviving as a couple in a world in which any morning could bring some new disaster. Incongruously, Rhonda wanted children—Walker couldn't see the point.

Aside from the screaming matches, it was an amicable divorce.

In 2020, martial law was instituted in parts of America to control riots over crime and massive goods shortages caused by the increasingly devastating global energy crisis. The petroleum-based calamity was a main contributor in the continuing decline of the economy from the previous decade. The nation saw a massive migration of population, unseen since the Great Depression, away from cold climates toward major cities and coastal towns. Personal transportation and ostentatious housing became a thing of the past. Many suburbs were unsustainable. America became littered with seas of abandoned suburban neighborhoods and overpopulation in the cities.

Walker's mother died and left him the house in the Hollywood Hills, which he embraced as a hermit's hovel. It was a lifesaver for him. By then, his job as a reporter had dried up and he was forced to take whatever he could get—such as covering crap for *Celebrity Trash*.

Further catastrophe struck in 2021, when the so-called "Knoxville Fever" erupted in Tennessee and quickly spread across the country. A particularly virulent strain of the seasonal flu, it moved across the population and wiped out six million American lives. The government was unable to appropriately respond. There were rumors that it was caused by an engineered virus from an unfriendly nation—but that was never proven. Nevertheless, with limited medicine available for most of the nation, the Fever remained a menace well into 2023. Knoxville, Little Rock, Memphis, and Akron became ghost towns as nearly the entire populace succumbed to the disease. Where the disease wasn't present, martial law eventually proved ineffective. Local municipalities took on responsibility for their own governance and security. Some locales did better than others, with the worst areas descending into violent anarchy.

All the while, immigration wars along borders raged. Mexican gangs wreaked havoc by conducting raids on U.S. border towns. Canada was forced to protect its borders from Americans fleeing a frail country.

Walker reflected that things had remained relatively stable since 2023. On the positive front, Korea had agreed to use converted cargo ships to return the American citizens from territories controlled by the Greater Korean Republic—which by then included Japan, Malaysia, Indonesia, the Philippines, Thailand, Cambodia, and Vietnam. On the negative side, the fact that the Greater Korean Republic existed at all was a worry on everyone's mind. The anti-American rhetoric, the aggressive takeovers in the name of "peace," and the military dominance in the Far East reminded historians all too well of a certain German dictator who had caused a bit of trouble in the mid-twentieth century.

Screw 'em, Walker thought. He had never liked the Koreans. His feelings harked back to an inherent mistrust of the race in Walker's family—his grandfather had died in the Korean War of 1950–1953.

Today it was all about getting through one day at a time. Walker, at thirty-four, had no living parents or siblings. Rhonda had remarried long ago and they rarely spoke. It was a good thing he owned outright his small house in the Hills. He had for years taught himself to cut back and require little in the way of small pleasures. He got by.

Walker arrived at the Arena in plenty of time before Saint Lorenzo's act. A good portion of the parking lots were still occupied by people living in beat-up cars and motor homes. They either had no other housing or were stranded because they couldn't afford gas to keep moving. The enclaves had become little communes with fences built around them for dubious protection. They may as well have been deemed "slums."

He waved his press pass at the three guards blocking the entrance to the *real* parking lot, and then drove to the area where other motorbikes were parked. He stopped, claimed a space, and chained it to the pole in the ground to keep it from being stolen. As he walked toward the front doors, Walker nearly laughed when he saw the huge line of fools who had paid hard-earned money to hear the kid speak. The crippled, the blind, the deaf, the diseased—all hoping for a chance to be "cured."

What a load of bullshit . . .

"You going in to see Saint Lorenzo?"

Walker turned to see a young man in his mid-twenties. Clean-cut, with some facial hair. Not a homeless person.

"I'm a reporter. I'm covering the show," Walker answered.

The man nodded and then indicated the line of misfits. "I was curious about him, you know, but after seeing all of them I'm having second thoughts."

"Save your money, pal," Walker said. "The boy's a fraud."

"Oh, believe me, I know he is. I thought maybe it'd be good for a laugh. Actually I met a girl last night at a bar and I'm supposed to meet her here, but I have a feeling she stood me up. I ought to just blow it off and head back home to Colorado."

This got Walker's attention. "Oh? How is Colorado doing? Any better than here?"

"Not much. Denver's a mess. The smaller towns are pretty much deserted. I live in Montrose, in the eastern part of the state. Not many people left there, either." He held out his palm. "My name is Jacobs. Robert Jacobs."

Walker shook his hand and introduced himself. "What brings you to LA?"

Jacobs laughed and rolled his eyes. "Would you believe a job interview? With the Korean Consulate here in the city, no less."

"No shit. Doing what?"

"They advertised for pilots. Why, I have no idea. I'm a former Marine helicopter pilot. When the military started cutting budgets, they gave us the option to retire early, so I did."

"I don't blame you."

Jacobs shrugged. "Flying for the Marines got boring, you know? We weren't *doing* anything. So I got out. Since then I've been working odd jobs in Montrose, and then I heard about the job posting. I figured maybe the Koreans could at least give me some work doing what I love to do. I don't much like the Koreans, but a job's a job."

"I hear you. How'd you get here?"

"Took the train from Colorado, and then public transportation around LA. God, the bus fares about broke the bank, so I'm heading back tonight unless that chick shows up and I get lucky."

Walker checked his watch and said, "Look, man, by all means don't waste any more of your money in the Arena. Forget Saint Lorenzo."

"Yeah, I thought you looked like a sensible person, so I thought I'd ask what you thought about it.

Thanks."

"Advice is free. Can't say it's worth any more than that."

Jacobs held out his hand again. "Nice meeting you, Ben. Stay safe."

"You, too, man, and I hope you get lucky tonight." They shook and parted.

Walker made his way to the front door, bypassing the eager throng of ticket holders, waved the press pass again, and slipped through. Inside the arena, one might have thought a superstar rock act or a championship game from a now-defunct pro sports team from the good old days was taking place. The crowd was in a near frenzy and Lorenzo hadn't even taken the stage yet. A warm-up musical combo performed hymns and religious folk songs for the noisy crowd, and nearly everyone was singing along and clapping in rhythm.

Walker took a position in the press section and prepared to be underwhelmed. He wondered if it might be possible to try and be a classic investigative reporter again by looking into Saint Lorenzo's background and exposing the kid as a fraud. It was probably the boy's parents who were behind the scam. Or a religious organization. Walker wouldn't put it pass the pundits.

It was something to think about.

Yi Dae-Hyun also came to the LA Arena to hear Saint Lorenzo speak. His objective, though, was not to pay any attention to the young charlatan. Yi was there to observe the mood of the public, assess the malleability of LA's citizens, and issue a final report to his superiors in Pyongyang prior to the momentous day of Korean Victory over the puny United States of America.

When Yi first came to California in 2021, he had successfully integrated himself into American society as a mild-mannered electronics salesman working for a Korean microchip manufacturer. He had taken an American wife—of Korean ethnicity, for he couldn't have abided bedding a Caucasian—and lived in a small house in Van Nuys.

No one knew that his code name was "Salmusa," after the Asian viper, or that he was a childhood friend of the Brilliant Comrade, Kim Jong-un. They had been born on the same day—January 8—in the same year. Yi's father had distinguished himself to the North Korean regime in 1983 by taking part in the bombing of Burma, a patriotic act that killed several South Korean officials. Thus, Kim's father, the former leader Kim Jong-il, granted Yi's family special status. Young Dae-Hyun was allowed to play with young Jong-un, and when they were of age, both were sent to the English-language International School of Bern in Switzerland. They studied martial arts together, conversed in foreign languages, and, while in Europe, were inseparable.

Yi always knew Kim Jong-un would be a better leader than his father. When Kim Jong-il died in 2012, Jong-un took over as dictator with the support of his uncle Chang Sung-taek. Jong-un immediately promised a new era of peace and prosperity. He announced, with great fanfare, that North Korea would give up nuclear weapons and seek peaceful reconciliation with South Korea. He even allowed United Nations inspectors into the country in the interest of complete disclosure of all its secret programs. Any domestic opposition in the country quietly disappeared with little notice from the public.

Then came the historic signing of the peace treaty between the North and the South in 2013. Yi was present at the monumental event. Kim Jong-un won the Nobel Peace Prize and was named *Time* magazine's "Man of the Year." Nicknamed "The Unifier," Jong-un was responsible for a fever of nationalism that overwhelmed South Korea. There were calls for the U.S. military withdrawal from the South, and the country's historical economic woes were blamed on America.

So America left.

In 2014, North Korea appropriated Western—including U.S.—technologies that were previously sold only to the South Koreans. The Korean economy reaped benefits from untapped mineral resources, as well as from an influx of educated, cheaper labor. Nevertheless, despite the best efforts of Unified Korea's propaganda arm, the peninsula continued to be referred to internationally as North Korea.

In 2015, Jong-un took direct control of the military without much protest. He immediately began an effort to upgrade equipment and standards. He made use of U.S. technology as well as arms bought from the Chinese and Russians. Meanwhile, Yi Dae-Hyun was given a job in a hidden cell of the secret police to help shape public opinion in the South. Opposition leaders were either engulfed in scandal or they suffered terminal "accidents."

It was an occupation Yi thoroughly enjoyed.

By 2016, Kim Jong-un enjoyed a cult of personality in his country. He was seen as the savior of the people, and a propaganda campaign depicted him as the man who would lead the New Juche Revolution. Yi watched with pleasure when, in 2017, the Korean government made formal protests against violence toward ethnic Koreans in Japan and demanded international condemnation. Meanwhile, North Korean Special Forces units took part in elaborate amphibious and airborne-landing training exercises. War against Japan was declared in 2018. The Koreans took control of a number of nuclear facilities in Japan. In an act to show resolve, they destroyed one of the reactors, killing thousands instantly and laying a death sentence on countless Japanese living within the radiation fallout.

Japan surrendered without firing a single shot. In a reversal of history, Korea occupied Japan.

Throughout 2019, Korea exerted its control in the Far East. The military took over Japan's Aerospace Exploration Agency and captured the latest M-V rocket, which was based on the Peacekeeper ICBM. The Koreans also established prison camps. Yi smiled as he reflected on how similar they were to those still in place in North Korea. Jong-un promoted Yi to a role overseeing public executions in Japan. At this point, the viper-like operative earned his code name, "Salmusa."

Korea obtained military equipment from Japan; thus, by the end of 2020, the growing armed forces began learning how to operate U.S. gear.

The Greater Korean Republic was formed in 2021, with the annexing of Malaysia, Indonesia, the Philippines, Thailand, Cambodia, and Vietnam. Once the alliance was in place, the propaganda machine doubled its efforts to blame the West in general, and the U.S. in particular, for continuing conflict in the Middle East. This was also the year Salmusa was sent to the United States to integrate into American society. His cover as an electronics salesman allowed him to quickly find a wife. Marrying Kianna further solidified his disguise while he implemented the beginning phases of the Brilliant Comrade's master plan.

The year 2022 saw the Koreans conducting various military exercises, such as using converted commercial cargo ships for moving troops between its allied nations in East Asia. They also began a convoy system, providing Aegis escorts for actual commercial cargo ships traveling to Mexico and back in the name of "protection against a U.S. attack."

The Brilliant Comrade came up with another ingenious idea in 2023—in order to obtain Korean citizenship and join the People's Party, one had to enlist in the military. The size of North Korea's regular military exceeded twenty million, including five million in the expedition force. They all marched under the banner of the Korean People's Army.

Finally, just last year, Salmusa's home country

reinvigorated its unmanned space program with the stated goal of rejuvenating the decaying global GPS system. The West was unable to justify a protest when the Koreans launched a satellite for this purpose.

Salmusa, the Asian viper, was one of the few who knew what the satellite really contained.

After Saint Lorenzo's ridiculous performance, Salmusa left the Arena in his Hyundai, the largest selling automobile in the world. He would miss driving it, but that was a frivolous emotion he had inherited by living in America. In two days, he would no longer care about it.

It was time for the Execution Phase of the Brilliant Comrade's plan, one that was set in motion years earlier.

Salmusa looked at his watch as he drove onto I-110. Less than twenty-four hours to go.

THREE

10:00 a.m., PST.

Walker had spent no more than an hour the previous night writing his piece on Saint Lorenzo. Basically he ripped the performance—and the kid—to shreds. He compared Lorenzo to the phony faith healers from yesteryear and described the scene at the Arena as nothing more than a "circus sideshow act."

After sending the article to his boss by e-mail, Walker had a glass of Jack Daniels and then, surprisingly, slept very well.

Thus, he felt relatively good as he chained his bike to a meter, swiped his Meter-Card, and then stepped around the homeless beggars camped out on Hollywood Boulevard. The famous Walk of Fame had deteriorated in stature and glamour during the past decade. The city no longer supported the Walk, allowing the various stars on the sidewalk to fall into disrepair. Most tourist-themed shops were long gone. Grauman's Chinese Theatre was now a homeless shelter. The Kodak Theatre was one of the government-run heating centers, although every now and then Hollywood's old guard attempted to put on some kind of live show once or twice a year. Very few people attended. Walker often wondered where the money came from to finance the production. He figured somebody, somewhere, had the cash to drop into the nostalgia bucket and satisfy his or her own personal need for old-style Tinseltown hoopla.

The *Celebrity Trash* offices consisted of two rooms in what once was a cinema bookshop. In fact, the place still doubled as a bookstore with much of the old stock still on the shelves—but no one had bought a book during the entire five years Walker had been employed there. Most of the time he worked from home. The state government encouraged folks who could to do so. It saved gasoline, power, and city utilities.

Johnny Slazbo, the owner and publisher of web-zine *Celebrity Trash,* stayed glued to his computer screen as Walker came in. (Walker referred to him as Johnny "Sleazeball" behind his back.) The boss didn't bother hiding the porn he was viewing. That was one industry that still seemed to flourish. People couldn't afford gasoline or food, but they still spent money on pornography. Walker often pondered the correlation between hard times and vices. Did immoral habits increase during periods of economic strife? He didn't know. It was a fact, though, that prostitution, drug addiction, and alcoholism ran rampant. There was something very wrong with that picture—the only people currently making real money were the porn stars, pimps, and drug dealers. Not since the legendary 1920s had organized crime become so powerful.

"Did you get my article on Lorenzo, Johnny?" Walker asked as he pulled up a chair in Slazbo's cubicle.

"Yep." The man refused to take his eyes off the

skin on his screen.

"I was thinking my next piece should be an exposé on the kid. You know, really dig into his background, his parents, his manager, his financial supporters. There's got to be some spicy stuff there."

Slazbo continued to study the action on the monitor. "Why would you want to do that?"

"Because the kid's a fake! Look, I don't want to hurt a ten-year-old, it's his handlers I really want to go after. They're selling bullshit to the public and I want to call 'em on it. Johnny, would you turn that off and talk to me?"

Finally, Slazbo punched something on his keyboard and the nasty video shut off. In its place was salacious computer wallpaper that was just as disgusting. The boss, who was in his twenties, turned to Walker and said, "I don't think our readers would appreciate that. Saint Lorenzo is a hot topic. We can get some good copy on him while he's popular. Maybe in a few months, after his fifteen minutes of fame dies down, then you can do that."

Walker expected that answer. "Okay, how about this? Let's go after the Koreans. I want to do a hatchet job on Kim Jong-un. That guy is a fraud, too. The propaganda coming out of the Greater Korean Republic is too Nazi-like for its own good. Look around outside. If it's not filth and trash and reminders of the sorry state of affairs, then it's signs of the Korean dominance in our marketplace and society. They're all around us, even after we've declared them to be a menace!"

Slazbo drummed his fingers on the desk. "Very passionate speech, Ben, but I'm gonna have to say 'no' to that one, too. Too political. We don't do political editorials at *Celebrity Trash*. It wouldn't be popular. I don't think anyone gives a shit about Kim Jong-un. Everyone is miserable. They just want something to laugh at, if they can. We try to provide a little bit of entertainment."

Walker didn't like that answer. "Jesus, Johnny, don't you care about what's happening out there? No one gets real *news* anymore. I'm guilty of dishing out the garbage, too. For the past five years, I've just been a hack, churning out these trashy stories about *nothing important,* and worse than that, I've stepped on a lot of toes and hurt people doing it. I don't have many friends left in this business."

"Damn right, Walker. And you know why? You're the best reporter we've got. I don't mind telling you that. You're unscrupulous. You'd sell your grandmother for a story. And that's what I like about you. We need that kind of no-holds-barred attitude around here. The only good reporter these days is one with a lot of enemies. And that's you. So shut the fuck up and get out there and find us another celebrity to interview."

Walker got up and left the cubicle. He hesitated at the front door before stepping outside, and then turned around and confronted Slazbo again. The man was already once again staring at the porn on his computer screen.

It was time to do what Walker had planned. There

was no turning back now. He'd given the boss one last chance to assign him something worthwhile.

"Johnny, guess what. I quit."

That got Slazbo's attention. "What?"

"I don't want to do this anymore. I quit. Please pay me what you owe me. I'm walking away."

Slazbo's mouth dropped. "Are you serious?"

"Yeah. I'm through."

The boss laughed. "Are you nuts? Where else are you going to get work? Have you seen what's going on in the streets?"

Walker leaned over the desk. "That's what I just said to *you* a few minutes ago!"

Slazbo just snarled. "Go on then! Quit! Your damn check's in the mail. Maybe it'll actually get delivered."

"No way, Johnny. I know damn well you keep cash on hand for tipsters and weed." He held out his palm. "Pay me now. You owe me."

Cursing, Slazbo grudgingly opened his desk drawer, unlocked a petty cash box, and counted out several bills. "Here. Don't slam the door on your way out." The man turned back to his computer, fuming.

Walker pocketed the money and said, "Okay, Johnny. Goodbye and good luck." He turned and left the building.

As Walker pulled the Spitfire into the gravel drive of his house in the hills north of Mulholland Drive, he saw his neighbors, the Gomezes, getting out of their old station wagon. Their house was the nearest structure to his, maybe fifty yards away. Walker had been lucky, having inherited the home from his mother. She had bought it in the late 1980s, just before Walker was born. Properties were not in close proximity this far north; the privacy and isolation suited him.

Rudy Gomez was a man in his forties. His wife Luisa was probably Walker's age. They had two children—a boy in high school and a girl a bit younger. Gomez had been out of work for over a year. Walker didn't know how they got by, but they did. Walker and the family often shared food and supplies. Once he even gave Gomez a five-gallon can of gas to help him out.

Apparently the Gomezes had taken a trip to the supermarket, for Rudy carried a single bag of groceries. The two kids and the wife appeared very downtrodden. Gomez was always glum. Walker couldn't blame him. The man lost a lucrative burger joint franchise when the economy went belly up. Just thinking about it made Walker's mouth water—he had loved those burgers. Hell, he would've settled for a Big Mac. Ironically, McDonald's was one corporation that barely hung in there. They had closed probably 85 percent of their stores worldwide; the few franchises left open were only in big cities and charged a small fortune for a Happy Meal. There was a handful in Los Angeles.

"Hey, Rudy!" Walker called. He waved. "Luisa. How's it going?"

Gomez just nodded in Walker's direction. Luisa answered for him. "We're fine, Ben. We bought some hot dogs—we'll have you over for a cookout this weekend!"

"That'll be nice. Let me know what I can bring."

The kids looked at him as if he was crazy. What could Ben Walker afford to bring? A bottle of mustard?

Walker considered asking Gomez if he wanted to share a drink with him, but then he decided the man looked too forlorn. It would be a downer. The guy had enough problems without Walker plying him with alcohol.

The Gomezes went in their house and Walker rolled his motorcycle in his garage. One thing he'd inherited from his late father was the pleasure of being an amateur mechanic. About the only possessions Walker was proud of were the many tools he owned. He had rebuilt the Spitfire when he was twenty-four and it still worked like a charm. It was fortunate he had stocked up on spare parts years ago, for today he wouldn't have been able to buy them. Walker was also good friends with Buddy Jenkins, a guy who ran one of the few open service stations north of Hollywood Boulevard. They had a deal—Jenkins saved a couple of five-gallon cans of gas for Walker with each delivery, and Walker paid him regularly in cash. Hardly anyone used credit cards anymore. The banks simply couldn't support them.

Could he keep up the gas payments now that he didn't have a job?

Inside the house, he turned on his computer to check e-mail and switched on the television for background noise. Walker then went to the kitchen, removed the last bottle of Jack Daniels, and poured a glass.

He wondered if it would *really* be the last bottle.

On the way to the living room, he caught a glimpse of himself in a mirror that hung on the wall. Walker stopped and stared at the unemployed joker looking back at him. His wavy brown hair always seemed to be too long. Those green eyes the chicks used to love when he was in college betrayed a frustrated, bitter melancholy. At least he had his killer smile.

Right.

11:00 a.m., PST.

Salmusa sat in front of the computer in his house in Van Nuys. Despite the anticipation of the day's events, he had slept soundly. His wife, Kianna, had not disturbed him when she'd left to go to work that morning. She had a job at a donut shop within walking distance of the house. Koreans ran the bakery and they did a modest business in the weak economy. Everyone still ate donuts, and they were inexpensive.

Salmusa pursed his lips. Kianna wouldn't have to work much longer.

He looked at his watch and brought up the web browser. Logging in to the encrypted URL with his password, he found his operatives already waiting for him in the chat room. They were physically stationed all over the United States, one each in New York, Washington, D.C., Chicago, Atlanta, Miami, Dallas, Houston, Denver, Phoenix, Seattle, and San Francisco. The men were under Salmusa's direct control. Other sleeper cell agents of the GKR scattered across the nation followed the instructions of different handlers who held the same status as Salmusa.

Well, not quite.

Salmusa was privileged with a special rank in the echelon of Korean spies in America. He was the only one who had direct access to the Brilliant Comrade. In fact, he was the only one of the agents who reported to Kim Jong-un personally. Salmusa looked forward to their communication later that day. He missed his childhood friend. It had been too many years since Salmusa had seen him.

The man once known as Yi Dae-Hyun shook his head in amazement when he considered how ignorant and unsuspecting the Americans were. The sleeper agents lived in the U.S. for years under the government's very nose, and no one thought anything of it. Ever since America washed her hands of the problems in the Middle East, Islamic terrorists left her alone. After time passed there was no need for the government to pour money into the anti-terrorist groups as they had in the past. The NSA downsized considerably. The CIA was in tatters. The FBI was a joke. By retreating into a state of isolationism, America left herself vulnerable. With the military reduced to a bare minimum, the power grid weakening, the social structure frayed, and the population hurting—it was the perfect time to strike.

Typing in Korean, Salmusa issued last-minute instructions to his operatives. At this point, it really didn't matter if they were caught performing their final task. They all knew going into it that arrest or death were possibilities. But if all went well, he and his comrades would soon be rejoined with their people.

On American turf.

"Dae-Hyun? What are you doing?"

Salmusa stiffened. Kianna had returned from her job early!

She stood behind him. "I thought you had to go to work today."

Kianna had insisted that they always speak English. After all, they were Americans. Well, *she* was.

Salmusa felt only the slightest touch of remorse as he spoke in Korean, "I *am* working, Kianna. Today is the most important day of my job."

She was confused by his switch in language.

"Darling? Is something wrong? What's that on your computer? Who are you talking to?"

Salmusa quietly opened the desk drawer in front of him and removed the Daewoo 9mm K5 semi-automatic. It was already equipped with a suppressor. He held the pistol close to his chest out of her view.

"Dae-Hyun? I asked a question. What are you doing?"

Salmusa took a breath and answered, "Preparing for the new dawn."

He then turned and calmly shot his wife in the chest.

The suppressor silenced the gunshot well enough. Surely no one outside the house heard it.

Salmusa stood and stepped over to his wife's body. Although blood spread across her blouse, she was still alive. Kianna looked up at him in surprise and shock.

He pointed the gun at her forehead and said, in Korean, "I never loved you."

The Greater Korean Republic's most senior sleeper

cell agent in America squeezed the trigger again, pleased that he didn't have to use the M9 knife he kept strapped to his calf.

It was time to commence Execution Phase One.

WALKER'S JOURNAL

JANUARY 15, 2025

I did it, just like I said I would. I quit my fucking job. Now I can sit down with my bottle of Jack and get drunk with no remorse.

Actually I feel pretty weird about it. Was I crazy? I don't know.

Hey, the old Ben Walker gut told me to do it, so I did. Sometimes the gut is right, and sometimes it isn't, but it's my gut and I usually listen to it.

Saw the Gomezes outside just a while ago. Ouch. Rudy didn't look too good. He's had a lot of shit happen to him, so I guess I can't blame him acting like Death. The only things missing were a black cloak and a scythe. Luisa and the kids seemed okay, though. Or else they're just good actors.

Hell, in the words of everyone else in the country . . . "Who gives a shit?"

Let's see, as I look at my digital clock in the kitchen, I see it's early afternoon. What else could possibly go wrong today?

Time for a drink. Or two.

FOUR

3:45 p.m., PST.

Salmusa parked his Hyundai near the intersection of Hollywood and Vine. Making sure the car was properly locked, he swiped the Meter-Card in the appropriate box. Even though in a few hours it wouldn't matter, Salmusa always made it a point to obey the city's traffic and parking laws. It had become a habit, simply because he never wanted to call attention to himself throughout his years of residency.

Walking to the boulevard, Salmusa carried a silver metal briefcase containing a package that had been delivered to him from Pyongyang. It had come through Ready-Electrics, the Korean electronics firm for which he worked when he was undercover. Similar briefcases were distributed to his operatives around the country. Salmusa felt confident his men were, at that moment, also carrying the cases to their targets.

He wanted to sneer at how easy it was to smuggle the C-4 explosives into the country. Salmusa had spent several months researching the efficiency of America's security operations and had determined that they were at an all-time low. After the RDX—cyclotrimethylene trintramine, the explosive ingredient in C-4—was combined with the binder and plasticizer, his company made several trial runs by transporting harmless electronic components in ordinary shipping containers across the Pacific. C-4 could be molded and shaped into any crevice or hole, so hiding the stuff inside electronic consoles was perfect. When the C-4 finally arrived, no one at the Port of Los Angeles examined the cargo. The manifests indicated there was nothing inside but parts, cellphones, the new holographic television sets (intended for those wealthy enough to afford them), video game machines, and other home entertainment odds and ends. The bombs inside the briefcases were assembled at Ready-Electrics and one was tested in the Mojave Desert just a month earlier. Salmusa was there to witness it.

It blew a hole in the ground the size of a strip mall parking lot.

In Salmusa's jacket pocket was a cellphone that acted as a remote control transmitter. An old-fashioned method, to be sure, but effective. All he had to do was punch the correct numbers and the timer inside the case would start.

He walked west on Hollywood Boulevard, wincing at the grime and filth that surrounded him. The city's smell had certainly grown worse since the cuts in utility services. Salmusa didn't doubt the reports that Hollywood had become rat-infested. There was enough garbage on the streets to feed all the rodents in China.

He smiled at the thought—*pretty soon rats would*

be the dominant species in America.

The Los Angeles Metro Rail services had deteriorated exponentially with the failing economy. Nevertheless, thousands of citizens still rode the trains daily. The Red Line, the oldest subway in LA, was a decrepit, often dangerous piece of junk, and Salmusa almost had to force himself to go down the steps at Hollywood and Highland to board. He grimaced as he observed how rundown and puny it was, especially compared to the clean and modern rail lines that now existed in Korea. Every surface was covered with graffiti. Bills that called for a revolution against the government, generated by radical groups, were glued on the walls. Product advertisements were obscenely vandalized. More homeless people camped on the platforms, begging more affluent waiting passengers for money or food. One hapless musician who played a violin surprisingly well was ignored, his tip cup empty.

A person took his life into his own hands riding the LA subway, and that was during daylight. Salmusa could only imagine what horrors lurked down there at night.

After dutifully paying the fare—an outrageous $9.50 for a single ride—Salmusa stood on the platform for the train heading back in the direction from which he'd walked. He waited only a few minutes before it screeched into the station. It was packed full of passengers, all looking harried, uncomfortable, and miserable.

Good.

He glanced at his watch. It was four o'clock on the dot.

Everything was going according to plan.

Salmusa stood at the open doors as a few people shoved their way off the train, and then he calmly boarded.

The car smelled of body odor, urine, and cheap perfume.

Disgusting.

As the train pulled away from the station, Salmusa set the briefcase on the floor and leaned it against the side of the car. He pushed it back with his foot, out of the way. There were so many people in the train that no one noticed.

He purposely avoided looking any passengers in the eye, but he could see who they were. Men and women, commuting to or from work. Some mothers with children. Teenagers—probably gang members—trying to look tough. And the usual allotment of homeless souls who had nothing better to do than ride the trains back and forth between stations.

Salmusa thought—*soon they'll be free of their agony.*

It didn't take long for the train to reach the Hollywood and Vine station. Salmusa allowed himself to be pushed out of the car with the exiting throng. Once on the platform, he made his way to the staircase and ascended to the street. As soon as he was outside, he removed the cellphone from his pocket and dialed the number he had memorized. Salmusa then held the phone to his ear, pretended to talk, and walked toward his car. Just another ordinary citizen.

Before the Red Line train reached the next station at Hollywood and Western, Salmusa heard the muffled, but distinctly devastating boom underground. The sidewalk shook as if another minor earthquake had hit Southern California. Pedestrians reacted to the noise, but they were clueless as to its origin. Salmusa stood by his car and waited to see what kind of pandemonium would erupt as soon as the news of what happened reached the street. For fun, he watched the seconds tick by on his watch. It took exactly twenty-five of them before black, billowy smoke gushed from the Hollywood and Vine subway entrance. This was quickly followed by people running and screaming from the station.

"There's been an explosion! Call 911!" someone cried.

Given the reputation of LA's emergency services, Salmusa knew the response would be slow and disorganized. But in an hour, the police and fire departments would have their hands full.

Perfect.

Now to give America a few hours to reel from what had just occurred in LA, New York, Washington, and the other cities where his operatives performed their duties. Then, in the midst of the chaos, Phases Two and Three would be implemented.

Salmusa got into his car and drove away before the sound of sirens penetrated the dark, cloudy air.

4:20 p.m., PST.

Dressed only in boxer shorts, Walker sat on the sofa

in front of the television, a glass of Jack in one hand, the remote in the other. Ever since he'd come home from the *Celebrity Trash* office, he'd done nothing but make a short journal entry and work on the whiskey. He'd had the sense to have a bite to eat, and now the crumbs from the microwaved pizza littered his lap.

There was nothing but crap on TV. If it wasn't an idiotic game show, it was a talking head blabbing about America's problems. Soap operas were a thing of the past, but there was still "women's fare" such as cooking shows in which housewives were shown how to make complete family dinners out of practically nothing. Religious-themed stations dominated the cable channels; even Saint Lorenzo had his own talk show. The movie channels broadcasted decades-old features. That was fine by Walker, but nine times out of ten he'd seen whatever was showing. The big three networks—NBC, ABC, and CBS—barely had the funds to keep operating, but they managed to do so. Nothing in their lineup was aimed at an intelligent audience anymore. Even the news programs were watered down, full of half-truths and feel-good pep talks about how "things were getting better."

At the moment, Walker was watching one of the so-called "entertainment" programs, on which undeserving celebrities were profiled or interviewed. He'd just poured another glass of whiskey when a news bar appeared at the bottom of the screen. As it rolled, he read: "breaking news—explosion in los angeles subway. authorities are investigating." Walker didn't think much of it. There was always something.

He continued to watch the program, but a few minutes later another news bar appeared. "breaking news—explosion reported in new york city subway."

Walker blinked and sat up.

This was immediately followed by "breaking news— explosion reported in washington, d.c., subway."

Hold on. What the hell?

Walker used the remote to change channels. He found a dedicated news station and the story was front and center. A popular anchorman relayed the disturbing news as images of fire, death, and destruction flashed on a screen behind him.

"—as we are receiving it. Again, we have reports that deadly explosions have occurred on at least three major U.S. city mass transportation systems. In Los Angeles, at approximately four o'clock Pacific Standard Time, a bomb exploded on the Red Line Metro. The death toll is estimated to be a hundred or more. In New York, a similar, simultaneous explosion occurred on the Number One subway at approximately seven o'clock Eastern Standard Time. In Washington, D.C., at the same time, a bomb went off on the—hold on." The anchor put a hand to his earpiece. "I am now receiving a report that a bomb has exploded in Dallas, Texas, on a DART train, and in Atlanta, Georgia, on a MARTA train. Wait—oh dear Lord, there's one in Miami, too. A Metromover in Dade County was . . . And in Denver, Colorado . . ."

Stunned, Walker sat with his jaw open. What the hell was going on? There hadn't been terrorist attacks in the country for over a decade. The fundamental-

ist Islamics couldn't be back, could they? And why?
America had left the Middle East. There was nothing
for them to bitch about.

Who was behind it?

For the next hour, he stayed glued to the set as
reports came in. Just when he thought it was over,
another city was named as a target. Obviously, well-
executed, well-planned, simultaneous attacks had
occurred all over the country. Twelve major cities,
all on mass transit systems. Most of the explosions
were on trains, a couple on buses, one on a streetcar.
Hundreds dead. Hundreds injured. Mass confusion
and panic. Emergency services were pushed to the
brim.

Somewhat sober now, Walker managed to stand,
walk outside onto his deck, and look over the hills
toward the city. He heard sirens in the distance. He
thought he saw a couple of dark clouds of smoke over
Hollywood, but compared to the haze that normally
hung over the area it was difficult to tell for sure.

Feeling a chill, he returned inside and went to his
computer. He browsed some of the blogger websites
that tended to focus on the realities of the world.
Discussions of the attacks were all over the Internet.
Conspiracy theories abounded. The fundamental-
ist Muslims were back. It was the Koreans. Angry
radical revolutionaries in America were responsible.
Washington was behind the attacks in an attempt to
rally the people to a common cause.

Behind him on the television set, the president
appeared to deliver a short address from the Oval

Office. He urged the public to remain calm and pledged that the government would do everything in its power to find the culprits and bring them to justice.

No one listened to the president anymore.

Walker grabbed his cellphone. He had a sudden compulsion to call his ex-wife, Rhonda, to whom he hadn't spoken in ages. But when he dialed the number, the network was busy. He tried again a few minutes later with no luck. He finally gave up the attempts after an hour.

He had a very bad feeling about it all. Somehow Walker knew this was just the beginning of something unprecedented.

FIVE

11:15 p.m., PST.

The day had gone well.

Salmusa sat at his computer in the Van Nuys home. He had carried his wife's corpse into the bedroom and left her there. He would have no further need for their home after today. If she was found by authorities, they wouldn't be able to locate him. Besides, they would have so much more on their hands without having to worry about finding the killer of an insignificant Korean American woman who worked at a donut shop.

In hindsight, Salmusa acknowledged that Kianna had been a good woman. It wasn't her fault she was an American. It was too bad she and her family had bought into the American lies and decadent lifestyle. She had served her purpose well as part of his cover. He wished her happiness in her next life.

Still, Salmusa felt no remorse for what he'd had to do. He had conditioned himself long ago to kill with calculated objectivity. If it was for the Greater Korean Republic and the Brilliant Comrade, then it was his duty. He would lay down his life for Kim Jong-un, and he would murder thousands for him.

He would never forget the pledge he had made to his friend when they were both eight years old. They were in Kim Jong-il's summer residence outside Pyongyang, where Salmusa had gone to stay for a few months with young Jong-un. His friend had read somewhere how the Italian mafia would swear blood oaths to each other. New recruits attended a secret ceremony at which the don or whomever would prick the newcomer's finger as well as his own, and the two men would ritualistically join their blood together in front of the entire group. Then the recruit guaranteed his loyalty to the "family."

Jong-un had been fascinated with tales of the Italian mafia. He admired how the "family" was controlled by a father figure, the so-called "don," and the organization beneath him was made up of lieutenants and captains and muscle. He had advisors, too, but the final word rested with the don.

Salmusa's friend likened the mythos to North Korea. His father, Kim Jong-il, was the don, and everyone else in the country was his family. Men had to pledge allegiance to him and act on the dictator's orders.

So, in private, on the banks of a stream near the summer home, Kim Jong-un and Yi Dae-Hyun pricked their fingers and held them together. They swore to be friends forever. Even though they did not know then that Jong-un would one day be chosen as his father's successor, Dae-Hyun pledged eternal commitment to him. Reciprocally, Jong-un vowed to afford Dae-Hyun a place of power in his organization.

Salmusa glanced at his watch. It was time to commence Phase Two.

He logged in to the private URL and chat room. All but one of his operatives were present. The man from Miami was missing.

Salmusa asked if anyone knew where he was.

The man stationed in Atlanta replied that the Miami operation was problematic. There were eyewitness reports from a survivor that a passenger on the Metromover noticed the abandoned briefcase and tried to stop the operative from leaving the train without it. Apparently there was some kind of struggle. The bomb went off with the operative still in the car. The survivor reported that the man attempting to leave the car was Asian.

Salmusa didn't think it was of any consequence. They had all known it was a dangerous task.

"We honor our fallen comrade," he typed. "I will see to it that his name is known to the Brilliant Comrade and appropriate tributes are made."

Enough of that.

"This will be our last communication, as Phase Two begins in minutes. Please verify that your snake is implemented and ready to strike."

The "snake" was Trojan spyware for which each operative was responsible. It had taken two long years, but the Koreans managed to hack into all U.S. networks and communication systems, including the military and Federal government agencies. Because 50 percent of all software and hardware in the last ten years was made in Korea or the member countries in the Greater Korean Republic, it was possible to compromise the Trusted Platform Module components that went into American government computers. The TPM was a security device that offered facilities for the secure generation of cryptographic keys, as well as authentication procedures for hardware. Since most of the hardware was manufactured by third party companies—many under Korea's control—it was possible to install backdoor Trojan access into the modules. Of course, not every computer in the Federal government was applicable, but a very high percentage was. Most important, the military networks had gone through a computerized upgrade within the last two years—one of the few things on which money was spent since their methods had become more automated. With the "new military" consisting of more drones and robots and less human deployment, the upgrade was necessary.

Nearly all of the computer equipment bought by the military indirectly came from Korean suppliers. The plan had been in place since 2016.

Each man answered, "Ready." The snakes were coiled and prepared for triggering.

Salmusa congratulated the operatives on the success of their mission, wished them well, and signed off. He then placed a video call to Pyongyang.

After the usual few minutes of security checks and verification of Salmusa's identity through two subordinates, Kim Jong-un appeared on the monitor.

"Brilliant Comrade, good day," Salmusa said.

"It is indeed a good day, Salmusa," the dictator replied. "The sun is shining and it's not too cold."

"I am happy to report that Phase Two is ready for implementation."

"Very good. I will send authorization to the appropriate administrators. How is the mood in America?"

"They are panicking like ants that have had their hill stepped upon. As you know, all twelve mass transit attacks were successful. We lost one operative." He relayed the man's name to Kim.

"I will inscribe his name in the Book of Honor and inform his family that he died serving our country."

"For the past seven hours, emergency services in the twelve major cities have been put to the test. It is time to enact Phase Two while the police, fire departments, and ambulance drivers are busy attempting to deal with our work today. And after that . . . Phase Three."

"Your safe house is ready?"

"Yes, my Brilliant Comrade. It is not far from here. I will abandon this house as soon as we sign off. I sacrifice my Hyundai in the name of the GKR."

Kim laughed. "I will see to it that you have another one day."

"I am sure the Volkswagen in the shielded garage will be fine. The Germans made good cars . . . once."

"Then this is goodbye for now, my friend. In three days we will talk again?"

"Providing the satellite data card in the safe house works properly. Do not be concerned. I will get a message to you one way or the other."

"Very well." Kim bowed his head. "Thank you,

Salmusa. Thank you, Dae-Hyun. You have done a great service for me and for Korea."

Salmusa felt a surge of great pride. "My service is not over, Jong-un. I will see my mission through as long as I am needed here. Thank you for the opportunity, Brilliant Comrade."

Then Kim did something Salmusa wasn't expecting. The dictator held up his index finger, the same one he had pricked many years ago. Then he smiled. Salmusa nodded and held up his own index finger. The scars had disappeared but the memories were still there.

The two men said goodbye again and signed off.

Salmusa looked at his watch. 11:30 p.m.

Time to go.

The North American Aerospace Defense Command, otherwise known as NORAD, provided advance aerospace warning, air sovereignty, and defense for both the United States and Canada. Located at the Cheyenne Mountain Air Force Station in Colorado, the facility remained on active status even after the downsizing of the U.S. military. NORAD's commander was also the head of USNORTHCOM, a Unified Combatant Command that supplied protection from air, land, and sea approaches to the contiguous States, Alaska, Canada, and Mexico, as well as the Gulf of Mexico, the Straits of Florida, the Bahamas, Puerto Rico, and the U.S. Virgin Islands.

While there had been significant cutbacks in staff of both NORAD and USNORTHCOM, a minimum crew of fifteen constantly monitored satellite communications, air traffic, and early warning systems.

At 12:30 a.m. Mountain Standard Time, the Senior Analyst on duty, Captain Jeffrey Peterson, was keeping an eye on the Korean satellite designated as "K101." Ever since it had positioned itself over the United States earlier in the day, he had submitted the appropriate reports to the Pentagon and his superiors. No one seemed to pay any attention. The satellite had passed over North America numerous times since the Koreans launched it in 2023. Everyone knew its purpose was to revamp the failing global GPS system. It was working, too. The past six months had shown significant improvement in international GPS mapping. It was believed the Koreans, for once, were actually doing the world a favor.

Nevertheless, Captain Peterson was concerned because the satellite hadn't moved in three hours. It remained in a stationary position, directly three hundred miles above Lebanon, Kansas, near the intersection of AA Road and K-191—said to be the exact center of the contiguous United States. Normally the satellite was always on the move.

Sergeant Melissa Davies turned away from her monitors, since nothing was going on there, and asked her boss, "Jeff, is that satellite still giving you the heebie-jeebies?"

Peterson slapped the counter and took a swig of his rapidly cooling coffee. "I can't understand why it's just *sitting* there. Has it malfunctioned?"

Davies got up, stood behind Peterson, and looked over his shoulder. "And it's been there for how long?"

"Going on four hours."

"And you've contacted the Pentagon? And the commander?"

"I got hold of the deputy commander. He said not to worry about it."

"No response from the Pentagon?"

"It's the middle of the night there. You know it's a skeleton crew until morning."

Suddenly, every monitor in the command center went blank. The other thirteen analysts simultaneously vocalized surprise.

"What just happened?" Peterson asked. He started fiddling with controls. "We're offline." He stood and called out to the others. "Is anyone online?"

Negative.

He picked up the dedicated hotline and made a call.

In the silent halls of the Pentagon, the men and women working the graveyard shift were just as panic-stricken. Every computer in the building had abruptly shut down. After a moment's hesitation, the staff scrambled to find out what went wrong.

The same thing happened at the White House. As inter-governmental communication failed, personnel relayed messages within the building by intercom and phone. The Chief of Staff was awoken and briefed. He personally strode to the president's living quarters to rouse him.

At the J. Edgar Hoover Building, the FBI experienced a lesser, but just as devastating computer breakdown. They lost connections to world databases and comlinks to U.S. civilian law enforcement agencies.

The digitally mechanized NSA was powerless. Before the full seriousness of the attack was known, a security agent commented wryly as he picked up the phone, "I have to dial the chief. How quaint."

The CIA's vast computerized network, including their remaining active stations in Europe, Asia, and the Middle East, were cut off.

Phones rang all over Washington, waking the Cabinet and key members of Congress. The government could not communicate with the branches of the Army, Navy, Air Force, Marines, Coast Guard, or National Guard. The various agencies could not converse with each other except by telephone.

Besides the inability to liaison, issue commands, and act on them, the military had no way to launch defense missiles.

Many computer networks associated with the FAA ceased to function. Control towers at airports all over the nation lost the ability to track commercial planes already in the air. Pilots could still speak to each other and to air traffic controllers, but ground radar was kaput. In short, they were flying without a net. At first the problem didn't seem to be *too* serious. In the middle of the night there was little air traffic; pilots could usually navigate aircrafts manually and land without the benefit of a controller's instructions. They all thought—*surely the glitch will be fixed shortly*.

By midnight, Pacific Standard Time, the realization set in that America's military and governmental computer systems had been hit by an unknown, seriously destructive cyber attack.

Perhaps it was best that the public at large had no idea what had occurred. The only computers affected were non-civilian. The average person was unaware that the country had been rendered defenseless in a matter of minutes, setting the stage for the *coup de grâce*.

SIX

JANUARY 16, 2025

12:05 a.m., PST.

After his conversation with Salmusa, Kim Jong-un, the Brilliant Comrade and leader of the Greater Korean Republic, sat in his private office. Lost in thought, he studied a map of the United States that hung over the planning table. A bull's-eye was marked on the strategic point in Kansas, above which the satellite the Americans called "K101" hovered.

What he was about to do would change the world.

For 250 years, the United States of America had dominated the globe. She had managed to thwart mighty Britain until the United Kingdom was a mere shadow of her former self. America defeated Germany twice, even pushing back the powerful Nazis and destroying Hitler's plans of world conquest. The North American country even stomped on Imperial Japan, reducing that proud nation to rubble until the Land of the Rising Sun became a subservient pawn in U.S. superiority.

Kim's father, the honorable Kim Jong-il, stood up to America time and time again. He was forced to withstand inequitable sanctions and criticisms from the international community due to lies and accusations regarding North Korea's nuclear programs. As a result, South Korea prospered while North Korea languished in poverty and pedestrian technology.

But now everything had changed. Ever since the favored son ascended to replace his late father to be the leader of the Democratic People's Republic of Korea, Kim Jong-un succeeded in turning the country's fortunes around. By reuniting with the South, he strengthened the land's financial pockets and military muscle. He conquered Korea's longtime enemy, Japan. He annexed other Asian countries to create the Greater Korean Republic. Kim Jong-un brought *respect* to what was once referred to as "North Korea."

Slowly but surely, chinks were made in the once potent American armor. The sworn enemy of Kim's nation was no longer a giant that policed the world. She was weak and vulnerable. Kim once heard a Western Biblical story concerning a boy named David and a giant named Goliath. The Hebrew boy was no match for this vicious and powerful adversary. But David surprised everyone by defeating the giant with a single slingshot. A tiny weapon against a strong warrior.

The analogy could be applied to Korea and the United States.

When Korea captured Japan's Aerospace Exploration Agency and took possession of the M-V rocket, Kim Jong-un saw that his dream to defeat America could become a reality. What the world didn't know was North Korea *did* have nuclear capabilities back when he allowed the United Nations into the country for inspection. They were simply well-hidden. By seizing the missing materials in Japan needed to build a nuclear weapon, the task was completed.

The satellite launched into orbit in 2023 carried a ten-megaton thermonuclear device. When detonated three-hundred miles above America, as it currently was positioned, the blast would blanket the entire country in an electromagnetic pulse—an EMP. Nearly every electronic device with an integrated circuit of any kind would immediately fail.

Phase Three.

Kim Jong-un knew fully well what the consequences of the act would be. The international community would condemn Korea. European allies would rush to America's aid, but given the current economic conditions all over the world—except in Korea—it might takes months or even years before help arrived. By then, it would be too late.

Korean warships were already crossing the Pacific on their way to Hawaii, set to arrive in forty-eight hours. Then, using Hawaii as a staging point, the world's largest Special Forces contingent would land a mix of troops on the West Coast shores of the United States. Airborne paratroopers would be dropped farther inland. The takeover of key targets of value—military bases, civic centers, and natural resources such as the oil shale in Colorado, which the U.S. lacked the technology to extract—would swiftly fall into Korean hands. Noncritical areas would be left to survive or fall on their own, assuming the people didn't try to retaliate or defend areas of Korean interest.

Kim's analysts assured him the American government would be helpless. After the initial transit attacks to demonstrate to the population how susceptible it was, and the cyber strike to convince the government and military that they, too, were defenseless, the EMP would catapult the country's level of technology back to the 1800s.

Kim Jong-un was well aware what this would mean.

A new world order, with Korea calling the shots.

He picked up the phone and gave the order to commence Phase Three.

12:30 a.m., PST.

Walker had fallen asleep on the couch. Jack Daniels had done its work, knocking him into a state of oblivion during the evening hours after the mass transit attacks. He was watching the news on television and eventually couldn't keep his eyes open.

A loud, rumbling noise shook him to his senses.

At first he was disoriented—and still drunk—when he opened his eyes.

The house was pitch dark. No lights anywhere.

He had felt something *odd*. As if a wave of vibration had passed over him. Was that what woke him up?

The flat screen television was off. He didn't remember switching it off, but perhaps he had.

The sound was growing louder. It was above him, in the sky. Something was coming closer. In his hazy state, Walker thought it might be an airplane.

An airplane?

He sat up too swiftly, causing his head to spin. Groaning, he put his face in his hands and rubbed. Sitting there quietly for a moment, he took some deep breaths until he was able to stand.

Walker turned toward the kitchen to see what time it was. The digital clock on the counter was unlit.

He glanced at his computer. It, too, was off. He never shut it down. The computer went into sleep mode after a period of disuse, but an indicator light always told him it was still on.

Oh, shit. Power outage.

He hated it when that happened. Damned Los Angeles Department of Water and Power. For the past several years, there had been numerous power outages. Usually they got it fixed in a few hours, but it was always a big hassle.

The noise in the sky was growing louder. Closer.

Oh yeah. The airplane.

Walker shook his head and stumbled to the glass door leading to the deck.

Wait a second.

The entire city was dark. No lights anywhere.

Even during power outages, there were always parts of the metropolis that weren't affected.

This must be one hell of an outage!

The noise above him rapidly intensified.

What the hell is that?

Walker leaned over the deck rail backward to look at the sky, past the eve of his roof.

Nothing.

Just a booming, soaring *whoosh* that sounded as if it was headed straight for him.

And then it appeared over the house.

A commercial airplane—no lights, no power—just zooming through the air.

Toward the city.

Oh . . . my . . . God . . .

It was as if time suddenly stood still. Walker couldn't move. He watched in horror as the dark, winged shape wavered unsteadily, clearing the hills and plummeting toward Hollywood like a gigantic paper airplane sailing to the ground in slow motion.

Walker felt his stomach lurch. A shiver went up his spine as he gripped the deck rail. He couldn't take his eyes off the phantom bird as it shrank away from him and the low rumbling noise diminished. The sight was surreal—only the light of the moon reflected off the plane's wings, highlighting it against the black city beneath.

A few more seconds . . .

Walker lost view of the plane. He held his breath.

A fireball of immense magnitude erupted on the streets below, followed by the horrible roar of death and destruction. The explosion lit up the sky, momentarily providing Walker with the vista of a Hollywood without electricity.

My God . . . My God . . .

What the hell just happened?

Leaning over the rail, he saw the Gomezes also in their front yard, watching the spectacle.

"Are you guys all right?" he called.

Rudy Gomez waved. "Yeah. What's happened? What's going on?" he shouted.

"I don't know!"

No one moved.

They stood and watched as the flames spread and formed into a massive inferno. The noise of the crash died down, leaving the night's eerie silence.

Wait a second, where are the sirens?

Wouldn't there be police cars, ambulances, fire trucks? Even during an outage, cars could be seen on the streets and freeways.

From his deck, Walker could see a small section of the Hollywood Freeway. The I-101 was full of cars, all right, but they weren't moving. No headlights were on.

He quickly rushed into the house, nearly tripped over the chair in front of his computer desk, and went to the kitchen. The outside blaze illuminated the room well enough for him to see what he was doing. He rummaged through a drawer and found the pair of binoculars he knew he had. Returning to the deck, he put them to his eyes and studied the small visible strip of the I-101.

Sure enough, cars were stalled on the road. Owners were standing beside their vehicles. Some held cellphones but were shaking their heads, the body language indicating there was no service. There appeared to be many collisions, too, as if the drivers had suddenly lost the ability to control their cars until they slammed into ones in front. Bumper Cars at an amusement park after the ride was shut down.

Walker swung the binoculars down to the blaze. He couldn't see the collision point, but from the angle and position of the conflagration, Walker guessed the plane had crashed into Beverly Hills.

What a nightmare. How many people were dead? How many more injured? Where were the emergency services?

He scanned what streets he could see. As before, automobiles stood still on the roads, some wrecked into each other, others crashed into buildings or light posts. Pedestrians shouted at each other, waving their arms in frustration.

Walker went back inside and picked up his cellphone.

It was dead.

Back to the deck. He scanned the horizon with the binoculars and pinpointed smaller fires here and there. Clouds of smoke, positioned intermittently, billowed up into the moonlit night sky.

Not a single electric light.

Dead quiet, save for the crackling of the blaze below.

In moments, though, the silence was replaced by distant screams.

WALKER'S JOURNAL

JANUARY 16, 2025

The world has gone to shit outside and my head is splitting with the hangover from hell.

Was it the Koreans?

We should have known.

The fucking government should have seen it coming. Maybe they did, and no one did anything about it. Perhaps no one could do anything about it.

No—the truth is that the bastards surprised us. Just like the Japanese did at Pearl Harbor nearly a hundred years ago.

And what was I doing those precious few hours before we lost everything? Sitting on my ass, getting drunk. I think I might have finished off the entire bottle of Jack. All I know is that it was empty the next time I noticed it, lying on the floor next to the couch.

Everything is fucked. I can't believe what's going on outside. It's the fucking apocalypse.

Fuck the bastards. Fuck the Koreans. Fuck the President. Fuck Congress. Fuck everybody and everything.

Jesus. I thought writing down my thoughts would ease my anger, but it's just making it worse, so I'm going to stop.

Fuck me, too.

SEVEN

JANUARY 19, 2025

Salmusa sat in what he called the "safe house," which was actually another small two-story home located within walking distance of the dwelling in Van Nuys he'd shared with Kianna. He purchased it a year earlier and made the necessary renovations to it in the months prior to the attack. First he insured the garage was shielded against the EMP. Stored inside was a fully gassed 1974 Volkswagen, ready to pull out and drive away anytime Salmusa wanted. Several five-gallon cans of gasoline were also hidden in the garage, the door of which remained locked.

The house itself was stocked with plenty of food and water to last several weeks, if necessary, although Salmusa knew he wouldn't have to stay there too long.

Most important, the house contained three generators that provided enough electricity to give him some light in the office, run a refrigerator, and power his EMP-shielded state-of-the-art computer. The generator ran off gasoline, but he was in no danger of running out before he had to abandon the safe house.

The computer was equipped with a satellite data

card that connected to the Korean spacecraft and back down to earth. Upon arriving at the house on January 16, when chaos ruled the streets, Salmusa tried out the computer to make sure it functioned. The data card connection worked only during specific times of the day, when the satellite moved over North America. There was a good three- to four-hour window in which he could communicate with personnel in Korea, including Kim Jong-un.

The Brilliant Comrade was pleased with the progress. While America "burned," the People's Army sailed across the Pacific in cruisers obtained from Japan and South Korea. They were scheduled to reach California in six more days. Just a day earlier, on the eighteenth, Korean troops landed on the western shores of Hawaii. The infantry quickly mixed with civilians and moved freely through the land. Before the day was over, Pearl Harbor was under Korean control.

The government on the mainland had no way of knowing this.

Salmusa received a report that the ship carrying "the package" would reach Pearl Harbor on schedule the next day, the twentieth. The package, he knew, was a high-yield nuclear weapon. The plan was to move the device on the back of a truck to the middle of a town square in Honolulu, where it would sit in plain sight, unguarded. The message was clear: once the American military learned of the takeover, they would be forced to stand down or Hawaii, and over a million inhabitants, would go the way of the Bikini Atoll.

As he made a hearty breakfast with a hot plate connected to one of the generators, Salmusa thought once again about Kianna's body lying in their old home. The country was littered with the dead. Hundreds, even thousands, died on the highways when the EMP struck. Many airplanes fell out of the sky, killing passengers and people on the ground. The Americans were lucky the Brilliant Comrade had decreed that the EMP occur at night, when most of the population was asleep. Otherwise the death toll would have been far greater. Kim Jong-un had shown great mercy and compassion. It was not his desire to murder Americans. Granted, the collateral damage was an unfortunate necessity—it couldn't be helped.

Salmusa took his coffee cup into the upstairs bedroom, which served as his office. Switching on the computer, which was more than most Americans could do, he opened his encrypted mail server and saw that an e-mail had come from Korea. Salmusa smiled, as it was from the Brilliant Comrade himself. He opened it and read.

Congratulations once again on a job well done. You have served the Greater Korean Republic above and beyond the call of duty. Of course, in the GKR, the call of duty has no ceiling. Dae-Hyun, you have made me proud that you are like a brother to me.

I need not remind you that for the time being you must lay low and not attract attention. Procedures for Operation Water Snake are underway. Once the KPA has established footholds in the United States,

you will be contacted to report to Military Command
to receive further instructions. I trust no other operative to take charge of Operation Water Snake. I
have attached coded, classified documents for you
to study. I suggest you become familiar with the
complete geography, from the north to the south of
the Mississippi River.

I hope to speak to you soon, Salmusa. Keep safe.

Salmusa felt honored and gratified. He knew all
about Operation Water Snake, but he had no idea
Kim Jong-un would choose him to implement it.
It was an important step in the exploitation of the
United States for Korean gain. The undertaking was
also complex and dangerous.

He immediately downloaded the documents and
printed them. He had hours to kill, but it was best to
get started. As the pages emerged from the printer,
Salmusa heard gunshots outside the house. He stood
and walked to the bedroom window, which faced the
street. He carefully pulled back the curtain to see what
was going on.

Two policemen on horseback rode by, obviously
chasing someone. One of the officers held a handgun.

Salmusa had seen the police in the neighborhood.
Since most cars didn't run, many of the cops had taken
to riding horses in the streets to try and maintain law
and order. It was a losing battle. Even though the safe
house was located in a relatively affluent area of Van
Nuys, looters, vandals, and thieves were everywhere.
Posted decrees warned that anyone caught attempting

to break into a home would be shot on sight.

The Korean shook his head and moved away from the window. He took the pages from the printer, sat, and began studying.

WALKER'S JOURNAL

JANUARY 20, 2025

I don't know how to put into words the things I've seen over the past three days. I haven't attempted to write in the journal since the EMP blast because I've been too busy trying to find out what the fuck is going on.

That's right, an EMP blast. An electromagnetic pulse, caused by a thermonuclear explosion. No one knows much right now, and there's no way to get news from other parts of the country, but the word on the street is that the Koreans did it. I'd say that's as good a guess as any. I can't think of anyone else who'd have the balls to do such a thing. I've been saying for years that Kim Jong-un and his "Greater Korean Republic" was Public Enemy #1. Our stupid government acknowledged the threat but they never really did anything about it. To be fair, they probably couldn't. Our country just didn't have the might and influence it once had.

Anyway, the first day—January 16—was a horror story. All of America panicked, I imagine. Los Angeles certainly did. In the morning, people woke up to the shock of their lives. Imagine this—there's

*no electricity, no running water, and you can't flush
a toilet. Your car won't start because all the circuitry
is fried. Telephones don't work—neither cellphones
nor landlines. Gas stoves and heaters don't work.
Needless to say, you can't check e-mail, get online, or
turn on your computer. And that's just in the privacy
of your home. Outside it's a nightmare beyond your
wildest dreams.*

*You try to go to work, if you have—or had—a
job, and you walk, hitchhike, or just don't go. If you
make it there, you find out your place of employment
is closed due to lack of power. So you go to the ATM
to get some cash, and guess what? ATMs don't work
either. Your money is stuck, FROZEN inside the bank,
which, of course, is closed.*

*You walk to the nearest grocery store and find
that, miraculously, it's open. Police are attempting
to keep hundreds of customers in a line that stretches
around the block. They take cash only. Credit cards
are worthless. Unruly folks get hit with a baton. Best
to stay away. Besides, everything will be gone in less
than 24 hours.*

And that's just everything I found out on the first day.

*On the second day, the 17th, I decided to take my
chances and walk two miles down the hill toward
Hollywood. I should have taken a weapon. I don't
own a weapon, but I should've taken something—a
knife, baseball bat, a hammer. I got down to Franklin
and saw throngs of angry people in the streets
up ahead. Hollywood Boulevard was a madhouse.
Looters were busy breaking in to shops and taking*

everything in sight. Liquor stores were hit the hardest. They tried to get into closed banks, but no one could get into the vaults.

Everywhere you looked, stalled or crashed automobiles sat blocking the roads. If you could imagine a giant kid playing with a bunch of toy cars and trucks, and then he dumped them all on the floor—that's what it looked like.

Police rode horses and did their best to control the crowds. I got there in time to see them throwing tear gas canisters at the mob. Someone told me the crowd overpowered three policemen in downtown LA. The cops may have been beaten to death, I don't know. I could only imagine what was going on in South Central and other poorer neighborhoods.

I hightailed it back to my house. I'd had enough adventure for one day. There was plenty of food in the pantry for, well, a little while. Maybe a week. I hope. Unfortunately, everything in my fridge is going to spoil. I went over to check on the Gomezes. Luisa told me Rudy is very depressed and won't get out of bed. I asked her if they had enough to eat for a few days. She didn't give me a straight answer, but it sounded as if they'd be okay. I could tell she was worried about her husband. The kids looked all right, just scared.

You know what? I'm scared, too.

That night, a policeman on horseback rode through the Hollywood Hills, shouting through one of those handheld loudspeakers. He told people to stay inside their homes. There was a curfew from 8:00 pm to 7:00 am. Looters would be shot on sight. Anyone caught on the streets after dark would suffer serious consequences. Questions asked later.

Apparently a lot of fires flared up around the city. As it's winter and not the warmest time of the year, some people actually tried to build a fire in their house—with no fireplace—and ended up burning the place to the ground. In other cases, arson was the probable cause.

I couldn't imagine what it was like in a cold city like Chicago or New York.

My God, is this Judgment Day? Is this what they were talking about when Revelations was written?

The next day, the 18th, I walked in a different direction, toward a strip mall area I thought would be more civilized. The convenience store there was empty, completely looted. A gas station had been torched. People milled around with looks of despair on their faces. I saw grown men crying.

I recognized a cop I know, a guy I used for tips when I was Celebrity Trashing. His name is McDaniel. I don't know his first name. Anyway, he recognized me, too, and we started talking. He gave me a leaflet from the mayor's office. They're circulating all over the city. That's how I found out about the EMP. It said there was a nuclear explosion over the United States. Since no one can get any information from anybody, anywhere, it's all speculation. But apparently some noted scientist-type issued a statement that the mayor adopted, so it was copied by hand on hundreds of these leaflets—and these are slowly spreading through LA with the help of the police.

The hard facts were laid out on the flyer: Our SCADA systems are dead. These are the Supervisory Control and Data Acquisition Systems. They control electrical transmission and distribution, water management, and oil and gas pipelines across the U.S. Additionally, the power grids all over the country are fried. When you think about how much of the minutiae in our daily lives depend on these things, you can see how we are up shit creek.

It was going to take months, maybe years, to repair it all.

But that was the good news. It CAN be repaired.

The leaflet urged any mechanics and electrical engineers to make their way to various listed locations in the city to begin work. Individuals who have the ability to fix automobiles were encouraged to rebuild the ignition systems in their cars. There were calls for volunteers to help with all sorts of other issues such as medical problems, street cleanup, and food preparation.

I asked McDaniel what he knew about other parts of Los Angeles. South Central, for example. He shook his head. Said the gangs are running rampant. One group killed several cops on horseback.

He told me some cars are working. Either they were parked in a shielded location, or the owners already had necessary parts and knew how to repair them quickly. He said the police force was pulling vintage vehicles out of "retirement" because they'd be easier to repair. Not many are in working order, though. I mentioned that I have a motorcycle with little to

*repair. The Spitfire's magneto for the 2 spark plugs
and the alternator to charge the battery were apparently immune to the EMP. The prospect of getting it
running cheered me up, if anything could.*

*McDaniel told me about the plane crash in Beverly
Hills. It destroyed numerous celebrity mansions.
Estimated death toll is 650. McDaniel said it wasn't
the only plane that fell out of the sky that night. He
didn't know what happened in other parts of the
country, but apparently there were PLENTY of awful
crashes near LAX. The pilots tried to guide the planes
toward the airport in the hopes of crash-landing on
a runway. One managed to do so, but it still killed
everyone on board. At least five hit residential neighborhoods. A couple overshot LAX and went down in
the Pacific past El Segundo. A private Gulfstream carrying one of the Lakers wiped out Santa Monica Pier.*

*My friend relayed more disturbing news. Asians
were being attacked in the streets. Koreans were the
targets, but it didn't matter. Japanese, Vietnamese,
Chinese—if someone is Asian, there's a strong likelihood that venturing into the street could be fatal.
McDaniel said a white mob stormed Koreatown last
night and tore it to pieces. They set fire to shops and
restaurants, chased Koreans out of their homes, and
even lynched a few. McDaniel feared we're on the
verge of an all-out race war. He said a lot of uniforms
were ready to write off anything south of Jefferson
and east of Figueroa as a lost cause.*

Everything was worse than I first thought.

And what about normal, peace loving, intelligent,

and sensible folks? Like me? How were we going to cope with the madness?

It was all so overwhelming.

Some of the parks are filling up with refugees. I guess that's the right word. Can you imagine being a refugee in your own town? Griffith Park is now a campground, and not a very safe one, either. Armed men alternate guard duty. The police turn a blind eye to weapons in the open if the bearer looks like a "normal" person who is simply trying to protect his family.

Shootings, however, happen everywhere. It's like we're back in the Wild West. McDaniel said some neighborhoods are already instituting local "sheriffs and deputies" who keep anyone off the block who doesn't belong. There's no way the police can handle it all. McDaniel hoped the National Guard will be called in, but he didn't see that happening for a while. The government has to figure out how to communicate again.

As I walked back to my house, I found my anger over what happened was still brewing, but different emotions were starting to take over. McDaniel's leaflet showed me there are still people who care and that something is being done about our situation. But nothing is going to happen overnight. The obstacles are monstrous. It's going to take cooperation and good will. No one can afford to be selfish.

So what did I do the next day, on the 19th? Nothing. I stayed home and brooded. I felt sorry for myself and for the rest of America. Now it's the 20th, and I'm about to go down to my garage and start tinkering on the Spitfire. Maybe I can fix it. Not sure what I'll do with it; someone would just try to stop me in the street and steal it. Probably kill me, too.

Where is the president? What's he doing right now? Is he alive? The East Coast is a fucking long way from here. Anything could have happened over there. The Norks might have nuked Washington or New York. How are we to know?

Do the Koreans, if that's who's responsible, really think they can get away with this? What do they expect to achieve? I can't believe they'd attempt an actual invasion—that just seems preposterous. Sure, I know they have the largest standing army in the world—but still, America is a big fucking country.

Nah, that's not going to happen.

But as I sit and write this and wish I had another bottle of Jack to keep me company, I'm starting to think it can.

Korea's not going to do something like this to us and then just leave us alone.

Would you?

EIGHT

A week after the EMP attack, Los Angeles was in a state of anarchy. An entire societal system had denigrated to a primal level in just seven days. It was extremely dangerous to venture into public. Gangs of thieves roamed the streets, robbing—and sometimes killing—anyone who looked as if they might be holding food or water. The police had all but given up. It was a losing battle. Without the benefit of squad cars, proper supplies, radio equipment, and manpower, law enforcement personnel were at such a disadvantage that most officers threw in the towel and went home.

Without electricity, hospitals and medical facilities couldn't cope with the sick and wounded. Patients who were already on dialysis or hooked up to life-support machinery had no chance. People died by the hundreds on a daily basis. Fear of uncontrolled disease and pestilence kept doctors and nurses away as well. It was as if the Black Plague had made a return appearance and no one wanted to take a chance of catching it.

A related problem was that the city was littered with corpses. Some were in their homes, many in the streets, others still sitting in their wrecked automobiles on the roads. Cleanup crews simply had not got around to removing all the bodies and properly disposing of them—and stray dogs were having a field day for meals. Since schools were closed, many high school gymnasiums were turned into morgues. The mayor finally issued a decree that corpses would be cremated in mass funeral pyres built in school football fields. Attempting to identify bodies was a lost cause. In most cases, however, no one cared about the carrion. The stench permeating the city was overpowering.

In area prisons, it was impossible to control the inmates' rage. When the EMP hit, prisoners were in their cells. But because cell doors operated by electricity, the guards had no way to open them; thus the prisoners were forced to remain locked up. They didn't like it, and after a couple of days they let it be known. In addition, the kitchens ceased to operate, so there was no food. The stronger inmates murdered weaker cellmates in protest. The guards, facing an intolerable situation, left the prisoners to live or die on their own. Survival of the fittest.

After seven days, even the city authorities became disenchanted. No one was on salary anymore—there was no way to get paid. With banks inoperable, all work was on a volunteer basis. The tasks, such as clearing corpses and disposing of them at the ad-hoc morgues, were thankless and disgusting jobs. Many well-intentioned souls gave it a couple of days' effort and then couldn't take it anymore. With police dropping out of the game, elected officials also threw up their hands in defeat and walked away.

No one was in charge.

* * *

Walker had spent the previous few days in his home, not venturing out except to get a bit of fresh air—but even that was in short supply. The stink of the city had grown worse with each passing day. With no city services at work, the sanitary conditions had gone to hell. Standing on his deck, the smell wafting up from Hollywood was nothing less than that of an overflowing toilet. He had heard portable latrines were distributed around the city, but without vehicles to carry them, it was a long and difficult process. Walker himself had to determine a way to get rid of waste. He was lucky in that he had a bit of yard in front and back of his house. He dug holes in the backyard and buried it. He supposed other home owners could do the same thing, but thousands upon thousands of people in the Los Angeles area lived in apartments. What were they supposed to do? There were over eighteen million people in the LA urban sprawl. In seven days, that many human beings could produce a lot of shit.

No wonder it smelled bad outside.

He'd also spent his time maintaining the motorcycle. He had all the parts and tools he needed in his garage, but because the bike was an older model, there wasn't serious damage. On the third day of work, it was ready. The Spitfire started on the first kick.

The sound of the motor was like music to his ears.

The rest of the day Walker spent considering his options. He was sick and tired of his house, even though he'd been stuck there only a week. Now that he had wheels, he could take off and leave the stench of Los Angeles behind him. But where would he go? The rest of the country was probably no better off than Southern California. But how did he know? Things might be better farther east.

On the other hand, how would he survive? The Spitfire held four gallons of gas. Would he be able to obtain more on the road? He had very little cash. Would it have value outside of LA? Walker also knew he was not a guy who liked to "rough it." He never enjoyed camping, didn't know jack shit about surviving in the wilderness, and couldn't start a fire without matches to save his life. He was a city boy, completely addicted to modern accommodations. He was good with tools and considered himself an amateur tinkerer, but he'd never be able to build himself a log cabin.

As afternoon eased into evening, Walker came to the conclusion he was better off staying put. Nothing worked in his home, but at least it was familiar. And so far, no one had bothered him. His house was remote enough that burglars and squatters had yet to make their way up into the hills.

But they could come one day. What would he do then? How would he defend himself and his property?

Walker had considered buying a gun a few years ago, when he'd had to do some reporting in questionable areas of the city. Now he kicked himself. At least a weapon would skew the odds of survival a little more in his favor.

Putting those thoughts aside, he went to the kitchen to take stock of what food remained. There were two more boxes of cereal in the pantry. He'd been eating the stuff dry. Wasn't bad. Three liters of bottled water left. The crackers were gone. Everything in the fridge was consumed. He'd even eaten all the candy in the house.

Not much left.

Walker thought of the Gomezes and wondered how they were getting along. He hadn't seen them in a few days. In fact, he'd seen none of his neighbors. He rarely saw them anyway, since the houses were so far apart—but it was unusual not to see the Gomezes every other day or so.

He decided to take a box of cereal over and share it with them. Maybe they had some other food they could trade. They all had to be humanitarians to survive, right?

Walker grabbed a cereal box and left the house. To get to the Gomezes, he had to walk down the gravel drive to the road and then follow it about thirty or forty yards to their drive. He noted that the smell wasn't so bad in front of the house, which faced the hills and countryside. The back of his home, and the deck, faced the city. That direction was what reeked.

He approached the Gomezes' house and went up the walk to the front door. He knocked and called, "Rudy? Luisa? It's me, Ben."

Silence.

He tried again, louder. Still no answer.

Had they left? The garage door was closed, so he couldn't tell if their old station wagon was inside or not.

Walker tried knocking one more time, a little harder— and this time the door pushed open. It wasn't locked.

He peered inside. Nothing in the front foyer and short hallway leading to the living room.

"Rudy? Luisa?" He couldn't remember the kids' names. "Anyone home?"

Well, hell, he thought. Might as well take a look. Maybe there was food in their pantry. If they were going to split and leave the door unlocked . . . And wasn't it better that a friend and neighbor raid their kitchen rather than some vagrant?

As soon as he stepped inside, a putrid odor bombarded Walker and made him gag. He heard the sound of flies buzzing around him.

Oh no . . .

In his heart of hearts, he knew what he would find inside the house, but he didn't want to believe it.

"Rudy? Luisa?"

Walker put a hand to his nose and mouth, and then he walked slowly toward the living room. The horror he found there made him drop the box of cereal and vomit on the floor.

Rudy Gomez was sitting in a comfy chair, but his head—what was left of it—was a gooey mess of dried blood and gray matter. He was still holding the shotgun between his legs.

After Walker recovered from his nausea, he stood and braced himself against the wall. "Oh, Rudy. What have you done?"

He turned toward the hallway leading to the bedrooms. Dreading what he would discover, he moved at a snail's pace toward the closed doors. He went to the master bedroom first. He placed his hand on the knob, took a deep breath, and opened the door.

Luisa Gomez was lying on the bed. Her brains were all over the mattress and wall behind her.

Walker closed the door and stifled a sob.

Trying the other bedroom doors was superfluous, but he had to do it just to bring closure to what he'd seen so far. Both Gomez children—the teenage boy and the younger girl—were dead in their own beds.

Gomez, in despair, must have killed his family and then turned the gun on himself.

It was too horrible to fully comprehend.

Walker rushed to the foyer and started to leave—but then he remembered the cereal box he'd dropped. Normally he might have run out of the house screaming, or perhaps dialed 911 *first* and then fled in terror. But the cereal was too precious a commodity to leave behind. He steeled himself to return to the sepulchre that was once a family living room and retrieve the box. He didn't dare glance at Rudy Gomez a second time.

Only after he got back to his house did Walker realize that a more valuable commodity would have been the shotgun, but he wasn't about to return to the scene of the crime and retrieve it. It was covered with Gomez's dried blood and who knew what else. Dismissing the thought, Walker dropped on his sofa and stared at the blank television. He knew he was in shock. Nothing he'd seen during the past week had prepared him for *that*. The hellishness of what he'd seen in the streets was *nothing* compared to what he'd uncovered next door.

And what was he going to do about it?

Nothing.

Absolutely nothing.

What could he do? The Gomezes were dead. There was no ambulance to call, no police to phone. He supposed he could dig graves in their backyard and bury them, but he didn't want to go near the bodies. They were bloated and putrefied. Probably been dead two or three days. It was Bacteria Heaven over there.

No, he wasn't going to do anything at all.

And that thought struck him profoundly.

He had left a revolting scene of carnage, simply returned to his home, and plopped down on the sofa. If he'd had a cold beer, he would have popped it open and turned on the television.

How could his soul have degenerated to such uncaring nonchalance?

Walker stood, opened the glass door to the deck, and stepped outside.

It would be dark soon. The only lights in the city below him were fires. The silence in the air was the sound of death.

It was time for a change.

Walker would risk it; he would take his motorcycle and head east.

WALKER'S JOURNAL

JANUARY 23? 24?, 2025

Okay, I'm ready to go.

Not sure what time it is, my watch doesn't work anymore either. It's either just before midnight on the 23rd or it's already the 24th. All I know is it's dark outside. Even though there's a curfew, I'm going to take the chance.

Where am I going? Hell, I don't know. I'm just heading east. I want to leave this godforsaken place.

I stuffed what I could take in a backpack—my remaining bottles of water, some baggies filled with cereal, a box of matches, a tiny first-aid kit with band-aids and ibuprofen, binoculars, some extra clothing, what toiletries I felt were necessary, sunscreen, some kitchen stuff—eating utensils, a few plastic plates, and a cup.

I strapped a metal toolbox, a sleeping bag, and two 5-gallon cans of gas on the back of my bike. It was all I could fit. I'm also taking a Swiss Army knife and the only other "weapon" I could find—a big blade meant for carving turkeys. I cut some pieces of canvas and stapled them together to form a sheath. This I tied around my right calf. If I have to, I can draw the knife *fairly easily. I hope to God it never comes to that.*

I have an LA Dodgers baseball cap, so I put that on. It's not going to provide much protection from the sun, but it's better than nothing. Maybe along the way I can find a cowboy hat or something.

Luckily I never threw out my paper folding maps of the LA area. They're out of date, but the main roads will still be there. I'm going to avoid the Interstates. That's where the worst trouble will be. I figure I'll go up to 134 and head toward Pasadena and then on to San Bernardino. Maybe conditions are better out that way. I have no idea what I'll find. There's an old Marine base out in the desert, north of Palm Springs and a town called Twentynine Palms. I know it's been closed for a few years, but maybe I can find some refuge there. Maybe there's still a military contingent there. It's a plan, at any rate.

So it's goodbye to Los Angeles, for now anyway. Hopefully someday I can return. Something tells me, though, that this is it. It's weird saying "so long" to all my stuff and the house my mom owned. I never thought this would happen, but I have to face facts. I'm out of here. Even though there are still millions of people alive in LA, I know I'm leaving a ghost town.

There's nothing here for me anymore.

NINE

Walker set out taking side roads up to Glendale. With a motorcycle, it was easy to navigate around the maze of abandoned cars in the streets, but it was slow going. He was forced to keep his speed under thirty miles an hour. It would have been impossible to escape the urban sprawl in a full-sized automobile.

He prayed he wouldn't run into policemen who might shoot him for being out past curfew. Worse than that would be to run into any of the roving gangs of "outlaws" he'd heard about. As it was the middle of the night, the odds were in his favor.

It was deathly quiet and very, very dark. Only the rumble of the Spitfire's engine broke the silence. The bike's headlight was the only illumination aside from the moon and stars.

The night air was chilly. Walker wore a brown leather bomber jacket, gloves, a scarf around his neck and lower face, and sunglasses. Goggles would have been better than the sunglasses, which made driving at night more difficult. He'd left a pair in his garage without thinking.

When he got to Glendale, he turned east on

Highway 134. Up ahead a bonfire raged on the side of the road. People huddled around it. Walker debated whether he should find an alternate route or take his chances and go on. He paused and idled for a moment as he dug into the backpack for his binoculars. Raising them to his eyes, he determined the folks around the fire appeared harmless. They were all middle-aged men, probably homeless, simply trying to keep warm. Walker put the binoculars away and rode forward. There was a clear path in the highway, allowing him to increase his speed. As he drove past the bonfire, the men shouted at him, pointing, amazed to see a vehicle that worked. They wanted him to stop but Walker kept going. No time to chitchat. Besides, they might not be as friendly as they looked.

As he reached Pasadena, the highway became Interstate-210. Many more deserted cars and trucks scattered the road, creating obstacles that slowed him down. It took nearly three hours to get to Arcadia, and by that time the sun was rising.

Nature called, so Walker risked stopping to take a leak. It didn't really matter where he halted; the web of cars on the highway provided plenty of privacy. He parked beside a van, stood in between it and another car, and did his business.

But just as he was zipping up, a gunshot cracked nearby. Walker flinched as he felt the heat of the round hit the side of the van near his head.

The road wasn't so private after all.

Walker ducked and rushed to his bike. Another shot shattered a window on the van. He jumped on, turned the key, and slammed his boot on the kick-start.

The cycle didn't start. The engine coughed as if it had emphysema.

Walker cursed and looked behind him. He made out three figures running toward him. One of them whooped and hollered, as if they'd caught themselves breakfast.

He kicked the start again. This time the engine revved—but died again.

What the hell was wrong?

Another gunshot punctured one of the extra gas cans on the back of the bike. Precious fuel poured out as if a spigot was turned on.

Walker stomped the kick-start again, and it caught on the third try. He gunned it, and the Spitfire shot forward between the obstacles in his way. The pursuers shouted in anger. More gunfire. It was the first time in his life Walker had to run from men shooting at him.

He didn't slow down until his hunters were mere specks in the distance. Steering more cautiously now, he was back to the excruciating thirty-mile-per-hour speed.

It was around Azusa that he stopped again to check out the damage to the gas can. He removed and shook it. It was empty so he tossed the can on the road and climbed back on the bike.

He figured he had less than a half tank. The other five-gallon can would help, but he doubted he could make it to the following day without filling up somewhere. The Spitfire got good gas mileage at higher speeds; the snail's pace was killing him.

Walker studied his map for an alternate route. It wasn't a detailed street map—it only displayed the major roads and highways. In the end he decided it was too risky to venture off the Interstate. There was no telling what the side streets were like and he wasn't familiar with the territory.

He took a moment's pause to eat a little breakfast. Walker had made a vow to exercise discipline and conserve his food and water. He took only a couple of handfuls of cereal, which left him hungrier than before he stopped. After one swig of water, he was ready to move on.

By mid-morning, Walker noticed more people walking along the highway, all headed east. There were groups of varying sizes consisting of men, women, and children. Some of the men carried rifles. Walker figured they were regular folks, just trying to get away from the horrors of the city. Many of them waved as he rode past. Walker waved back.

By noon Walker was in San Bernardino. The plan was to take I-210 as it curved to the south and merge onto I-10 toward Palm Springs. Once there, he'd take Route 62 up to Twentynine Palms and look for the Marine Corps training grounds at Camp Wilson. Walker was aware it was probably a desolate, empty hellhole in the desert, but there was a chance some military personnel might be present along with a little more law and order.

As Walker rode past Redlands, the labyrinth of abandoned cars on the highway diminished. There were still enough to keep him from increasing to a speed over forty, but the road wasn't nearly as dense with derelicts. To his surprise, he encountered a group of three men and two women with a working Toyota, likely a model from the early 1990s. They had stopped to push a BMW out of the way so they could drive past it. Walker was amazed they'd managed to navigate through the network of dead automobiles this far.

He stopped to help them.

Together, the six of them tipped the BMW on its side and rolled it over. This provided enough space for the Toyota to get through.

"Much obliged," one of the men said.

"You have any food?" a woman asked.

"I'm sorry," Walker answered. He knew if he started sharing what little cereal he had with anyone on the road, it wouldn't last through the next meal.

At Moreno Valley, Walker passed a makeshift road-side eatery run by Mexicans. They had erected a picnic umbrella and had a portable tamale cart. A big sign read: Tamales—$10 each. A few walk-up customers sat at two picnic tables by the stand. Apparently the Mexicans were doing fair business.

The price was outrageous, but the thought of tamales made Walker's mouth water. He hadn't had hot food in a week. It was too tempting to pass up.

Rather than taking the chance of losing the motor-cycle, Walker got off at the next exit, turned into a closed gas station, and rode around to the back. There was nothing there but a couple of junker cars without wheels and a lot of garbage. He stopped, cut the ignition, and chained the bike to the axle of one of the cars. He then walked to the feeder road and headed back the mile-and-a-half to the tamale stand.

There was a family of three at one of the picnic tables—a man, woman, and a boy who appeared to be around six. Two older Hispanic men sat at the other table. They were all chowing down on the food, which smelled delicious.

A Mexican couple manned the stand. The man greeted Walker in Spanish and seemed friendly enough. Walker ordered one tamale. It was small, but he was hungry; a hot tamale was manna from heaven. The couple also sold warm soda cans for five dollars each. Walker decided to splurge.

He approached the family of three and asked, "Mind if I join you?"

The patriarch replied, "Be our guest."

Walker sat across from them, opened the soda can, and took a sip. Even warm, the cola was like nectar from the gods. The tamale was hot, fresh, and perfect. He took his time, savoring small bites so it would last as long as possible.

"Where you headed?" the man asked.

"I don't really know," Walker answered truthfully.

"I noticed you came from the east. Where'd you come *from*?"

"Oh, I—" He started to tell them he was traveling away from LA, but he didn't want to reveal ownership of a motorcycle. "Uhm, I live right here in Moreno Valley. I was holding out spending any money all week, but finally the thought of a hot tamale got the best of me. So here I am."

"Is it true about the gangs in this area?"

Walker wasn't sure what to say. "Gangs?"

The man looked at his wife and nodded. "We've heard there are motorcycle gangs between here and Palm Springs. Outlaws. They stop people and rob them. If you put up a fight, they kill you."

"Or worse," the wife added.

Walker understood what she meant. "I haven't seen any. They have motorcycles that run?"

The man took a sip of his own soda and answered, "More and more people are repairing their cars and trucks. It's not that hard, especially on older models. It's the newer computerized ones that are the problem."

"I wonder how long it's going to take to get the country back in order."

The man shot Walker a look. "Are you crazy? The country will *never* be back in order. It won't ever be the way it *was*, that's for sure. The Norks really did a number on us."

"We're certain it was the Koreans?"

"Yeah. I have a buddy in Burbank—that's where we're from—who has a ham radio in his basement. The EMP didn't affect it. He told me he heard a broadcast every now and then by someone with the Emergency Broadcast System. I don't know how they're able to transmit any messages because the entire radio network across the country is wiped out. But there must be transmitters here and there that somehow happened to be protected. They were in a shelter or something. Anyway, he said it was confirmed by Washington that the Koreans were responsible."

"That's what I thought, too," Walker said.

"There's a rumor they've landed in Hawaii."

"Really?"

The man shrugged. "It's just people talking."

Walker ate in silence for a few minutes. When the meager meal was finished, he asked, "Where are you folks going?"

"We're gonna try and make it to Phoenix. Nancy has family there." He indicated his wife.

"By the way, I'm Ben Walker." He held out his hand. The man shook it and introduced themselves as the Pattersons. Walker glanced at the two Hispanic customers at the other table. They had finished their meals and were now smoking cigarettes, refusing to make eye contact with him or the other Caucasians. It wasn't surprising. Race relations had deteriorated in the LA area over the last couple of decades due to anti-Immigration laws and hostile sentiment. Walker didn't think it made much difference now. What was happening in America was going to seriously affect Mexico and Canada—not to mention the rest of the world. It was more important than ever for people to try and get along.

As Walker rose to clean up and throw away the trash, the sound of motorcycles attracted everyone's attention. From the feeder road, coming from the east.

"Uh oh," Mr. Patterson said.

Sure enough, it was a gang of seven rough-looking guys on Harleys. They were heavily tattooed, big and overweight, and carried automatic weapons.

Holy shit.

Everyone at the tamale stand froze.

The one leading the pack held up his arm to signal a turnoff. The seven bikes slowed and stopped in front of the tamale stand.

"What did I tell you?" Patterson whispered.

"Shhh," Walker said.

The men were dirty and greasy—probably hadn't bathed since before the EMP. Their rank odor permeated the area, even outdoors. The leader was missing an eye and didn't wear a patch.

"What have we here?" he bellowed. "Tamales! Boys, we're having lunch on me!" The men cheered and got off their bikes.

Walker glanced at the Mexican couple that ran the stand. They smiled nervously at the gang members.

One-Eye approached the stand while the others assumed positions. Two men watched the road in both directions. One guy with a badly pock-marked face stayed with the leader. The other three kept watch on the customers at the picnic tables.

"How many tamales you got in there, amigo?" the leader asked.

The proprietor opened the cart and counted. He answered in Spanish.

"I'm sorry, I didn't quite get that. Can you speak *English* like an *American*?"

The Mexican couldn't.

Walker answered for him. "He said there were twenty-three left."

One-Eye slowly turned toward Walker and gave him a long, hard stare. Walker thought it best to look away and sit quietly.

"*Thank* you, buddy. I guess you're one of them immigrant-lovers, seein' as how you know their language and everything." He turned back to the couple. "We'll take all the tamales and all your sodas. We're mighty hungry." The men murmured in agreement.

The owners grabbed plates and started piling on the food.

"Uh, we want those *to go*," the leader said.

The Mexican understood that. He nodded quickly and pulled out brown paper bags while his wife wrapped the tamales. In a couple of minutes, the leader distributed the food to his men. Then the proprietor made the mistake of telling the biker how much it cost.

"What was that? I didn't quite catch what you said."

The Mexican grabbed a little notepad and pencil and scribbled "$310," tore off the slip, and handed it to One-Eye, smiling broadly.

Walker winced as the other customers at the tables shared worried glances. The tension was palpable.

The leader turned to his gang and said, "Boys, we owe the man three hundred and ten dollars. Anyone got their credit card handy?"

The men grunted.

One-Eye turned back to the Mexicans, crumpled the "bill" in his fist, and dropped it. That was a cue for Pock-Face to draw his semi-automatic and point it at the Mexican couple. The woman shrieked and they immediately raised their hands. The owner shook his head and spoke in Spanish, pleading with the biker not to rob them.

"Hand over what cash you have," One-Eye commanded. "At ten dollars a pop, I suspect you've made quite a killing."

The little Patterson boy started to cry. His mother did her best to shield his eyes and keep him quiet.

The vendor continued to babble in Spanish. One-Eye turned to the fattest of the men watching the customers and jerked his head. The minion moved to the couple behind the stand and said, "Out of the way." He pushed the couple to the side and dug into the box where they kept the cash.

The Mexican's voice turned threatening as his wife attempted to stop him. She beseeched her husband to move back but he shrugged her off. Cursing at the bikers in Spanish, the man drew a revolver from underneath his loose jacket, pointed it at the fat man, and fired before anyone could react.

The fat man screamed as the round drilled through his shoulder blade, perforated his massive chest, and exited his breast with such speed and force that it also hit Pock-Face. Blood spurted over the tamale stand and money. Pock-Face flinched and reflexively fired his pistol into the air.

The Mexican swerved the revolver at One-Eye, but by then the rest of the gang had their weapons out.

Walker shouted, "Get down!" as he leapt for the

ground. The Pattersons and the Hispanic customers followed suit just as a hail of bullets caught the tamale stand vendors, both man and wife. The barrage was deafening. Walker kept low, covering his ears and shutting his eyes in terror. It seemed as if the gunfire lasted for minutes.

Finally, there was silence, save for the moaning of the one man who was wounded. The fat man was flat on the ground, dead. The Mexican couple lay in a rapidly spreading pool of blood, their bodies dotted with holes from head to toe.

Walker remained where he was. His ears rang.

"The rest of you, get up!" the leader shouted.

Walker felt a boot kick him in the side. He looked up to see the remaining bikers pointing their weapons at the customers.

Oh God, this is it. I'm going to die.

"Stand up!"

They all did as they were told. The Patterson woman held her son against her leg and hip as he sobbed. Walker, Patterson, and the two Hispanics raised their hands.

One-Eye surveyed the small group and focused on the two Hispanics.

"Looks like we missed a couple of illegal immigrants, boys," he said. Without warning, he raised his pistol and shot both men in their heads—*one, two*. The Patterson woman screamed again. Her husband grabbed hold of his wife and son and hugged them close. Walker was too shocked to move.

Pock-Face now didn't seem bothered by what was

apparently a minor wound in the arm or shoulder. One Eye ordered, "Search 'em." With bloody hands, Pock-Face went through the dead Hispanics' pockets. He took what money was there and gave it to One-Eye.

The head biker then turned to the Pattersons and Walker.

"Empty your pockets, folks."

They had no choice but to comply. Walker placed his wallet on the picnic table. He took a gamble by not handing over the Spitfire key, though. Hopefully the bikers wouldn't notice it.

Patterson also handed over his cash. He gently prodded his wife to place her purse on the table.

"Empty the purse, lady."

Patterson did it for her. It contained a few makeup supplies, a small photo album, and a billfold. One-Eye took all the wallets and removed the money. He knew the credit cards were useless. The man then turned to the Pattersons and focused on the woman. He reached out and touched her cheek. She trembled in fear.

"You're kinda pretty, lady," he said. "Why don't you ditch this guy and come with us. I guarantee we'll have a lot more fun."

Patterson wisely didn't say a word. His wife wouldn't look at the biker.

"No? Suit yourself." One-Eye then turned to the fat man's motorcycle. "Guess we don't need this anymore." He aimed his pistol at it and shot both tires flat and blew a hole in the gas tank. He then turned to the Pattersons and Walker and said, "Oh, could you have used that? I'm sorry. I wasn't thinking."

The other men laughed. They didn't seem to care about their fallen comrade.

One Eye glared at his victims. "You know we outta shoot all of you. Shouldn't leave any witnesses, you understand. But seein' how there's no law and order anymore, I doubt anyone's gonna come after us. So you have yourselves a nice day."

With that, he jerked his head at his men. They all boarded their Harleys with bags of tamales in hand, kick-started the bikes noisily, and rode away.

The Patterson boy wailed. Walker realized he'd been holding his breath and finally exhaled. They all sat, too shaken to respond.

An eternity passed.

The silence finally got to Walker, so he stood, nodded at Patterson and said, "Good luck to you." Not waiting for a reply, he walked east toward the gas station where he'd left his bike. The Pattersons remained where they were.

The Spitfire pushed onward, southeast on I-10 toward Palm Springs. Still stunned by what had happened at the tamale stand, Walker had to stop and vomit. Perhaps it was because of whatever was in the tamales. Could have been dog meat for all he knew. On second thought, he figured he'd have been sicker if that was the case. This was nerves.

After resting a minute, he moved on. The highway remained covered with deserted automobiles, although every now and then Walker noticed one contained a body or two. Most likely the corpses had been there since the blast.

The sun was low in the sky when he reached Palm Springs. He stopped and emptied what was left of his last gas can into the Spitfire's tank. Now he was out, which was worrisome. Every gas station he'd passed was shut down. He hadn't seen any black market dispensaries in abandoned stations that entrepreneurs had set up before the blast. Hopefully he'd catch a break and find something the following day.

As it was getting dark and he was dead tired, Walker had to consider where he would sleep that night. The trek had been much more difficult than he'd imagined. With the stress of navigating the tricky vehicle-littered roads, the sudden release of adrenaline at the tamale stand, getting sick, and not having enough food, Walker felt shaken. He had to call it a day.

He got off the highway and rode into Palm Springs. The resort hotels would be closed, of course, but Walker wanted to find a place off the beaten path—it would be safer. He passed the usual assortment of homeless people standing around burning barrels. Some waved, most didn't. The town itself was dead, which he hadn't expected. Where was everyone?

At one point he passed an ancient graffiti-covered billboard that advertised the dew drop motel. It was three miles down a side road. Walker wondered if it still existed. Even if it was closed, maybe there was a vacancy. He almost laughed at the thought.

He turned and followed the street to an eerie, dilapidated business zone. But sure enough, the Dew Drop

Motel still stood. It looked as if no one had stayed there since before the Millennium.

It was perfect.

He drove around to the back and stopped. Walker got off the bike, picked a ground floor room, and kicked at the door. It took three tries, but the lock finally broke. He rolled the bike into the room and shut the door. He dug into the backpack for the matchbox. He lit one and examined his accommodations. A mattress and box springs—no sheets. Tattered drapes covered the window. That was good. The musty, moldy smell he'd have to live with. He checked the bathroom. Surprisingly, the toilet bowl had water in it, even though it was brown.

What? No towels? No television? What kind of a place is this?

"I want my money back, god damnit," he muttered aloud, and laughed half-heartedly.

He spent the next five minutes shoving the dresser against the broken door so no one could surprise him. Once he felt safe, Walker took off his clothes, unrolled the sleeping bag on top of the mattress, and climbed inside.

He was asleep in minutes.

TEN

JANUARY 24, 2025

It started with two gunshots and shouting.

Salmusa heard the commotion outside and checked the time on a battery-powered clock. It was close to eleven-thirty. Dressed in his pajamas, he got up and cautiously looked out the safe house's upstairs bedroom window. Two horses carrying policemen stood next to each other in the street. Studying the officers' body language, Salmusa determined they were looking for someone.

For some reason, thieves had run rampant in Van Nuys. Salmusa thought more affluent areas of the city would have been targets; perhaps they were, but he never expected this middle-class community in the San Fernando Valley to have so much crime. The house across the street was broken into a few days ago while occupants were inside. The intruders killed the family before ransacking the place. Police on horses arrived just in time to shoot the bandits as they exited with the loot. Salmusa watched the whole thing from his window. It was better than what used to be on American television.

Apparently the criminals were becoming bolder, but they had yet to try and break into the safe house.

Now, however, Salmusa wondered for whom the police outside were looking. Apparently hoodlums were hiding somewhere in the neighborhood.

One officer turned his horse to the east and cast a bright handheld flashlight up the street, scanning the houses. The other cop did the same thing to the west. Then they both rode off in their respective directions for closer inspection. At that same moment, as the policemen left the front of the house, Salmusa's keen eyes caught three silhouettes dart across his front yard.

So! They were using the safe house as cover.

Salmusa moved away from the window, grabbed his Daewoo pistol, and went out the bedroom to the top of the stairs. He listened carefully—and heard muted whispers outside the front door down below. One of them tried the doorknob.

The Korean operative smiled. *Let them try and break in . . .*

Swiftly and silently he descended the stairs and slipped through the swinging door into the kitchen. The burglars made a lot of noise tinkering with the lock. Salmusa thought they must be using some kind of lock-pick tools or screwdrivers. He sat at the kitchen table, placed the handgun on top, and calmly waited in the dark for his guests.

There was a distinctive *click* as they succeeded in unlocking the door. The three men entered the house and stood in the foyer, talking softly.

"Is there anyone here?"

"It's quiet."

"You—go check the rest of the house."

"Fuck that. Let's see if there's anything in the kitchen. Eat first, kill later."

"I'm for that."

"Got your flashlight?"

Sudden illumination spilled into the kitchen from the slit under the swinging door. Salmusa was impressed that the hoodlums had a working flashlight. He picked up the Daewoo and quietly screwed the suppressor in place.

The sound of footsteps came closer.

The door swung open. The man with the flashlight entered and cast the beam on the kitchen table. Salmusa fired in its direction before the burglar could gasp. Instead he yelped in surprise and pain. The flashlight dropped to the floor and rolled into the kitchen.

Salmusa squeezed the trigger a second time.

The second man emitted a muffled grunt. As both men's legs crumpled, Salmusa leapt from the chair and onto the floor, still pointing the Daewoo at the open door.

The third man was armed. He fired two rounds at the kitchen table where he thought he'd seen someone. Without a suppressor, the discharge was deafening.

Salmusa blasted the intruder twice in rapid succession. The man dropped the gun and fell backward into the living room.

All of this had occurred in two seconds.

The operative stood, placed the Daewoo on the table, and picked up the flashlight. It was still on. He moved the beam over the bodies and saw that the burglars were African-American men in their twenties. He didn't care about having to kill them, but the racket of the third man's gun was problematic. Would the loud noise attract the attention of the policemen outside?

He stepped over the bodies, moved to the kitchen window, and carefully peered through the drapes. Sure enough, one of the policemen had ridden his horse closer to the house. He had definitely heard something.

Salmusa hurried out of the kitchen to the foyer and discovered that the burglars had left the front door wide open. Not good. No wonder the cop was curious.

There was no time to go back to the kitchen and retrieve his handgun. The officer dismounted, drew his sidearm, and approached the front porch.

Salmusa stealthily slid into the living room and crouched in the shadows beside the open door. The M9 knife he always kept strapped to his right calf was already in his hand.

The policeman turned on his flashlight and pointed it inside the house. The beam swerved through the foyer. The living room archway was to his left. The kitchen door was to his right.

A body lay sprawled on the floor, blocking open the swinging kitchen door.

The officer cautiously stepped inside and saw the arm of another body just inside the kitchen. He moved forward and faced the crime scene, his flashlight running over the three corpses.

"Wish the damn radios worked," the officer mumbled. Then he hollered as loud as he could. "Carl? Carl, can you hear me?"

The cop headed back toward the front door to find his partner.

"Hey, Carl! I found—"

Salmusa's blade prematurely ended the officer's call for backup with a swift slice across the man's throat. As he fell back, the Korean caught him and gently laid him on the floor. The officer struggled and choked helplessly. Blood gushed from his wound. Salmusa quickly stepped outside and looked up and down the street. There was no sign of the other policeman. The horse stood obediently in the yard.

Salmusa approached the animal and slapped its rear. "Go!" he commanded. At first the horse wasn't sure what to do. Salmusa slapped it again, harder. This time the beast whinnied and bolted off the property.

The Korean went back inside and shut the front door. The lock needed repairing but that could wait. For now, he had to make do by moving a heavy chair from the living room against the door. When he was done with that task, he opened the crawl space hatch, located directly under the stairs.

Still wearing pajamas, Salmusa dragged the first body across the floor, smearing blood as he went. It didn't matter. He would abandon the safe house very soon. Salmusa stuffed the corpse through the crawl space opening, then moved it farther inside by pushing it with his bare feet. He repeated the steps with the other two burglars. The police officer went in last.

Salmusa finally went up the stairs, removed the blood-stained pajamas, and dropped them in the laundry basket. It would have been nice to take a shower, but he managed with the water basin and soap he'd been using since moving in to the house. He then put on a clean pair of pajamas, brushed his teeth, and went back to bed.

ELEVEN

JANUARY 25, 2025

Walker awoke to voices outside the motel room. At first he didn't know where he was. It was the room's stale smell that brought it all back. He was so exhausted the night before that he hadn't noticed how bad it was. He rolled over on his side and coughed into his hands, trying his best to stifle the noise. Then he took a minute to breathe through his mouth as he slowly sat up.

The voices outside were very close, just beyond the door.

Walker immediately went on full alert. He grabbed the kitchen knife, which he'd set on the nightstand next to the bed.

A man said, "Hurry up and get the blankets."

Walker stood and went to the window. He carefully peered through the tattered drapes and saw a beat-up 1970s-era Chevy Nova parked a couple of rooms down from his own. A man of about forty was loading something in the trunk. After a moment, a teenage girl appeared with an armful of blankets and handed them over. The man threw them in the back seat. The girl went back inside the motel room, and pretty soon she returned with a boy a little older than she.

A woman's voice called, "Billy, you left your socks."

The man winced and said, *sotto voce,* "Betty, keep your voice down!"

They were a normal family who had done the exact same thing Walker had done—they broke into a motel room and spent the night. They probably didn't realize he was there.

Walker threw the knife on the bed, pushed the dresser out of the way, and opened the door. The teenage girl shrieked. The man drew a pistol from nowhere.

"Whoa!" Walker said, holding up his hands. "I'm sorry, I didn't mean to scare you! It's okay. I'm friendly. I'm a good guy."

The man narrowed his eyes. "Come out with your hands up. Don't try any funny moves. Becky, run inside. You too, Billy."

The two kids shot into the motel room.

"Shut the door," their father commanded. When that was done, he addressed Walker. "You alone?"

"Yes, sir. Really, you can lower the gun."

"Close your door behind you. With one hand."

Walker did so. "I'm alone. I promise. The only thing inside is my motorcycle." Keeping his hands up, he nodded at the Chevy. "We must have had the same idea. I broke into the room last night. I didn't even hear you guys arrive. I was really out."

The man studied Walker's appearance and finally decided there was no threat. "Okay, you can put down your hands." He holstered the pistol.

"Thanks." Walker tried some levity. "Some

accommodations, huh?"

The man wasn't having it. "Where you headed?"

"I'm not sure. I thought I'd check out Twentynine Palms. It's not too far from here." Walker held out his hand. "Ben Walker. I'm from LA."

The man cautiously shook it. "Gary Franklin. We are, too."

"Where you going?"

"Mexico." Franklin turned toward the motel room. He waved at them to come on out. The door opened and they appeared, along with a woman in her late thirties. The Franklins were a handsome family, although it was apparent they were in the same condition as Walker—stressed, hungry, and frightened.

"This is Billy, Becky, and my wife, Wendy."

Walker smiled and introduced himself. Franklin said to his wife, "Why don't you finish getting our things together. I'd like to get out of here."

She nodded and went back inside. The kids stood and studied Walker.

"Tough times," Franklin said.

"Yeah. What do you know about Mexico? Is it safe down there?" Walker asked.

"I have no idea. I just figure it's got to be better than here. I bet they never thought they'd get illegal immigrants going the other way."

Walker nodded. "Have you heard anything about the old Marine base at Twentynine Palms? Is anything still there?"

"I couldn't tell you. But I do know there are gangs on these highways. Dangerous, desperate men. They ride motorcycles and some have cars."

"I know. I ran into some of them yesterday."

Franklin looked him up and down. "And you're still alive?"

"I was one of the lucky ones."

"I see." Franklin gestured east. "They may be on Route 62, Mr. Walker. I hear they stop anyone with a motor vehicle and kill them for it. Women are raped. It's like they've decided it's the end of the world so anything goes. I don't know what's happened to the police. I haven't seen a cop since we left LA."

"Me neither."

"You have a weapon?"

"Not really." Walker laughed wryly. "A kitchen knife."

"Wish I could help you." Franklin patted the pistol on his belt. "It's all I've got."

"I understand. What I really need is gas. Have you seen any black market guys selling any?"

"Nope. I think on this stretch of road, the outlaws would kill 'em for it."

Walker rubbed his chin. "I've got about a quarter tank. I don't know how far that's gonna get me."

Franklin turned his head and stared off in the distance for a moment. He rubbed his unshaven chin and then said, "I tell you what." He moved to the back of his car and opened the trunk. "Come here." He reached inside and pulled out a five-gallon gas can. "Here you go. It's only half full."

Walker's jaw dropped. "Oh my gosh! How much you want for it?"

Franklin shook his head. "Take it. I have a bunch."

Walker joined him at the back of the Chevy. The trunk was filled with five-gallon cans.

"I guess I'm one of those end-of-days fanatics," Franklin said with a sheepish grin. "I always kept supplies for emergencies. I even had a bomb shelter back at our house. I've had these cans for over a year."

"Mr. Franklin, I can't take your—"

The man held up a hand. "Nah, nah. These days most people are likely to be mighty selfish. I believe it's a time when we need to be neighborly."

"Well, thank you. Thank you very much."

"You're welcome. Ben, is it?"

"That's right."

"Call me Gary." They shook hands again. "I don't know how much farther those two extra gallons will get you, but it's better than nothing."

"I'll say. Thanks again."

"We're gonna get going now. Good luck."

"You, too."

A low, harsh rumble in the distance caught their attention.

"What was that?" Walker asked.

It happened again, a little louder.

"That's gunfire," Franklin said. "Tanks. Big guns."

"Oh my God." They turned toward the noise. "Where do you think it is?"

"I don't know. Not too far away. A few miles."

Walker gasped and pointed. "Look."

Planes. Flying toward them in formation.

"Where did *those* come from?" Franklin asked. "I

think they're ours!"

"I have some binoculars in my room."

"Go get 'em!"

Walker retrieved the pair and brought them to Franklin. The man raised them to his eyes.

"Oh, Lord," he said.

"What?"

"They're ours, all right. U.S. Air Force transport carriers."

"That's good, isn't it?"

Franklin lowered the binoculars. His eyes betrayed his fear. "They've got Korean insignias on them."

"What? Let me see." Walker grabbed the glasses and looked.

There were at least a dozen of them. The planes were flying low enough to the ground that he could make out details. As they passed directly overhead, Walker saw the red flags with blue top and bottom borders and a star inside a white circle. These were affixed over the U.S. Air Force emblems.

"How can that be?" Walker asked. "How do they have our planes?"

The carriers continued eastward until they disappeared in the clouds.

Franklin looked at him grimly. "Dear God, we've been invaded."

TWELVE

JANUARY 25, 2025

Despite Franklin's warning, Walker set out on Route 62 heading north from Palm Springs toward Morongo Valley, where the highway would then bend eastward toward Twentynine Palms. Walker considered why he was so intent in finding the Marine base. There was no reason for him to believe it would offer any solace or protection. The base was shut down years ago during the military's cost-cutting spree. It could be a huge mistake. After all, Twentynine Palms was at the southern edge of the Mojave Desert. Would there be water? Food? Was he insane? Walker thought perhaps he should have followed the Franklins down to Mexico. At least there was a civilization across the border. Who knew what Walker would find in the desert.

Maybe it was a death wish.

As the motorcycle zipped through the ghost town of Morongo Valley, Walker convinced himself it was his gut that told him to go to Twentynine Palms. Throughout his life he had trusted that gut. Professor Shulman once told him that when a door shut behind him, a new one always opened in front. That had usually been the case. Most of the time Walker's gut guided him toward those new doors. And for some unknown reason, he had a good feeling about the Mojave Desert. There was the possibility that a military contingent was there. It made sense to check.

There were fewer cars stuck on Route 62. Walker increased his speed to fifty miles per hour as he rode past the Little San Bernardino Mountains on his right. Whatever had happened to the nation in the last twenty years, the land itself hadn't changed. The vista was gorgeous. Walker had always found beauty in the deserts and mountain ranges of California. He wasn't far from the awe-inspiring Joshua Tree National Park, where he had once attempted a bit of rock-climbing as a teenager. Walker ended up breaking his arm. He never was the outdoor rugged type—until now.

Walker stopped at the small town of Joshua Tree around noon. It, too, was deserted, which didn't bode well for Twentynine Palms. In fact, he hadn't seen any human beings since he left Palm Springs. He was beginning to wonder if this was all just a huge mistake.

He emptied Franklin's gas can into the Spitfire's fuel tank, which brought the level up to near where it had been when he'd started out that morning. After a bit of lunch—cereal again—and a few swigs of water, he continued the journey. The water supply concerned him. His body required much more hydration than he'd originally calculated. The sun was quite hot for January, but then he *was* in the desert. It would be very cold at night, but the days could be just as brutal as they were in the summer.

In an hour he finally reached Twentynine Palms,

and Walker's spirits sank. There wasn't a soul in sight. The town was desolate and empty; it had most likely been that way for years prior to the blast. He drove the Spitfire up and down the streets looking for any signs of life, but he found nothing. There was, however, an Indian reservation east of town. The Twenty-nine Palms Band of Mission Indians of Coachella Valley, California, were Chemehuevi that had prospered in the 1990s by opening a casino in Cabezon, which stood at the southern end of the reservation, southeast of Palm Springs. The Twentynine Palms entrance was technically the "back door," and it was well-guarded. The Native Americans had constructed a fence and gate to keep the outside world away. Walker wondered how life had been on reservations around the country since the economic crises of the past decade. It can't have been good. No wonder there was a barrier.

Walker stopped and turned off the bike. He walked toward the solid steel gate and knocked.

"Anyone home?" he called.

No answer. Nothing but the wind.

He banged on the gate again. There was no intercom or mail slot or window. It may as well have been a fortress. Maybe that's what it was meant to be.

Walker turned back to his bike. Just as he was about to mount, a gun discharged behind him. The cartridge kicked the dirt on the left side of the Spitfire, scaring the hell out of him. He jumped behind the bike and saw a Native American standing on a platform at the top of the fence, rifle in hand. It was pointing straight at Walker.

"Go!" the man shouted.

Walker raised his hands. "Wait! I'm a friend. I just—"

The gun recoiled again. The round hit the ground even closer.

"Fine, fine," Walker said. He got on the bike and kick-started it. As he rode away, he looked back to see the Native American had been joined by two others. They must have had their fair share of trouble with motorcycle gangs and weren't taking any chances with white men like him.

Walker supposed he couldn't blame them.

Disheartened, Walker drove to the north end of town toward the old Marine base. If that turned out to be a dead end, he didn't know what else to do. He didn't have enough gas to get back to Palm Springs.

"You fucked up, Walker," he said aloud.

He reached the turnoff for Route 62 and a road heading north. An old graffiti-smeared sign indicated it was the way to the Marine Corps Air Ground Combat Center Twentynine Palms. Three miles ahead. He physically crossed his fingers and said, "Please," and revved the bike. But before Walker could cross 62, he noticed dark specks on the road to the west, distorted by the heat waves wafting off the hot asphalt.

Vehicles—headed his way.

Walker didn't know whether to greet them with joy or run and hide. He pulled out the binoculars and took a look.

Motorcycles. Another gang of outlaws.

One of the men pointed at him. They increased their speed.

Walker cursed, turned the bike around, and sped back into town. He pulled into a residential street and scanned the houses as he drove past, looking for one without a fenced backyard. He located a candidate at the end of the block, swerved in between the houses, and rode around behind the structure. Walker shut off the bike and waited.

The engine noise grew closer. They must have seen him turn into the neighborhood. Walker clenched his teeth as his heart pounded in his chest. He heard the gang ride past the house in front. Someone whooped and hollered, though he could barely hear it over the deafening din of the bikes. He couldn't tell if they were staying in the same spot or not.

What were they doing? *Go away!*

Then the noise diminished as they moved on, and Walker breathed a sigh of relief. The bikers must have gone on to the next block or turned the corner or something.

Now to get out of there and back to the Marine base.

But just when he thought it might be safe to leave, he heard the revving of their engines *increase* in volume. They were returning. Once again, there was shouting and motor racket in front of the house. Walker got off the Spitfire, not sure if he should try to hide—there wasn't any place where he could—or run. He drew the kitchen knife from the jury-rigged sheath on his calf.

So this is what sheer terror felt like . . .

The bikes were at the side of the house, coming closer. They'd found him.

Four serious motorcycles roared into the backyard— a couple of Harleys, a Kawasaki, and a Triumph, all heavy touring models. They carried seven men—two rode double on three of the bikes—all whooping like American Indians circling the covered wagons.

This is it. They're going to kill me.

The bikers shut off their rides and got off. The one man who was riding alone was bald, had the build of a professional wrestler, and had tattoos up and down his bare arms. All of them wore black leather jackets with the sleeves cut off.

"What a shitty ride you got, mister," he said, walking around the Spitfire. "How old is that thing?"

Walker swallowed and tried hard to keep the nervousness out of his voice. "It's a nineteen-sixty-seven model."

The biker pointed to Franklin's empty gas can. "Any gas in there?"

"No. What I've got is in the fuel tank."

"Got any money?"

"Not much."

"Food? Water?"

Walker removed his backpack and threw it on the ground in front of the man. "There. Take a look. What you see is what you get."

The bald leader turned to his men and said, "I think we got ourselves a smart-ass." He looked at Walker. "Are you a smart-ass?"

Walker was scared to death, but at this point it didn't matter what he said. "I try not to be, but sometimes my true nature comes out."

The bald biker snorted. "He's a comedian, too!" He picked up the backpack and threw it to one of his pals. Two of them started going through it, removing the water bottles, the rest of the cereal, and the other items. The leader unstrapped the tool box on the back of the Spitfire and opened it. He nodded, pleased with the contents, and strapped it back on. He didn't touch the sleeping bag.

"Where's the key?"

Walker's stomach lurched. "In my pocket."

"I'd like you to hand it over to my friend Rascal here." He gestured to one of the other men who'd been riding double. Rascal, a bearded ugly son of a bitch, grinned broadly, revealing a set of yellow teeth with three missing.

Walker dug in his pocket and tossed the man his beloved key.

"Better empty all your pockets."

They ended up taking everything. His wallet, motorcycle, backpack, tool kit, and even the kitchen knife, which they found amusing.

"He's a tough guy! Carries a big knife!"

One man grabbed the Dodgers baseball cap off his head and put it on. Another man claimed the sunglasses.

Walker prayed they wouldn't take his clothes.

Instead, the seven men decided to have a little fun and beat the tar out of him. The bald leader delivered the first punch directly into Walker's stomach, doubling him over, winded and in agony. Rascal then kicked him in the face, knocking him to the ground. Another man grabbed hold of Walker's shirt to raise him just high enough to punch him in the nose, breaking it.

A fourth man kicked him in the ribs.

A fifth kicked him in the kidneys.

They each had a turn and then started all over again.

He didn't know how long he was unconscious. The sun had dropped considerably but it was still daylight. He lay on the dirt and rocks of the backyard where the bandits had beaten him senseless. Bolts of pain assaulted his entire body. His face and torso felt as if they'd been crushed in a vise.

Slowly, excruciatingly, he got to his hands and knees and spit blood. His left side was in agony. Walker suspected he had one or two broken ribs. He didn't want to see his face. His nose, he knew, was busted. It was clogged with dried blood and mucus. But he still had his teeth. And his clothes.

And he was alive.

Walker got to his feet and supported himself against the house. After a pause, he stumbled to the back door and tried the knob. It was locked, of course. He didn't have the strength to kick it in. He went to a back window and looked inside. All he could determine was that it was once someone's home.

Dazed, Walker went around to the front and started walking back toward the highway. He remembered it wasn't far. Looking up, he saw what appeared to be a buzzard circling over his head.

One of us thinks dinner is on the horizon . . .

It took an hour, but eventually he made it to the crossroad of Route 62 and the road to the Marine base. He continued north, forcing himself to keep going. Pretty soon it would be dark.

Another hour later, Walker passed a closed gas station. The door and windows were boarded up, vandalized by graffiti, but there was a hole in the garage door. He didn't think much of it, just continued on. He could see the Marine base up ahead, surrounded by a high chain-link fence with barbed wire along the top. The gate was chained and padlocked. A large metal sign on the gate displayed the legend: closed—no trespassing—u.s. marine corps property—danger—violators subject to arrest.

Through the fence, Walker saw many neglected buildings—barracks, a mess hall, and who knew what else.

How could he get in?

He studied the fence and barbed wire. There was no way he could climb over it. The chain and padlock were impenetrable.

Walker wanted to cry. He banged on the fence with a fist and cursed. He kicked and shouted, picked up a rock, and threw it at the metal sign.

He turned and walked back toward town. But when he passed the closed gas station, he stopped.

That *hole* in the garage door . . .

He crossed the street and looked inside. Dark. But there was *stuff* in there. And the hole was big enough for him to crawl through. So he did.

Walker took a minute to let his eyes adjust to the dim light. It was a typical service bay garage, littered with tires, machine parts, and garbage. But there were also plenty of tools on the benches. Walker found a tool box and went through its contents.

Wire cutters. Strong ones, too.

He left them in the box and looked for other items he could use. Found a flashlight, but the batteries were dead. Dropped it in the box anyway. Satisfied, he carried the tool box out and headed back for the base camp.

Rather than cutting a hole in the fence right by the gate—where passersby might see it—he moved farther along the fence, into the brush, where it would be hidden. He snipped the steel mesh, a piece at a time, until he could bend a section back to allow egress.

He was inside.

The sun was nearly gone.

In its heyday, the base was a small city with nearly nine thousand inhabitants. Because of its desert location, the Marines built training facilities to prepare soldiers for warfare in Iraq, Afghanistan, and other rough terrains. The vast expansion of land contained obstacle courses, "practice towns" for assault instruction, schools, family and bachelor barracks, entertainment facilities, equipment storage buildings, and administrative offices.

Walker moved through the village-like community, found an old you are here map on a wooden post, and navigated his way straight to the Mess Hall, which was still indicated as such. The door was locked, so he opened the trusty tool box, grabbed a hammer, and smashed the jam. Once inside, he explored. It was a large space with long tables and benches, meant to feed a couple hundred men or more at a time. There was a full professional kitchen with all of the equipment intact. Just for kicks, Walker tried the tap water in the sink. Nothing. He turned on the gas stove. Nothing. He shrugged. It was worth the attempt.

One wall was lined with several pantries, the doors of which were fastened with small padlocks. Kid stuff. Using the hammer again, he broke one off and opened the pantry.

Walker about shit in his pants.

The shelves were completely stocked with packaged and canned food and bottled water.

Unbelievable.

No, a fucking *miracle*!

He grabbed a large can of pork 'n' beans, looked around the kitchen, spotted an opener, and almost tripped trying to get to it. He placed the can under the opener, spun it around, and threw the lid across the room.

Sure enough, the can was full of pork 'n' beans.

After shoving three handfuls into his mouth, Walker went back to the pantries and opened them all. There was enough food to last months. *Months*. And it was all his! He took one of the prepackaged dried beef and noted the expiration date. Okay, so what if it was four years old? It couldn't be *that* bad.

Walker decided he'd stay awhile.

FEBRUARY, 2025

As the days went on, Walker regained his strength and his wounds healed. He'd wrapped his rib cage with bandages found in the Medical Unit; the pain in his side diminished over time. He found it surreal that the Marine base had been left in such an untouched condition. The Mess Hall was a godsend, of course, and he had mastered the art of lighting a fire in the grill. Collecting kindling wasn't a problem, seeing that desert shrubs and Joshua trees were plentiful. Walker discovered many other desirable amenities; for one thing, nearly all the barracks still had beds with pillows, sheets, and blankets. He picked what he thought was an officer's quarters for his "home." In the Recreation Center there were pool tables, dartboards, and decks of cards to occupy his time. A library contained hundreds of books. Some of the barracks contained left-behind personal items such as old portable CD players, televisions, and exercise equipment. Of course, there was no electricity, but Walker could use the gym for weight-lifting and running. In several of the barracks he found utility uniforms of all sizes. Walker was surprised by how loose and comfortable they were. After a while, it was all he wore. He even found batteries for the flashlight, the electronics of which were miraculously intact.

One drawback was the almost unbearable heat. Without air conditioning, the barracks were incredibly hot. But as time passed, Walker got used to it.

Every day he explored a different part of the base, dressed in the olive-colored camouflage uniform.

It was as if he were the last remaining Marine in America, and he wasn't even a Marine.

One day he found a heavy, padlocked footlocker under a bunk in one of the bachelor barracks. Something was inside. Since he'd found even better tools in the base machine shop, Walker got the locker open in no time.

His jaw dropped when he saw the contents—an M4 assault rifle and boxes of magazines.

Gingerly he pulled it out of the footlocker and held it. Walker didn't know a thing about guns, especially military-issue automatic assault weapons like this one. He had no idea how to load it or fire it.

But he was going to figure it out.

He carefully examined all the various switches and buttons on the rifle. It was obvious where the magazine went in and what direction it should face. Walker gave it a try and managed to correctly lock a magazine in the well. He went outside and aimed the rifle at one of the buildings in the distance. He squeezed the trigger and . . . nothing happened.

Was there a "safety"?

Walker once again pored over the machine, looking for the correct button. He found the select-fire switch—safe, semiautomatic, and burst fire. The gun still wouldn't shoot when he flipped the switch away from "safe." Finally, after much experimentation, he discovered the charging handle, a T-shaped device at the top of the receiver. He realized he had to pull it back and release it to "cock" the rifle.

The gun had a negligible kick. He was mighty pleased with himself that he had fired an M4. He was so thrilled that he emptied the magazine in seconds, and then spent the next ten trying to figure out how to release the magazine from the weapon. (It was a button just above the magazine well.)

Over the next week, Walker took advantage of the practice range and pretended he was a real soldier. He ran through the obstacle course and fired the M4 at imaginary adversaries. He set up targets and shot at them. He timed himself to be quick at loading a magazine, pulling the charging handle, and releasing burst fire in rapid succession. By the end of the month, he felt confident he could at least handle the weapon like an amateur. He may not have been an honest-to-God Marine, but maybe it would be enough training to keep him alive.

It was not a bad existence and, aside from missing a hot shower and an occasional female companion, Walker was content.

Then one morning he saw the planes again. The roar overhead woke him at the crack of dawn. Walker thought he was under attack, so he grabbed the M4 and rushed outside in his skivvies to see U.S. Air Force C-17s flying overhead in formation. He retrieved his binoculars to get a better look, and a shiver ran down his spine. The U.S. emblems were covered up as before, but this time by flags depicting a red-washed American flag with the North Korean coat of arms superimposed on top.

Walker knew it signified that America was now occupied and under the control of the Greater Korean Republic.

THIRTEEN

APRIL 8, 2025

Salmusa had been busy.

Ever since the Korean People's Army invaded the United States in January, he was given special assignments involving security, intelligence, and what the Koreans called "American compliance."

In late January he left the safe house in Van Nuys, drove the Volkswagen to San Francisco, and reported to KPA Military Command. The ad-hoc headquarters was set up in city hall after twenty thousand troops stormed the city and captured it. U.S. military resistance was strong at first, but the Americans were heavily outnumbered. The Koreans had come well-prepared, for they were trained in the use of American equipment and brought much of it along with them after having acquired it from Japan and South Korea. The U.S. forces were also in disarray after the years of downsizing and unfocused leadership. It took only two days for San Francisco to fall. Los Angeles, because of its massive sprawl, took four, although Edwards Air Force Base was secured in twenty-four hours. San Diego was under Korean control in only eight hours.

At the same time, C-130H troop transport planes captured at Hickam Air Force Base in Honolulu carried paratroopers inland. KC-135 and KC-10 tanker aircraft, also seized in Hawaii, provided the extra fuel so the C-130Hs could return. KPA troops were dropped in Nevada, Arizona, Utah, Colorado, Wyoming, Montana, Idaho, New Mexico, and Texas.

On January 27, Koreans flew C-17s from Edwards Air Force Base to drop troops even farther east, beyond the Mississippi River to the East Coast.

Salmusa admired the Brilliant Comrade's plan. It was ambitious, for America was a large country. The key was capturing strategic targets that gave Korea undeniable leverage against the puny American resistance. San Diego, Los Angeles, and San Fran-cisco, as shipping ports, were the obvious primary objectives, followed by Seattle and Portland. Heavy tech areas, such as oil refineries, were also priority goals. Whatever natural resources could be exploited, the Koreans wanted them. In a speech delivered to the inner leaders of the Korean Workers Party, Kim Jong-un stated, "Consider America a rotting warehouse filled with vermin. We must take all that we can from it before it falls in on itself. It must be stripped clean." He finished the speech with a rousing, motivational statement regarding the Korean strategy of a growing occupational foothold by saying, "The smallest germ, once planted, can spread to kill the largest giant."

Over the next three months, that germ had grown considerably.

The Korean military set up different Areas of

Responsibility similar to the Unified Combatant Command structure the U.S. had used worldwide for decades. These areas were designated around general purpose output and potential for KPA use. Hawaii and West Coast cities were obvious export hubs for oil and technology to Asia. Rocky Mountain and Midwestern states were divided into areas for agriculture, machinery, oil, and ores industries. While the Korean troops only occupied pockets of various states, they set up several Interest Zones under more direct authority, with a heavier number of troops.

It was Salmusa's job to oversee population control and implement plans to counter civilian opposition in these centers of weighty Korean presence.

Approximately eighty thousand suspected dissidents such as thought leaders, local politicians, bloggers, and student protesters were rounded up and killed during the initial invasion. Salmusa ordered that mass gravesites be dug in Sunset Park in Las Vegas, Hayden Island in Portland, the Glendale Golf Course in Salt Lake City, and Dodger Stadium in Los Angeles. He also instituted the decree that any American could be detained indefinitely without trial upon the order of a Korean military officer with the rank of captain or higher.

Salmusa was currently in the process of setting up detention centers, most of them on the sites of former prisons. West Coast tech and engineering personnel who refused to work with the Korean government to dismantle the U.S. infrastructure were sent to Alcatraz Interrogational Island for "rehabilitation." Low-level prisoners and common criminals were placed in the Pasadena Rose Bowl. Cobb Park in Fort Worth became a "camp" for wives and children of oil workers in Texas and the Gulf Coast to make certain of the loyalty of "American employees." Grants Pass, in Oregon, was enclosed by barbed wire and acted as a death camp for undesirables from the northwest cities of Tacoma, Portland, and Seattle.

And then there were the executions. The different Areas handled the process in different ways. For example, Salmusa allowed the Korean Commander of Area One to hang condemned prisoners from electricity poles in their local townships. The Commander of Area Three often conducted executions at night with the disposal of bodies done by cremation. Americans in this area often never learned what happened to a missing loved one or a family member.

California State Prison in Lancaster, a small community north of Los Angeles, was the newest Korean-operated detention center. Originally an all-male state prison that housed close to five thousand inmates with varying levels of security, half of the facilities were relegated to hold the types of prisoners the Koreans referred to as "dissidents." They weren't particularly dangerous civilians, but their ideas were. People who had been negatively outspoken in public toward the rise of Korean influence in the world fell into this category. Some of them were celebrities. Most were intelligent, college-educated citizens with strong opinions and the ability to organize, spread

anti-Korean propaganda, and persuade the population to fight back. In Salmusa's opinion, this made
them more treacherous than armed resistance fighters.

In order to make room for these enemies of the
Republic, half of the original prison inhabitants had to
be released. Salmusa forced the American warden to
decide who deserved to remain incarcerated due to the
heinous nature of crimes committed, and who might
be eligible for release. Once the list was compiled, the
warden was confined with the dissidents. He didn't
know that Salmusa delivered a death sentence to all
of the Level IV prisoners—the ones under maximum
security. Under the false pretense that they were being
released, nearly two thousand men were burned alive
by flame thrower-yielding KPA units in the prison
exercise yard. The Koreans had no use for American
criminals, so it was best to exterminate them altogether. Then, the newly arrived dissidents were moved
into the maximum security housing, while the original lower level inmates remained in the more relaxed
dormitories without a secure perimeter.

Salmusa arrived that morning for an inspection.
He was also due to visit the detention center at the
Pasadena Rose Bowl, having been given orders to
come up with a "deterrent" to resistance. But first
things first.

After touring the prison, Salmusa told the Captain-
in-Command he would like to interrogate a certain
dissident prisoner. He wanted to hear first-hand what
the man had to say.

His name was Horace Danziger. He was brought

into a bare room and tied securely in a chair that occupied the middle of the floor. One other chair faced it; that was Salmusa's seat. A noose hung menacingly from the ceiling above the prisoner's chair. It was attached to a pulley capable of raising or lowering the intimidating stretch of rope.

Danziger was a man in his fifties, but the strain of the past few months had taken its toll. He now looked seventy. The dissident was dressed in standard prison overalls.

Salmusa stared at the man for a full minute without saying a word. Danziger attempted to hold the gaze, but he couldn't help glancing up at the noose a couple of times.

"What? What do you want?" Danziger asked.

Finally, Salmusa said, "Your name is Horace Danziger and you have had many things to say that are insulting to our Brilliant Comrade, Kim Jong-un."

The man sighed heavily. He'd been through this dozens of times with other Korean interrogators. "Unlike your country, in America we have—or we had—the freedom of speech. We can say anything we want, not only about Korea, but our own country as well. That's what happens in a democracy. Our Constitution protects that right."

Salmusa opened a manila folder in his lap and studied it. "I understand you had a website where you called the Brilliant Comrade a 'pig in sheep's clothing.' I don't understand. I always thought the expression was a '*wolf* in sheep's clothing.'"

"I meant what I said."

"The Brilliant Comrade might not have been so insulted if you'd kept to the original expression. He *is* something of a wolf. But he is not a pig. That was insulting."

"I didn't think he'd see it."

"Why not? It was on the Internet. Anyone could see it." Salmusa examined more reports in the folder. "Before the invasion, you posted several blogs warning the American public about Korea. Why? Most people in America paid no attention to us."

"Why? It was obvious what you were up to. I knew it was only a matter of time before you tried something. Somebody had to say something."

Salmusa paused. "I understand you had your own television talk-show. You are famous."

Danziger looked away. "Whatever."

"Most Americans know who you are, am I correct?"

"I guess. Depends on if they watched TV."

"Even now, three months after our occupation of much of your country, the man on the street mentions your name. The people wonder where you are. If you are safe. If you are alive."

"Do they?"

"They do. I have seen illegal homemade posters pasted on buildings in Los Angeles. They say 'Free Danziger.'"

"That's nice to hear. I don't suppose you're going to do that, though, are you?"

Salmusa smiled.

Danziger's eyes flared. "Where are my wife and daughter? Huh? Where are they? I haven't seen them in three months, you bastard. *Where are they?*"

"To tell you the truth, I don't know. They were taken to another facility when you were arrested. I am sure they are fine. Tell me, Mr. Danziger, if there is one thing you could say to the American people right now, what would it be?"

The man thought about it. "I'd tell them to fight you bastards in our streets and neighborhoods. I'd say pick up any weapon you can find and kill the first Korean you see. I'd tell 'em to organize into resistance groups and give you hell. And I'd wish them luck."

Salmusa nodded. "All right. We will distribute your words along with your photograph to the American people. We will drop thousands of them from airplanes, all over the country. How about that, Mr. Danziger?"

The dissident frowned. "I don't believe you."

"Wait right there. Oh, forgive me. You can't go anywhere, can you? I'll be right back." Salmusa stood and went to the door. He opened it and clapped his hands. Three men in KPA uniforms entered, one rolling a small wheeled table with a laptop computer on it. The other man carried a camera. The third soldier went straight to the pulley and lowered the noose level with Danziger's face.

"Oh, Jesus," Danziger said. "What do you want from me? What do you want me to tell you?"

The soldier slipped the noose over the prisoner's head and slipped the knot tightly around his neck. Meanwhile, the Korean with the computer typed on the keypad. Salmusa addressed him, "You heard and got his words down verbatim?"

"Yes, sir."

Salmusa examined the monitor, which displayed a recently-created layout of an 8 1/2 by 11–inch flyer. The designer had placed text at the bottom—horace danziger died for these words: "fight the bastards in our streets and neighborhoods. pick up any weapon you can find and kill the first korean you see. organize into resistance groups and give them hell. i wish you luck."

"Very good. Let's see if Mr. Danziger approves."

The operator turned the laptop table around so the prisoner could see it. He shut his eyes and gasped. "Please, don't do this. Please . . . "

"I'll take that as 'approved,'" Salmusa said. "You see, Mr. Danziger, this will teach the American public that *anyone* who spouts treachery and disrespect will suffer the same fate as you." He then nodded at the soldier operating the pulley. The man flipped a switch. The rope grew taut and slowly lifted Danziger, and the chair, off the floor.

The photographer stepped forward and snapped several shots of the dissident hanging by his neck.

Salmusa didn't wait until the prisoner was dead. He ordered, "Pick the best one and paste it on the flyer. Then take it to the distribution center for printing and allocation. If this doesn't strike fear in the hearts of our enemies, I don't know what will."

He then left the room and made a call to the Pasadena Rose Bowl on the Captain-in-Command's working radio.

"This is Salmusa," he said when Pasadena's captain answered. "I have thought about the deterrent. I don't have time to come down to Pasadena today, so this is what I want you to do. Select a hundred prisoners at random and hang them from street lamps all along Hollywood Boulevard. Make sure each of them has a sign around their necks that reads: 'Anti-Korean Dissident.' I want the task completed by the end of today."

The Captain-in-Command knew not to refuse Salmusa's orders.

WALKER'S JOURNAL

MAY 20, 2025

It's hard to believe I'm alive—against all odds—and I'm in the company of a wayward National Guard unit.

Out in the middle of the Mojave Desert.

I know I haven't been writing much in the journal. I spent almost four months at the Marine base, all alone, and not once did I lift pen to paper. What can I say? I didn't feel like it. I had other things to do, like learn how to fire a friggin' M4 rifle! To tell the truth, I was living like a hog in slop. I had enough food to feed an army, books to read, a gun to play with, and a vast obstacle course and miniature town to run around in.

I didn't want to leave, but I had to. The goddamned Koreans came.

It was toward the end of February when the planes flew overhead and dropped flyers everywhere. I don't think they thought anyone was at the base; they were probably just carpeting the country with them. They wanted every American citizen to see their propaganda.

The first drop was a simple flyer urging the population to migrate toward "food shipment centers" in the big cities like Los Angeles. "Displaced persons" *programs had been implemented so everyone could get food, shelter, clothing, and other necessities. Supposedly the Koreans were "hiring" American workers to bring back the power grid and other utilities. The leaflet claimed there had been a "peaceful exchange" between governments and that the Norks were in our country to "help" us.*

Right.

I knew then and there that if the Koreans were running these programs, I wanted no part of them.

If the leaflet hadn't been so scary, it would have been funny. Whoever wrote the thing needed a better command of the English language. One sentence read, "Make bathroom waste drops at local supermarket deposit facility for clean happyness." WTF??

Then, in March, planes dropped a slightly thicker document—a small twelve-page book wrapped in plastic. It was lightweight, but I'm sure it injured a few people when it hit them on the heads. The cover was all red, had that bastardized American flag with the Korean coat of arms plastered over it, and was titled: DEMOCRATIC PEOPLE'S REPUBLIC OF AMERICA – OATH OF LOYALTY AND ASSIMILATION HANDBOOK. *Well, this so-called handbook was nothing but bullshit. It was supposedly written by the "North Korean Liberation Assistance Bureau" for "Bringing America Back to Greatness." Yes, there was an oath of loyalty that every American was expected to learn. Throughout the book were stupid pictures of Korean soldiers overlooking "happy" American families in their homes, or "friendly" Korean doctors and businessmen saying, "We are here to help you."* There were lists of new holidays, such as Kim Jong-un's birthday, his father's birthday, his grandfather's birthday, and so on. And there were the rules, such as curfews run by the Koreans rather than our own people. At the end was a list of "helpful phrases" in Korean, but if you ask me, none of them were particularly helpful. They were subservient. How do you say, "I will obey," in Korean?

At least the English grammar had improved.

Well, after this, I fully expected the Norks to come rolling up to the base and making themselves at home. But for some reason, they never showed up . . . until the beginning of May. They must have been too busy taking over military bases that were actually functional, with stuff to steal. Since the Twentynine Palms base had been closed years ago, they must have figured there was nothing here but buildings. But now that more Koreans were in the country, they needed the housing for their troops.

It was midday on May 2. I heard the rumble of tanks and marching troops. Using the binoculars, I spotted them in the distance heading up the road from town. I knew I had to get out of there, and fast.

I grabbed my backpack, which I had already stuffed with emergency supplies—water bottles and food packages, first-aid kit, some extra Marine utility uniforms—the M4 and ammunition, and a cap, and I ran like hell to the northern end of the base. Luckily I had the presence of mind to bring the wire cutters. So, as the Koreans blew off the gate on the southern fence, I cut a hole in the northern one. I slipped *through and ran northeast—straight into the boiling hot Mojave Desert.*

I was there for two weeks.

Jesus. Looking back, I realize how idiotic that was. There were a few days I thought I'd rather be a prisoner of the Koreans. I about died, I kid you not. For one thing, the food lasted only five days and the water lasted ten. Zip. Gone. And I was lost. I didn't know where the hell I was. There were mountainous ridges all around me. Nothing but sand and dirt and cactus and prickly brush and snakes and spiders and big giant ants and my old friend, the buzzard, flying over my head the entire time. He knew if he waited long enough, he'd get man meat. But I never gave him the satisfaction. Fuck you, buzzard!

And then there was the sun. My God, I never thought the sun could be so hot. I took to finding holes at the bases of cliffs to sleep in during the day, and I walked at night. Then it was cold as shit.

I shot a jackrabbit one day. Managed to build myself a fire and eat the damned thing. I tried my best at skinning it, but I still got a mouthful of fur. Yuck. I was no frontiersman. I didn't know a damn thing about surviving in the desert. I had to wing it, you know what I mean? And it was tough. One day I just sat there and cried. And I'm sure that son of a bitch buzzard was up there laughing at me.

Well, I lost track of the days, but it must have been ten or eleven since I left the base. I was barely moving. I was weak from hunger, dehydration, and heat-stroke. Nevertheless, I successfully fashioned a little den out of a tiny cave inside an outcrop of big rocks. I nestled in there and waited to die. I cursed the day I made the decision to leave Los Angeles. I cursed the Norks again and again. I prayed, even though I never went in for that stuff much. I became delirious. I had weird hallucinations and talked to desert spirits and thought I saw God.

Then, three days ago, on May 17, a National Guard unit happened to stroll by. They picked me up and saved my life. I'm still recovering from heatstroke and dehydration, and it'll be some time before I'm completely well. But I thought I'd write down what I could since all I can do is lie here inside one of their tents. Anyway, I'm tired now so I'm going to sleep. If you see that buzzard, tell him to go fuck himself.

Later, man.

FOURTEEN

MAY 21, 2025

Walker opened his eyes and saw a man standing over the cot, one of the National Guardsmen that saved his life. A man in his forties, dark hair with gray at the temples. Lean and fit. Intelligence behind the eyes.

"You awake?" he asked.

Walker nodded. Tried to sit up.

"Whoa, it's okay, just stay down. You need to regain your strength." The man handed Walker a canteen with a straw in it. "Have some water." Walker sucked it greedily. "Easy. Gotta make it last. We're in the desert, remember?"

The tent interior was very warm. Walker saw through the flaps that it was daylight.

"What time is it?"

"It's ten o'clock in the morning."

"What *day* is it?"

"It's Wednesday, May twenty-first." The man took the canteen away and held out his hand. "I'm Captain Michael Hennings. I'm in charge of the unit here."

Walker shook his hand. "Ben Walker."

"I know. We met when we first found you, but you were in pretty bad shape." He indicated the journal and pen lying on the ground by the cot. "You must be feeling better. You've been writing."

"Yeah, it's just a . . . I don't know what it is. A journal of sorts."

"Are you a Marine?" Walker shook his head. "You mind telling me how you came to be all alone in the Mojave Desert with an M4 rifle and Marine uniform on?"

"You got some time? It may take awhile."

"We've got all day. When we found you, the men were exhausted and about to drop like flies. Two guys have heatstroke, like you. I decided we needed to camp for a few days so *everyone* could recover. We're not going anywhere, *yet*. But pretty soon we have to pick up and keep moving."

Hennings unfolded a wood-and-canvas stool and sat by the cot. Walker proceeded to tell him his story, beginning with the day of the EMP blast. He covered the short time he spent with the Spitfire, his encounters with gangs on the highway, and his breaking into the Twentynine Palms base. But in the end he had more questions than answers. "So where do we stand, Captain?"

"That's quite a story, Walker. You're lucky to be alive. I take it you're not up to speed with what's happening in our country."

"Like I said, I figured the Koreans invaded. I have one of those bullshit documents they dropped from planes, some kind of loyalty handbook."

Hennings nodded. "I have one of those, too. Information is being pieced together by word-of-mouth because there's still no official communication between our government and the people. Comlinks are down and the military has no way of talking to each other. What news we get is from the Norks, and that's only through dissemination of their propaganda."

"So nothing still works? Electricity? Phones?"

"Nope. The Koreans have instituted teams of American manpower—or I should say *slavepower*—to repair some of this stuff in the big cities. But it'll all be for the Koreans' benefit, not ours."

Walker blinked. "Christ. So how did this happen?"

"As you know, on January 16, the Koreans detonated a nuclear device over America. That caused the EMP. Two days later a massive force landed in Hawaii. They took our Joint Base Pearl Harbor-Hickam, you know, our military hot spot. There's a rumor going around that they've planted a nuclear weapon in Honolulu and are holding our government hostage with it. Threatening to set it off, if our military strikes back. I don't know if that's true or not, but we have to act on the assumption that it is.

"Anyway, on January 25, they attacked the West Coast. Simultaneous landings in LA, San Francisco, and San Diego. Our own carrier planes from Hawaii dropped paratroopers farther inland. After a couple of days, they secured all of our active military bases in California and got their hands on C-17s to send paratroopers all the way across the United States, dropping troops in key cities. We're not even sure what they're holding. They're well organized, well trained, and they mean business. They've set up martial law in the occupied cities."

Walker shook his head. "My God. It's unbelievable. This is America, for Christ's sake."

Captain Hennings shrugged. "America hasn't been on top of the world lately. The last ten years took a few chinks out of our armor. We were vulnerable. Sitting ducks."

"What about our own military? Where are they?"

"Actually, every branch of the military—and the National Guard—put up a pretty good fight at first. There were some fierce battles in California, Oregon, and Washington. I don't know what happened in cities farther inland. One of the problems is the Norks captured a lot of our equipment and weapons. They brought along American stuff they'd obtained from Japan and South Korea, and then added more in Hawaii. When they took over our bases in California, they just slapped their flag over the American insignia, and now they have our tanks, planes, Humvees, you-name-it. It's ironic, really. We're fighting against our own technology. I hate to say it, but our military strength is simply not what it was. They clobbered us, Mr. Walker. They sent units running. In our scattered and fractured state, we couldn't drive them away.

"By March, it was pretty much a done deal. Army, Air Force, Marine, and Navy units had to act autonomously, so they went into hiding. The National Guard units did the same. That's what we're doing, although we have a purpose. We're not running, we're regrouping. It's gonna be a different kind of fight from now on."

"What do you mean?"

"This is a war that's gonna be fought by the people, Mr. Walker. There are resistance cells sprouting up all over. They're made up of soldiers who didn't run away, National Guard units like us, policemen, firefighters, Texas Rangers, and plain, ordinary folks who want to take up arms and make a stand. Take us, for example. We were stationed in San Diego. Got our asses whipped. We moved out and fought two more battles on the road. Lost half the unit. But we received some promising intel, so we're actually now on our way to a hardened complex in Utah, near Bryce Canyon, where a resistance cell is supposedly operating. Apparently, this place was shielded from the EMP, so they're supposed to have radios and tanks and vehicles. We're gonna join up with them. But it's a long, hard trek through the desert. It was the only way to go without the Koreans spotting us. They keep a close aerial watch on the major highways. I guess they figure no one is crazy enough to cross the desert."

Walker thought about what Hennings had said. "It's like Vietnam, or Afghanistan, in reverse. We couldn't win those wars because the enemy fought with guerilla tactics. That's what we have to do."

"You're right, Mr. Walker. This is *our* jungle and we know it a lot better than the Koreans. This war's gonna be won in our cornfields, in the streets of our cities, and in the suburbs—what's left of them."

"Does anyone know anything about Washington? Where's the president?"

"We don't know if he's alive or dead. Last I heard, he was holed up somewhere safe. Another rumor is that he's in England. No one knows. Hell, we don't know if the Koreans are *in* Washington or anywhere else on the East Coast. But we have to assume they are." He handed Walker the canteen again. "Want some more?"

"Sure."

As Walker took a sip, Hennings said, "We lost our doc in the last battle, but we knew enough about heatstroke to take care of you. You were pretty delirious when we found you. Thought you were gonna start shooting that M4 of yours, but you were too weak to pick it up."

Walker sat up and put his feet on the ground. "I'd like to try standing."

"All right." Hennings helped him, but Walker felt his knees buckle. "Just lean on me." They moved to the tent flap and Walker pulled it open. The intensely bright sun almost blinded him, but after a moment he could focus on the campsite—eight tents, a burned out campfire, three Humvees, and several horses standing under a canvas lean-to to protect them from the sun.

"Wow, where did you get the vehicles?"

"They were in a shielded garage at our base. Not every piece of equipment fell into Korean hands. The horses we picked up at a ranch in Escondido. They don't like this heat. Have to keep 'em hydrated, and they drink a hell of a lot more water than we do."

"Where's all your men?"

"Sleeping, I guess. We've been moving at night. Too

hot in the daytime. I came to check on you, but I'm going back to my bunk in a minute."

"How are you on supplies? Food and water?"

"We're good. The Humvees are full of stuff."

Walker felt dizzy and said, "I'm gonna lie down again." Once back on the cot, he asked, "How bad is it in the cities?"

Hennings shook his head. "Bad. The Koreans are doing what they can to feed everyone, but the rules they've imposed are harsh. It's like Nazi Germany. People have to carry their identity cards on them at all times, and you can be arrested for nothing. They've created detention facilities that are more like concentration camps. The Norks have no problem executing civilians. They hang people from light poles. Families are missing loved ones and don't know what happened to them. They force qualified people to work— you know, engineers, mechanics, programmers—to help rebuild the infrastructure. A lot of civilians are forced to be Quislings."

"What?"

"Quislings. Individuals forced to work for the KPA. They keep things running in the occupied territories."

"Collaborators?"

Hennings shrugged. "The difference is they're being forced to do it. The Koreans have their families in a detention center or somewhere with the threat of violence hanging over their heads. The Quislings have no choice but to cooperate. Unfortunately, because they're at a low level and have no official title in the Korean hierarchy, they often become scapegoats if something goes wrong."

Walker sighed. "I don't know what to say. It's worse than I thought."

"Oh, and then there are the race riots. You know about them?"

"No. Wait, yeah, I did hear something. About a mob attacking Koreatown in LA and burning it down?"

Hennings nodded. "That was the beginning. It's been going on for some time now. Anyone obviously not part of the KPA who is Asian is a target. It's crazy. Instead of fighting the real enemy—the KPA—the people are taking it out on American citizens who happen to be Asian. Now younger Korean Americans and other Asians are fighting back against the mobs. Americans attacking Americans. It's become an all-out war, and both sides are fighting the wrong enemy."

Walker rubbed his forehead. "Jesus, what a mess."

Hennings sat on the stool again. "So, listen, Mr. Walker. Once you're able to get around, what are your plans? You said you had to escape from Twentynine Palms when the Koreans got there. Where were you going, anyway?"

"I didn't have a plan. I just headed out here 'cause I didn't think the Koreans would follow me. I was hoping I'd make it to Vegas or somewhere."

Hennings nodded. "We can give you a compass and a map. That might help."

"Thanks."

The captain stood. "Well, I'll let you get some rest. We may pull out tonight, so we'll leave you the tent.

We have plenty since we lost so many of our guys. I'll see you before we go."

Hennings started to leave, but Walker got up. "Captain, wait." He was unsteady on his feet, but at least he could stand without help. "Take me with you."

The man shook his head. "Can't do it. You're not trained. You'd be a liability."

"I learned how to shoot the M4. I've gotten pretty good, too."

"You're not trained to be a soldier, Walker. If we run into a squad of Norks and get into a firefight, I don't want to have to babysit you. Sorry."

"Wait. Look, I'm a journalist. A reporter. What if I became your embedded correspondent? You know, it's done all the time. Reporters tag along with army units to give first-hand accounts of what's happening. We need that. Americans need that. I want to find a way to get the *truth* to the people. I may not have a way to disseminate it right now, but I can start compiling stories. Eventually we'll come across radios that work or something. Somebody out there is broadcasting information—I know that to be true. A guy I met told me about an underground network of folks with repaired radios, or maybe they were shielded from the blast. As time goes on, more and more people will have access to repaired equipment. You need me, Captain. I can be your *voice*."

Hennings pursed his lips and looked at Walker. "You're not in any shape to move. You still need recovery time."

"Don't some of your other men, as well? Are they ready to leave tonight?"

"They're gonna ride in the Humvees until they get better."

"Is there room for one more?"

Hennings opened the tent flap and looked out. "Let me sleep on it. I'll let you know tonight." With that, he left and walked across the campsite to his own quarters.

Walker returned to the cot, willing himself to feel better. There was no way in hell he was going to let the Guardsmen leave him alone in the desert again.

FIFTEEN

JUNE, 2025

As time passed, Walker and the other two Guardsmen with heatstroke eventually recovered. The unit moved northeast across the Mojave at a snail's pace, simply because it was too hot to travel very far during the day and too cold at night. The trek was especially difficult for the horses, which weren't used to desert conditions. As Captain Hennings once remarked, "After all, they're not camels." The unit of nineteen men clocked, at best, twelve miles a day.

Once Walker felt better, he got to know the other men. There was Johnson and Hodge, Kowalski and Masters, Drebbins and Mitchell, Marino and Goldberg, and others whose names he never remembered . . . and then there was Sergeant Kopple, who took the journalist under his wing. On the day the group set off again, he introduced himself.

"You Walker? I'm Sergeant Wally Kopple," he said. "I've been given the dubious task of taking you through basic training on-the-go, so to speak."

"Call me Ben. Thanks, I could use the training."

"Never call men by their first names. You're Walker. And I'm Sergeant Kopple. Got it?"

"Sure."

Kopple was a crusty military lifer in his late forties. His longish gray hair, mustache, and facial hair were a direct contrast to the more traditional buzz-cuts and clean-shaven appearance the other men had, although most of the soldiers hadn't shaved or had haircuts in weeks. Hennings, on the other hand, used a straight razor on his face every other day, without water or lather.

On the first day that Walker felt able, Kopple instructed him to bring the M4 to a "practice range" a few meters from camp. He coughed hoarsely and said, "The beauty about the desert is the entire place is a practice range." He pointed to a cactus shaped uncannily like a human being standing twenty yards away. "Shoot that guy's head off."

Walker held the rifle up and peered through the scope.

"Hold on, hold on, wait a sec," Kopple said. "You're holding your breath. Relax and breathe."

Walker had never thought of that. He'd always unwittingly anticipated the recoil and fought against it. He raised the rifle again.

"Hold on, hold on, wait a sec. First of all, you need to ask yourself, is that a long range target, a medium range one, or a short range one."

Walker guessed. "Medium?"

Kopple coughed and shrugged. "Sure. Some instructors might say it's short range. That's about twenty yards so it could go either way. One rule of thumb for short and medium range targets is the more rounds, the better. Use burst fire."

"If you say so."

"Why don't you try your three-burst mode and blow the shit outta that cactus."

Walker flipped the switch up and aimed. When he squeezed the trigger, the rifle popped three times in rapid succession. The cactus remained intact.

Kopple coughed and said, "Don't worry, you're doing fine."

"I missed it completely."

"You're tensing up. You're doing what I call 'spray and pray.' In other words, when you're spraying, don't panic. Keep your aim controlled. You may want to aim slightly lower than the head or torso to compensate for that itty-bitty recoil."

Walker tried again. This time he blew away the upper third of the cactus-man.

"Excellent!" Kopple said. "We just might make a soldier out of you yet. Let's try some long range shooting." He coughed again.

"Wally, er, Sergeant Kopple, that cough sounds kinda bad. Are you all right?"

Kopple waved him away. "Don't worry about it, it's probably cancer. It's been like this for almost a year. All kinds of crap comes up sometimes." He pointed to a group of cacti fifty yards in the distance. "See those guys over there? That's a squad of Koreans, aiming right at you. What do you do?"

Walker raised the gun.

"Hold on, hold on, wait a sec. What firing mode you gonna select?"

"Spray fire?"

"That might work, but I find that single-shot mode

is pretty good for long range. I guess it depends on how many of the enemy you're facing. Let's say it's just one guy instead of six. Try shooting the cactus on the far left with just one shot."

Walker aimed. He did his best to place the crosshairs on the cactus' "head." He squeezed the trigger—and missed.

"That's okay, that's okay. Try again. Aim a little lower. You'll get used to it."

"I thought I *was* used to it. I've been firing this thing for a couple of months!"

"Try it again. Go for a body shot."

Walker raised the rifle, aimed, remembered to breathe, and squeezed the trigger. Sure enough, most of the cactus was gone.

"Wow." Walker stuck a finger in his ear and wiggled it. "It's loud. My ears are ringing. I still haven't gotten used to that."

"You need some ear plugs, although during a firefight you'll need to be able to hear your mates. Now this time use the three-burst spray on those other guys. Put that slight recoil to good use. For that much distance, it's best to aim for the upper chest. Not only will your target suffer the damage from a bullet to the chest, the recoil of the second or third shot will probably take the head off. Or you could try a strafing technique, but I don't advise it because it wastes ammo."

Walker nodded, crouched on one knee, and aimed.

"Hold on, hold on, wait a sec. Why are you down on one knee?"

"My aim is steadier when I do this."

"Yeah, that may be, but crouching *really* makes you an easy target. If you're facing one guy, that's probably okay. But not against a group. Nuh uh."

Walker stood. "Okay."

"Now blast the hell out of those Norks over there."

He aimed, fired three bursts at the cactus on the far right, pulled to the left but skipped a cactus, fired three more rounds, moved to the right to hit the target he jumped over, and continued until all five remaining "Koreans" were in tatters.

"Not bad."

"Not bad? I obliterated them!"

Kopple shrugged and coughed. He glanced at the position of the sun and back at the camp. "We should get back and get some shut-eye. We'll do some more tomorrow."

"Okay."

As they walked back to the tents, Walker noticed a familiar shadow moving along the ground. He looked up—and there it was.

"Goddamned buzzard," he muttered. He raised the rifle and aimed, following the bird as it circled over its intended prey. "I don't like being followed, you mangy bastard!" Walker allowed the buzzard to lead his aim until the sun wasn't in his eyes, and then he squeezed the trigger. The buzzard jerked in the air, seemed to float motionless for a second, and finally dropped with a faint *plop* some fifteen yards away.

He lowered the rifle, proud of himself. "That thing's been on my ass ever since I left Twentynine Palms."

* * *

JULY, 2025

The unit moved faster when it reached the area of the Mojave Desert known as the Devils Playground. The relatively flat plains contrasted to the terrain of the Bristol Mountains, which delayed the National Guardsmen's progress for nearly a month. There was a compromise for the increased speed, however. Dunes and salt flats spread for miles; they reflected the direct sunlight, making the heat more brutal than before. One horse collapsed from heat exhaustion. Captain Hennings shot the animal. Morale was low. Several men questioned the wisdom of crossing the desert. Maybe it would have been better to have taken their chances on the highway and confront the enemy rather than bake for three months in hell.

Walker continued his training with Sergeant Kopple by working on stealth exercises and combat movement. One of Kopple's adages was, "Don't run around like an idiot." Walker practiced advancing with the rifle up and aimed, never taking his sight off a target. He caught on quickly, and Kopple grudgingly admitted the journalist was a better newbie than most recruits.

As June rolled into July, a mysterious virus struck the unit, a few men at a time. At first the captain thought their food had gone bad, but the symptoms went beyond simple food poisoning. As soon as the sick men felt better, another group fell ill. For three weeks, the men lay in their tents, barely able to move. Simple acts of drinking a little water, consuming cold broth, and relieving oneself were monumental tasks. Kopple, who had spent time in Africa and Southeast Asia, opined that it was a strain of the Knoxville Fever that struck America in 2021.

Three men died. Then, toward the end of July, the Guardsmen started feeling better. The virus had run its course and the hearty ones survived. Nevertheless, four soldiers remained sick for another week and Hennings didn't think they were going to make it; but just as the outlook appeared the grimmest, they, too, showed signs of recovery.

Weakened, but eager to move on, the National Guardsmen pushed forward, determined to cross Nevada and reach Utah by September. There were now sixteen men, including Walker, and seven horses. The Humvees never broke down the entire time. One of the vehicles carried nothing but fuel and supplies. The other two were armed, one with an M2 .50 caliber heavy machine gun, the other with an MK19 grenade launcher, both controlled by Common Remotely Operated Weapon Stations within the Humvees. The CROWS enabled the fighting crews to acquire targets and fire from inside the vehicles.

They finally reached a bluff overlooking Interstate-15, the preferred highway between Los Angeles and Las Vegas. From a quarter-mile away, they could see that a small number of empty, abandoned cars still littered the road. Hennings, riding one of the horses, ordered the men to stay back until a scout performed a reconnaissance. Kowalski rode ahead, spent ten minutes looking up and down the road with binoculars, and returned.

"Captain, there's a caravan of vehicles heading our way from the west. I think they're Korean. One IFV and two Humvees."

"How far away?"

"Maybe two miles."

"What kind of IFV?"

"Difficult to say, sir. Looked like one of ours. LAV. Twenty-Five, maybe."

"How many men?"

"Impossible to say, sir. However many could fit in all three vehicles would be the worst case scenario."

"Are the Humvees armed?"

"Didn't appear so, sir."

Hennings turned to Kopple, who was the second highest-ranking soldier. "What do you think?"

"We can take out an IFV. I think. I hope he's right about the Humvees not being armed. Then we'd just have to worry about the men inside and whatever they're carrying."

Hennings took the binoculars and scanned the highway. "I see them. They're moving at a steady pace. We'll have to hurry if we're gonna do this." He lowered the binoculars and made the call. "I want the designated riders to remain on their horses, everyone else in the Humvees. We go for the IFV first. Plan Reach-around, okay?"

"Got it."

Hennings instructed the six other riders to follow him west along the bluff so they could attack the Koreans' flank. As they took off, Kopple turned to Walker. "You should stay back here."

Walker was incensed. "No way, man, I'm going with you."

"You're not ready for a firefight."

"Sure I am. I'm not staying back here. I mean it."

Kopple coughed and spit brownish phlegm on the ground. "Suit yourself. Don't run around like an idiot."

The remaining men poured into the Humvees—two in the supply carrier and seven in the armed ones. Walker followed Kopple into the Humvee with the MK19. Johnson manned the gun. The sergeant sat in the front seat and issued the order to roll.

The three vehicles bolted forward, down the bluff, and toward the Interstate. The Koreans were moving perpendicular to the National Guardsmen at the same rate of speed—both sides right on a collision course to intersect at the highway. At the same time, however, the seven horsemen, armed with M4s and M16s, galloped diagonally toward the road *behind* the Koreans.

When the Humvees reached within a hundred yards of the Interstate, the Koreans reacted. Their three vehicles halted and the IFV's M242 Bushmaster 25mm cannon swiveled around to face the attackers. Its two M240 machine guns immediately started blasting at the Guardsmen's Humvees.

Johnson commenced firing the grenade launcher. The first M430 round struck the front wheels of the LAV-25 and exploded in a cloud of black smoke. At the same time, though, the IFV's Bushmaster fired a shell. The Humvees' drivers swerved to avoid the hit—just barely—as the shell blew a crater in the ground. The force of the blast lifted the side of one Humvee and almost flipped it over, but the driver managed to keep the vehicle moving, balanced on its right wheels, until the elevated side dropped a few seconds later.

The smoke in front of the IFV cleared, revealing that its front treads were disabled by the grenade. It wasn't going anywhere.

The doors on the Koreans' two Humvees opened and four KPA infantry, armed with automatic machine guns, poured out of each. They had seen the advancing horsemen.

Walker had never witnessed anything like the firefight between the Korean infantry and the Guardsmen on horseback. The image suggested a strange hybrid of a Western and a War movie—the good guys galloping on horses in a circle around the vehicles, albeit with contemporary automatic weapons in hand, and the evil enemy hunkered down around modern military machinery to return fire. It was totally surreal.

Johnson launched another grenade. This time it hit the Bushmaster cannon assembly, obliterating it in a massive explosion that rocked the IFV. The machine guns continued to fire, but they inflicted no damage to the Humvees.

Kopple gave the order to halt the vehicles—they were close enough to the Koreans.

"Take out those machine guns!" he shouted to Johnson.

The MK19 fired another high-explosive round at the IFV, this time knocking out the rear treads. Meanwhile, the Korean soldiers took positions behind the Humvees and shot at the horsemen. One animal went down, spilling its rider. The Guardsman bounced back unharmed and charged the enemy on foot. The Korean operators of the IFV's machine guns must have realized that shooting at the Humvees did no damage, so the guns swerved toward the riders. The spray of bullets hit two more horses and men.

"Damn it!" Kopple shouted. "Come on, Johnson, take out those guns!"

Another launch struck the side of the IFV, blasting a hole near the top. Smoke gushed out. Whoever was inside was certainly injured, for the machine guns ceased firing.

"Keep at it, Johnson. I don't want to take the chance that one of them bastards is still alive in there. The rest of you—go, go, go!"

The men piled out of the Humvees, shouting war cries: "Land of the free!" "Long live America!" "Remember Pearl Harbor!"

With four remaining horsemen and nine Guardsmen rushing the Koreans, the enemy was outnumbered. Their targets were split, coming from two directions, providing the Americans with the advantage. Walker then understood the meaning of Hennings' "Plan Reach-around."

The last one out of the Humvee, Walker felt simultaneous surges of energy and fright. Was he really about to go into *battle*? He was thirty-four years old, way too young to die. Not once in his short life had he ever envisioned himself performing military service. Yet, here he was, in the middle of the Mojave Desert, about to join a bunch of National Guardsmen in an ambush against the worst enemy the United States had ever faced.

"Christ," he murmured, and then he, too, cried out for "Glory!" and ran forward with the M4 raised to his eye as he'd been instructed.

The grenade launcher fired again twice in succession, this time knocking out the IFV's two machine guns and blowing another hole in the top of the vehicle. The four remaining horsemen rode around to the opposite side of the road and strafed the sides of the Humvees, hitting several of the enemy. No longer shielded behind cover, the standing Koreans were pinned against their vehicles. They fired recklessly at the aggressors while attempting to run for nonexistent protection. The horsemen had no problem mowing them down.

One man bolted toward the Americans on the other side, wildly shooting anything in sight. He hit two men and headed straight for Walker.

Oh my God, he's coming right at me!

As Walker met the enemy's eyes, time seemed to slow down. What was in actuality the span of two seconds felt like an eternity. He hesitated. Could he kill a man? Really kill him?

The running Korean, his face contorted with desperation, raised his rifle and pointed it at Walker.

Squeeze the damned trigger, you fool! Don't run around like an idiot!

Walker couldn't bring himself to do it. That was a human life running toward him.

But he's going to kill you if you don't act first!

Everything happened in slow motion. Walker couldn't make his finger move.

It was finally the heat of other bullets whizzing past Walker's head that motivated him to act. He remembered Kopple's words.

Short Range: three-burst spray.

Walker squeezed the trigger and the rifle kicked three times.

The rushing Korean jerked violently, fired his weapon, *missed*, and toppled to the ground. Walker wasn't sure where he'd hit the man, but the guy wasn't moving. He ran forward, gun ready, and examined his handiwork. Two out of three. One round had gone astray, but the other two had hit the Korean in the chest and side of the face. Instead of a cheekbone, there was an ugly, red, wet hole.

Holy shit. I've killed a man.

Walker experienced an immediate knee-jerk reaction and froze as a wave of conflicting emotions swept through his body. On the one hand, he was frightened, shocked, and appalled that he could take another human life. On the other, he felt exhilaration. Was that wrong?

Remember, he told himself. *This man was an enemy of my country. He was one of many who tried to destroy our way of life. He deserved to die.*

"You gonna stand there staring at your buddy or are you gonna help us clean up?"

Walker looked up to see Kopple in front of him.

"Huh?" He realized there was no noise. The gunfire

had ceased. It was over. "How long were we fighting?"

"What?"

"How long did the battle last?"

Kopple looked at Walker as if that was the strangest question he'd ever heard. "Two minutes. Not even that."

"Seriously?"

"Yeah, why?"

"That's fast. I thought it would take longer. I thought we'd be out here for an hour, battling it out until we were either dead or our ammo ran out."

Kopple shook his head and coughed. "It ain't like that. It always happens so fast that if you don't keep ahead of the seconds going by, you get killed."

Walker took a deep breath. "Did we win?"

"You bet your ass. Got ourselves a prisoner, too."

Walker surveyed the scene. All of the Korean infantry were dead. Their IFV was useless. Two Guardsmen pointed guns at a lone Korean on his knees with his hands behind his head. His uniform was charred and his face was black from smoke. He must have been inside the IFV.

Three horses were dead.

"Did we lose anyone?"

"Two. Masters and Hodge."

Walker saw them lying on the ground. Another two Guardsmen were wounded but were on their feet.

"We gained two more Humvees and some supplies," Kopple said. "This was a successful mission." He coughed, spat phlegm, and clapped Walker on the arm. "You done good, Walker. For a newbie. And you didn't run around like an idiot."

Kopple walked away and joined Captain Hennings, who was talking to the Korean prisoner. Walker kept his distance, but somehow he knew what was going to happen.

Hennings drew a handgun from a holster on his belt, pointed it at the Korean's left temple, and blew the man's brains out.

Normally Walker would have been shocked and appalled, but he wasn't. It was then and there that he knew something had turned inside of him. There was no way he would ever again be the man he was six months earlier.

As the men regrouped and examined the contents of the Koreans' Humvees, Hennings caught Walker watching him. The captain shrugged.

Walker didn't have a problem with that.

SIXTEEN

AUGUST 5, 2025

The Guardsmen reached Las Vegas during the morning hours, when once upon a time in "Sin City" most citizens and tourists would be sleeping off a wild night on the town while the hardcore gamblers would already be shouting "Jackpot!" on the floors of the big hotel casinos. However, during the past decade, Las Vegas as a destination hot spot declined with the country's failing economy. The glorious and gaudy establishments that lined the Strip closed down, but the shells remained intact, a ghostly reminder of America's decadent prosperity. The spectacular neon lights and signs, which used to operate even during daylight hours, stayed dead 24/7. There were no more live shows, no showgirls, and no stand-up comics. It was a real drag.

That's what the city was like the last time Walker visited Vegas, at least three years before the EMP blast.

But as the small caravan of horses and Humvees rolled along Las Vegas Boulevard, Walker could see that something had changed. For one thing, plenty of people were on the streets and they didn't appear too downtrodden. Some of the population waved and cheered at the soldiers, but it seemed to Walker that most of them were *busy,* walking somewhere with *purpose.* Some were laughing. Families were out for a walk. Couples held hands. Surprisingly, there appeared to be a lot of activity in front of the derelict hotels. The Guardsmen passed the iconic buildings of the Luxor and Excalibur, New York New York, the old Planet Hollywood, the Bellagio, and Bally's, and it was as if the casinos had reopened and were doing a booming business. People walked in and out, and there was a bounce to their steps. Most remarkable of all, they looked *clean,* as if they'd showered that morning, and their clothing appeared to be freshly-laundered.

My God, Walker thought. *These folks look relatively happy!*

Another striking aspect was that the Strip was clear of abandoned vehicles. It had become a pedestrian walkway, although Walker was astonished to see a few working automobiles puttering along.

When the caravan reached the front of Caesars Palace, a man in a sheriff's uniform stood in the middle of the street, waving his arms for the Guardsmen to stop. He looked to be in his late fifties, had a paunch, and was as well-groomed as the civilians. The Humvees came to a halt and Captain Hennings dismounted from the lead horse. Many of the men got out of the vehicles, including Walker. The big man held out his palm.

"I'm Sheriff McConley, but everyone calls me

Sheriff Mack. Welcome to Las Vegas. Where are you boys from?"

Hennings shook his hand. "We're a National Guard unit from Los Angeles, on our way to Utah. I'm Captain Hennings."

"I gotta say, you're the first military outfit we've seen since February. Are you just passing through or are you planning to stay awhile?"

Hennings looked at his men. It was clear they wanted to stop.

"I imagine we'll take a rest here, if you don't mind."

"Well, Captain, I'm gonna have to ask you to move your Humvees over to one of the hotel parking lots. Don't worry, they'll be safe. I believe there's room in the Caesars Palace lot behind the hotel. As for the horses, there's a nice shady fenced corral where we've got some of the other animals from the old circus shows. Don't worry, there are no tigers or anything like that. It's two blocks north, to the right, off of Sands Avenue. You'll see the golf course. The corral is right there."

Walker spoke up. "Sheriff, what's going on here? Aside from the obvious lack of electricity, it looks like you're all doing pretty well."

The sheriff shrugged. "We're getting by. Why don't you park your vehicles and come over there—" he pointed across the street to Harrah's—"I've set up my office in the lobby. I'll give you the lay of the land."

The Guardsmen deposited the Humvees in the designated lot while four men rode the horses to the corral. On the walk back to Harrah's, the soldiers were well aware they stood out from the crowd—their uniforms were filthy, they hadn't bathed or shaved in months, and probably reeked. Johnson remarked, "Man, oh, man, have you checked out the *women*? They all look so fresh and . . . *beautiful*!" Walker agreed. It was a sight for sore and weary eyes.

They all met back at the sheriff's place. One of the privates who'd been to the corral was amazed that there were people actually playing golf on the course. He said the horses acted as if they'd died and gone to heaven when they were let loose with the other animals.

The sheriff sat them down and said, "I can see by the looks on your faces that you're impressed by what you've seen so far."

"I'll say," Kopple said. "Were you guys not hit as hard as the rest of the country?"

McConley replied, "We were at first. But then the Koreans took over Hoover Dam and Boulder City. Over the past four months or so, they repaired much of the damage on the dam. It's probably for their benefit, but they got the water going. And that means we have running water in Las Vegas."

Walker nodded. Everything made sense. That's why everyone looked so good. It was extraordinary what a little thing like running water could do to make a difference in a civilization.

"That doesn't mean everything is rosy," the sheriff continued. "The housing situation was bad before the Koreans hit us. Unemployment was at sixty-five percent in the city. After the EMP there was a mass exodus to LA or San Francisco or Denver. It's rough getting any kind of supplies from the outside, seeing that we're stuck in the middle of a desert. Without electricity, there's still a lot of stuff that doesn't work. No one's been able to access their money out of banks since January sixteenth. There's no money changing hands, which in Las Vegas, I know sounds ridiculous. But we've worked out something else. We have our own little economic system going and so far it's worked pretty well."

"What's that?" Hennings asked.

"Casino chips. We're using them as currency."

Walker wanted to laugh. "You're joking."

"No, sir. Don't get me wrong, they don't get you very far. It's not like real money, they're more like credit tokens. We use them to keep food vendors in business, run some essential services like law enforcement, and for, well, entertainment."

"Entertainment?"

"The casinos are open, my friends. There's no electricity and everyone plays by candlelight. The slots don't work, of course, but all the games that didn't depend on electricity are active. You know, card games, craps, roulette, that kind of thing. No one bets with real money; they use the chips." McConley shrugged. "It satisfies the heavy gamblers' addiction and it gives the rest of us something fun to do. Believe me, living here isn't paradise. As you know, it's hot as hell. Without AC the buildings are like furnaces. We keep all the windows in the hotels open. Oh, and most people have moved in to the hotel rooms on the lower floors. The mayor finally made it a free-for-all town after a couple months of people living on the street. So feel free to pick a hotel, select a room, and take a shower. I have to say you boys, ahem, need one."

"Sounds like paradise to me," Johnson said.

"What are you doing for food?" Hennings asked.

"We have four communal mess halls in the city. The one over here on the Strip is at the Bellagio. They're only open for breakfast and dinner, seven to nine in the morning and six to eight in the evening. You'll need casino chips to buy a meal. We have a big greenhouse where we grow vegetables. There's no meat, but we have chickens that lay eggs so you can have yourself an omelet. We don't kill the chickens, there's not enough of 'em. And that brings me to some of the other rules. No thievery of any kind. We deal with that crime severely. Because you're military you can hold on to your weapons, but you better not fire them. I suggest you don't leave them in your hotel rooms. Even though we have strict rules on theft, someone just might like to have one of those automatic machine guns. We also have a strict limit on the amount of alcohol anyone can have, mainly because we're in short supply. It's another commodity we have to ration. There's a two-drink *maximum* in the casinos."

"That's a first," Kopple remarked.

Hennings asked, "So there's no Korean presence in the city?"

McConley shook his head. "Hard to believe, but it's true. They've ignored us. I guess they figure there's nothing here for them. In my opinion, Las Vegas represents the old decadence and capitalist spirit of

America, so they don't want to soil themselves by
setting foot in it. I'm just guessing. I keep thinking
any day they're gonna show up, but until that happens we're trying to make do with what we've got
and enjoy ourselves. I'm quite proud of the way we've
adapted. We all came together and cooperated to
make it work."

"This is remarkable," Walker said.

Hennings leaned forward. "Tell me, sheriff, do you
know anything about a resistance group operating
in Utah near Bryce Canyon? We're on our way to a
hardened complex there."

"I'm aware of resistance cells around the country,
but I don't know of one near Bryce Canyon. That
doesn't mean it doesn't exist. Without communications . . . " The sheriff held up a finger. "However!
We *are* able to receive some radio transmissions."

Walker's eyebrows went up. "How?"

McConley checked his watch. "You're in luck; it's
just about time for a broadcast. I have a ham radio
I kept in my basement at home. It wasn't damaged.
I have it here in the other room, come take a look."

The men stood and followed the sheriff into a small
space containing a table, three chairs, and a ham radio
that appeared to be circa 1980s. There was a portable
generator beneath the table that he fired up.

"We're utilizing every engine-generator we can for
essential needs, like at the hospital. My department
took control of the gas and we ration it. We have no
idea when we'll get more. I run the generator once a
day to check for any new broadcasts."

"Broadcasts?" Walker asked.

"The Emergency Broadcast System plays a recorded message five times a day. I don't know where it's being broadcast from. They've been playing the same message since early June. I'm hoping it'll change someday soon." He switched on the radio and the various old tubes lit up. Static filled the room through a speaker as McConley fiddled with the knobs to tune in on a signal. After a few seconds, a steady tone replaced the noise. Fascinated by the machine, the men crowded around the table as if it was the first time they'd ever seen such a miraculous device.

The sheriff looked at his watch again and said, "Should start any second."

Walker leaned against the wall and focused on the radio. Ideas brewed in his head but he couldn't quite pinpoint exactly how to interpret them.

Then, a woman's voice came through loud and clear. "This is a broadcast from the Emergency Broadcast System of the Federal Communications Commission of the United States of America. This is a recording made May twelfth, 2025, and it will be broadcast daily at the following hours, Eastern Standard Time: eight a.m., noon, five p.m., ten p.m., and two a.m. The message was recorded by the president of the United States from a safe and secure location."

Walker was all ears. He hadn't heard the president speak since weeks before the attack.

Sure enough, the familiar voice came through the speaker. He introduced himself and began. "My fellow Americans, we are in a state of crisis and your government is fully aware of it and acting upon it. You should know that the vice president, the Cabinet, and I are safe. I cannot reveal the location for obvious reasons, nor can I confirm or deny that we are on U.S. soil. Nevertheless, I want to assure you that we are doing everything within our power to alleviate our situation. I have received official communications from our European allies, and they have all pledged to come to our aid. Unfortunately, due to economic factors that have affected the entire globe, it's going to take some time before this occurs. I cannot estimate what the time frame will be. As some of you know, the Koreans are holding the state of Hawaii hostage with a nuclear device. They also have thousands of Americans locked up in various locations, so-called detention centers, all over the nation. Our military is helpless to attempt retaliation. I urge you all to sit tight and knuckle down. If you are living under direct control of our Korean occupiers, I implore you to do what you can to survive. If cooperation will keep you and your family alive, then do it. If you are hearing this, pass along what I've said to someone who has no access to a working radio. As soon as there is more news to relate, this message will change. We will get through this, my fellow Americans. Pray, keep well, and stay alive."

The recording ended and McConley turned off the radio and generator. "And that hasn't changed since May."

"That's not good," Kopple said with a cough. "Fuck, he could be dead. Everyone in charge could be dead."

There was a sobering silence in the room until Walker asked, "Are other people broadcasting? Ordinary citizens, I mean."

McConley nodded. "Every now and then someone manages to get something across. Usually it's about how bad conditions are in their town and they're asking for help. Sometimes they sound pretty desperate. They're hard to listen to. You know, the only people who can hear this stuff are the ones who've repaired their radios or kept them in shielded environments, like I did."

"Don't you think by now the number of repaired radios would be pretty high?"

The sheriff shrugged. "Maybe."

Kopple looked at Hennings and asked, "So what now, Captain?"

Hennings scanned the eager faces of his men. "Okay, we'll stay a few days. We'll meet here in Harrah's lobby once each morning after the breakfast hours at 0930 starting tomorrow. By the end of the week, though, I'm going to want to move on."

As they walked outside, Kopple looked at Walker and asked, "What are you going to do?"

"I think I'm going over to Caesars and find me a room where I can shower, shave, and relax. Then I'm gonna hit the tables. What about you?"

The sergeant coughed and answered, "Probably the same, except I'm gonna sleep in a real bed for the next twelve hours or so. *Then* I may hit the tables."

They shook hands. "See you around then."

Walker held a hand up to his brow to shield his eyes

from the blistering sun and crossed the street. Inside Caesars lobby, he immediately felt the heavy warmth and stuffiness of the place, but it was better than being outside. A white-haired woman in her sixties or seventies standing behind the old Reception desk handed him a paper fan. He noticed everyone he saw had one and was using it. Behind her on the wall was a huge whiteboard with room numbers and names written on a grid.

"I'll bet you want a room with a shower," she said, eyeing him up and down.

"That would be lovely."

"First two floors are full. There are some empty rooms on the third and fourth. The higher you go, the hotter it is, so I don't recommend anything above the fourth, but it's up to you. And you have to take the stairs. Elevators don't work."

Walker pointed to an empty space on the whiteboard. "Is 322 taken?"

"Nope."

"I guess that's mine, then."

She asked for his name and then wrote it on the space.

"There are no keys. They used to be electronic, you know, so we're all on the honor system. You don't go in anyone else's room unless you're invited. Anyone caught doing so is immediately evicted and reported to the sheriff's office."

"Gotcha."

She picked up a fan and used it on herself as she smiled and batted her eyes. For an older woman, she still had a good figure. Walker thought she might have once been a showgirl.

"Oh, and there's no maid service, obviously," she said. "You'll find linens and such on a table near the elevators on each floor. You're allowed to wash the linens and your clothes by hand in the basement once a week. Or you can use your bathtub any time you want."

"Thank you very much."

"I bet you want some fresh clothes?"

"Is that possible?"

"We have T-shirts and shorts and flip-flops. We charge you in chips but since you don't have any yet, I can give you the clothes now on credit and a starter set of chips—the first ten are free."

Walker was flabbergasted. "Are you for real?"

"I'm afraid so." She went back into the office and returned with a box of ten red chips, T-shirt, shorts, flip-flops, and a one-page contract. "I guessed your size. Bring 'em back if they don't fit. Sign here; it says you owe us twenty chips for the clothes."

He did so gladly.

"You in the army?" the woman asked.

He was still wearing a Marine uniform. "No. I was traveling with a National Guard unit."

She held out a hand for him to shake. "Enjoy your stay at Caesars Palace, buddy. You'll be a nice-looking fella after a bath and a shave."

Six hours later, after that shower and shave, and the best nap he'd ever had, Walker went downstairs in his new T-shirt, shorts, and flip-flops. Ten casino chips were burning a hole in his pocket.

Aside from the modern dress of the occupants, the scene in the casino was like something out of eight-teenth- and nineteenth-century paintings of gambling parlors. The entire room was lit by candles that basked the dealers and players in a soft, magical glow. Shadows danced across the high ceiling. Most of the old Caesars Palace pseudo-Ancient Roman decor was still intact, which, combined with the lighting, cre-ated an other-worldly effect that conjured up a time and place long forgotten. Gone was the cacophony of slot machine noise; in its place was a subdued, almost tranquil, ambience. A jazz quartet even played acous-tic instruments on a stage at one end of the vast hall.

No wonder the residents spend their time in the old casinos, Walker thought. Compared to what he'd experienced since January, this *was* paradise.

He toured the room and watched players at craps, roulette, and blackjack and poker tables. Some high-rollers played baccarat. Walker finally settled on tak-ing a seat at an empty blackjack table, behind which stood a tall, gorgeous female dealer. The brunette appeared to be in her early thirties and wore a T-shirt and shorts like everyone else. Walker thought the shape of her body was exquisite.

"Is there a minimum bet?" he asked.

"Two chips," she answered and held his eye. "New here?"

"Just arrived today." He placed two chips in front of him on the table and she dealt cards. Walker had a six showing and a five underneath. He asked for a card and was given a three.

"Not many people *come* to Las Vegas anymore, they mostly leave," she said. "How did you get here?"

"With a National Guard unit. Card."

"You a Guardsman?"

"Nope." She dealt him a four. He waved his hand. She turned her hidden card, revealing two face cards.

"Twenty," she said.

"Aw, shucks," he said as she flipped over his five.

"Eighteen. Too bad." She took his two chips. He placed two more on the table.

"So you just hitched a ride with them, or what?"

"More or less. I'm a journalist. From LA."

She dealt the cards. He had a face card hidden and a two showing.

"I hear it's pretty bad there."

"When I left it was. It's not so bad here. In fact, it's pretty nice. Card."

She shrugged and dealt him an eight. "We're surviving." He waved his hand and she revealed her cards. "Nineteen." She flipped his and made a face of approval. "Twenty. That's two I owe you." She gave them to him.

"Made my money back. What's your name?"

"Kelsie. Kelsie Wilcox." She held out her hand and he shook it.

"Ben Walker."

"Nice to meet you, Ben."

When she dealt the next hand, Walker made note that she wasn't wearing a wedding ring.

* * *

The casinos shut down during the meal hours so everyone had a chance to eat. Walker asked Wilcox to accompany him to the communal mess hall and "show him the ropes." He had won a total of forty-two chips at the blackjack table, tipped her seven, and walked out with thirty-five, which she guaranteed was more than enough to buy a meal.

The mess hall was a large circus tent, under which rows of picnic tables could seat over a hundred people. On one side of the space was a buffet line of sorts where customers could order whatever was available, pay for it in chips, and take a plate to a table. The evening's fare consisted of oatmeal; a variety of fresh fruit; tossed salad with lettuce, carrots, cucumbers, and tomatoes; and vegetable lasagna cooked over a fire. For dessert one could have watermelon or s'mores—melted marshmallow and chocolate between two graham crackers.

"I have to say," Walker commented as he and Wilcox grabbed seats in the crowded space, "you people have really done something incredible. I can't believe how you've managed to make lemonade out of lemons, so to speak."

Kelsie smiled. "It's kind of like what my Grandma Wilcox did when she was young. She was one of those hippies you read about, you know, the teenagers with long hair that lived in communes in the sixties? She once told me all about living on a farm and having free sex and stuff. She ran around with rock musicians and smoked marijuana. Loved the Grateful Dead and Jefferson Airplane."

Walker laughed. "Geez, Jefferson Airplane. I haven't heard about them in ages. She sounds like a cool grandma."

"Yeah. She passed away in 2003. She contracted MS when she was in her forties. Her last decade of life was pretty awful. It was sad."

"I'm sorry."

"It's all right. You know, Sheriff Mack does a great job. I love the guy. We all do. I think he knows everyone in town by name." She took a bite and said, "So tell me about your experience so far. I want to hear about it."

Walker shook his head. "Not tonight. I've been through a lot of crap. But I'll tell you about it if you're still talking to me tomorrow."

She laughed. "Was that a pick-up line or something?"

"No! I'm sorry, I didn't mean it that way." He turned away, embarrassed. "I meant if I'm still *here*, if I *see* you tomorrow, if you don't decide you can't stand me *tonight* . . . I didn't mean—"

Wilcox laughed again and touched his smooth cheek. "Don't worry, I got it. I'm kidding you."

At that moment Walker was struck by how naturally lovely she was. Her large brown eyes exhibited intelligence and wit, and her full lips betrayed a hint of desire. She was taller than him by an inch or so, and he hoped that didn't matter to her. Her fingers on his recently-shaved face felt wonderful.

"Tell me about you, Kelsie. Are you from Vegas?"

"No, not originally. Believe it or not, I'm from

Houston, Texas."

"You don't have a Texas accent."

"Nah, I lost it somewhere after we moved. When I was twelve, my dad lost his job and we started moving around a lot. I think I must have lived in fifteen different states in the next six years. As soon as I turned eighteen, I left. We were in Chicago at the time. But I graduated from high school, even though I spent it going to six different schools, and I went to college at MIT."

"MIT! Jesus, are you some kind of genius? One of those Mensa chicks?"

"Now *that's* a pick-up line!" she snorted endearingly. Walker loved the way the skin around her eyes crinkled when she laughed. "No, no, I'm no genius. Well, I mean, I earned good grades and was on scholarship, if that counts. That was the only way I could go to MIT."

"What did you study? Quantum physics?"

"Dream on. Electrical engineering."

"You're kidding."

She shook her head and smiled wryly. "And here I am dealing blackjack at a casino in Las Vegas."

"Well, what happened?"

"Life happened. The bad economy happened. The price of oil went up. You *know* what happened."

"How did you come to be in Vegas?"

"Well. I *thought* I had a job, at Hoover Dam no less. I *did* have a job. I moved to Boulder City and was all prepared to start work—when the U.S. Bureau of Reclamation cut seventy percent of the jobs.

Naturally, all the newbies got axed. I was left high and dry. So I came to Vegas and got a job at Caesars Palace. That was just before *it* went under. Even when the city started going down the toilet, I stayed. And then the Koreans invaded. Now I work for the city's reorganized Casino Management Company. The mayor and some other like-minded individuals got together and presented this wacky plan to the people—use casino chips for currency and rebuild the town communally. It smells of socialism, but you know what? It's working."

"Obviously. I wish there was a way to show the rest of America what you're doing. It would be very inspiring."

"But I am using my electrical engineering skills in other ways."

"How's that?"

"I'm part of the team that's working on restoring the city's power grid. I do that when I'm not at the blackjack table."

"Any progress on that?"

She shook her head. "It's going slow. We don't have enough experienced people."

Walker had a thought. "Say, do you know anything about radios?"

"What do you mean?"

"You know, *radios*. Like what the sheriff has in his office. AM/FM. Broadcasting."

"Do you mean the physical object? How to build one?" Walker wasn't sure if that's what he meant, but it sounded good. He nodded and she smiled. "Funny you ask. One of my class projects in school was to build a radio from scratch. So, yeah, I know how to do that. Providing I have the parts."

"Are there parts to be had in the city?"

"There's a communal depot for salvaging electrical components near the hospital, a few blocks north of here. I thought about working there, too, but I figured they could use me more efficiently on the power grid. Anyway, that's where people are bringing appliances and stuff to try and get fixed. There are also a couple of places in town where they fix cars."

"I've noticed some folks driving around." He slapped his head. "Boggles the mind!"

She laughed again. "Why do you ask? About the radio, I mean."

"An idea I have brewing. I'll tell you about it later." He looked at her plate. "You done?"

"Yeah. I have to get back to the casino."

"Well, come on, I have to win some more chips."

They walked to Caesars Palace together. The sun was setting; despite the absence of the classic Las Vegas neon skyline, the Strip was beautiful.

"Where do you live?" he asked.

"At Caesars."

"What floor?"

"Is that a pick-up line?" She laughed at her own joke, but he could hear the flirtation in her voice.

WALKER'S JOURNAL

SEPTEMBER 17, 2025

I haven't made a journal entry in a few weeks. Maybe it's just not what I'm into anymore. I have other things on my mind.

Like . . . I'm in love. That's right, me, Ben Walker, am head over heels in love with a woman named Kelsie Wilcox. I met her last month when the National Guard unit I was traveling with passed through Las Vegas. I was expecting Vegas to be a real dump after everything that's gone on in the country, but boy, was I surprised. Las Vegas is friggin' heaven! Not only have they got their shit together in Vegas—of all places—but that's where I met her.

She's tall—taller than me—and she's gorgeous—better looking than me—and intelligent—a helluva lot smarter than me. We live together in a room at the old Caesars Palace hotel casino. After a month of awkward "dating" (do people still use that word?), she moved in with me. And I can't believe it, but it's working. After my divorce with Rhonda, I never thought I'd have another serious relationship, but that's what it's turning out to be. God, we get along, we make each other laugh, and the sex is incredible!

The National Guard unit moved on a week after we arrived in August. I could tell Captain Hennings felt bad about taking the men away from such an idyllic place. The guy I'm really going to miss, though, is Wally. Sergeant Kopple. We finally got to where we were calling each other by our first names, and he never does that with anyone. I'm worried about him 'cause he's got a bad cough. Sounds serious. I hope they have a real doctor where they're going so he can have it checked out. Of course, with the state of the union being what it is, medicine could be hard to come by. He wouldn't be able to get X-rays. So, what the hell . . . anyway, I wish him well.

At any rate, I didn't have to go with the Guardsmen because I wasn't a National Guard. I elected to stay. I couldn't think of any place else that might be in as good a shape as Vegas. And besides, Kelsie had caught my eye. Big time.

Later, man.

NOVEMBER 8, 2025

I'm now a radio DJ, can you believe it? I'm known as "DJ Ben."

The idea began in September when Kelsie and I went to the electronics parts depot and got a bunch of junk to make a homemade radio. I also picked up an old CD player and some CDs. A little later, Kelsie and I went in together and bought a portable engine-generator. Cost us 3000 chips. So Kelsie and

I built our own transmitter and receiver. It's really a jury-rigged transistor board. Actually she's the one who did all the work. Anyway, it's really this circuit board thingy with tubes on it, and it can plug into an antenna that she made out of aluminum. Now we can receive stuff like that tired old recording by the president (which hasn't changed since May) and even some reports from other folks who have repaired or rebuilt radios. So far we've heard from seven people. There's a guy who calls himself Yankee Doodle—he's in Washington State somewhere. There's a guy in Texas called Max. Depending on how clear the sky is, we can receive stuff from as far away as Missouri.

So then I wanted to start broadcasting on my own. Kelsie fixed the transistor board so we can plug the CD player into it and actually send out music over the air waves. Add a microphone and—voila! Introducing DJ Ben!

At first I did it to amuse myself. I'd play some of my favorite oldies and do a sort of smooth DJ voice. After a while, I started giving news reports. I relayed what I learned from some of the other guys making broadcasts. Mostly I did the whole "peace and love" thing, trying to get people to cooperate with each other, 'cause that's the only way we're going to get out of this mess.

Then, around Halloween, lo and behold—I started receiving messages! "Hey DJ Ben, play some Led Zeppelin!" "Please DJ Ben, play Frank Sinatra!" "Keep it up, DJ Ben, you're making us all feel better!"

Well, that made my day. If playing music boosts morale around the country, then that's what I'm going to do.

DECEMBER 24, 2025

It's Christmas Eve!

Don't have much new to report. It's been a pleasant four months in Vegas. Kelsie and I keep busy playing around with the "radio station" and spend the rest of the time between the sheets.

I've been making friends over the airwaves. I'm in regular contact with Yankee Doodle and Max. I've been able to share information about the Occupation they've told me, and vice versa.

Did I mention how crazy I am about Kelsie?

Now if the Koreans will just stay away and leave us alone, everything will be great.

Merry Christmas to all!

SEVENTEEN

JANUARY 12, 2026

"You're live," Wilcox said as she adjusted the frequency on the transmitter. They sat in their makeshift "station" in one of the upper floor rooms in Caesars Palace. They'd found that the higher up they were, the better the transmission.

Walker winked at her and spoke into the microphone. "This is Radio Free America broadcasting to you from the edge of darkness. Greetings to all of you out there in Korealand. Have you had your daily serving of kimchi? Ha ha, just kidding. This is DJ Ben bringing you another hour of uninterrupted, commercial free news and music. Tonight we have a special treat for you. I'd like to be able to say I have Miles Davis himself in the studio this evening, but I've only got a CD of his classic 1959 album, *Kind of Blue*. It's nice and moody, not just a little melancholic, and oh, so exquisite. And what a band, too. Not only Miles, but John Coltrane, Cannonball Adderley, Paul Chambers, Jimmy Cobb, and Bill Evans. Amazing stuff.

"But before I get to the music, I want to thank everyone who's been broadcasting news to me. I've tried to assimilate the information and intel I've been receiving and am dedicated to delivering it to you, America, just in case you didn't hear it from the original sources. So keep your stories coming in, folks, and I'll do my best to get 'em out there. Now for the news."

Wilcox placed Walker's notes in front of him and kissed his cheek. He smiled at her and studied the sheet.

"I don't know how old this is, or when this actually occurred. I'm afraid we've had a major setback in our fight against the Koreans in San Pedro, California. Locals are calling it the 'San Pedro Firestorm.' Apparently a small group of workers, aided by a squad from the U.S. Army Corp of Engineers, managed to cause a series of major explosions at the Conoco-Phillips Oil Refinery just southeast of Los Angeles airport. The Koreans had control of the refinery, and our boys decided they'd rather destroy the oil than let it fall into the hands of the enemy. Unfortunately, the fires were driven by heavy winds and moved south, engulfing the Long Beach Naval Complex before shifting west. Two weeks after this report was made, areas of San Pedro were still burning. Well, folks, as I said, I don't know how old this report is, so hopefully those fires are out now. Nevertheless, I think the refinery workers and the Corp of Engineers should still be commended for their bravery. Here at Radio Free America, we try to impart only the truth, but seeing that I'm DJ Ben and all, you're also going to get a little bit of editorializing."

Wilcox handed him the next report.

"This next piece just came in from Yankee Doodle, our correspondent in Washington State. First, a little background to the story. In the days following the Korean invasion—God, was that almost a year ago?—the city councils of both Seattle, Washington, and Portland, Oregon, staged nonviolent 'sit-ins' on the steps of both city halls. The Korean military responded by hanging these government officials from downtown light poles."

Walker paused to take a breath and adapted a more serious tone.

"I'm sure those of you in the big cities have seen atrocities like this. It pains me to report them, but as I said earlier, the truth must be heard. At any rate, in the weeks and months that followed, rebels in the two cities instigated a series of arson events against the main shipping areas to keep the Norks from using them. On January second of the New Year, five Elliot Bay cargo facilities were destroyed. The Occupational government then announced a dusk-to-dawn curfew with a strict shoot-on-sight policy for any Americans caught out during that time. This extreme imperative was brought home to Seattle Americans when three days ago, on January ninth, an ambulance crew was stopped and executed by Korean military forces while attempting to answer a midnight call for help. Yankee Doodle reports that both Seattle and Portland have become lawless areas after dark with civilian authorities unable to respond to any crimes or emergencies. So, my friends, it's probably best to stay indoors during the curfew hours. One day we *will* take back our cities from these Korean dickheads."

Wilcox suppressed a laugh; the testimony was too

sobering to act otherwise.

"I suggest to those of you listening that on the anniversary of the attack, on January sixteenth, get together with as many of your family, friends, and loved ones, and hold a vigil. Organize it as you think best. If it's prayer you're into, then go for it. If you want to burn effigies of Kim Jong-un, knock yourselves out. If you just want to hold hands and be silent for a few minutes, that works, too.

"That's our news for this evening, January twelfth, 2026. Keep that truth coming in and I'll do my best to get it out there. Once again, this is DJ Ben. And now, here's Miles Davis and his sextet, performing the album *Kind of Blue*."

Wilcox hit the CD player button and the jazz standard "So What," began it's plaintive, soulful groove. Walker switched off the mic.

"How'd it sound?"

"You're getting better and better," she answered. "You know, I think you could parlay this new talent of yours into something bigger."

"What do you mean?"

"Right now you're very entertaining. You're fun to listen to and you play good music. But when you read the news, especially the more serious stuff, I see and hear a passion that might be very useful. To the Resistance, I mean."

Walker creased his brow. "I don't understand. Isn't reporting these things useful to the Resistance?"

She shrugged. "I don't know. I'm just thinking out loud. Maybe we need to establish a stronger transmitter so we know you're reaching the entire country. Then I think you could really do some good. You're very inspiring, Ben. I think you need to become something a little less frivolous than 'DJ Ben.'"

Walker rubbed his chin. "I'm flattered. Let me think about it. In the meantime, sure, let's make a better transmitter. But first, let's go to bed."

"Isn't it a little early?"

He wiggled his eyebrows. "Who said anything about sleeping?"

She slapped his arm and laughed.

JANUARY 21, 2026

Salmusa removed the "Iron Fish," a specially-designed iron-lined radioactive repellent suit supplied by the People's Nuclear Transport Company. It was much like a scuba outfit, only baggier. The face mask resembled any other protective gas mask except that it, too, was iron-lined and contained eye goggles made of an unbreakable plastic, originally designed by NASA, used for windows on space shuttles. The suit was not completely efficient. A man wearing the Iron Fish could not be exposed to the Cocktail Materials for more than five hours, or he could be contaminated. Contamination meant death.

After depositing the suit in the decontaminator, Salmusa stepped naked into the shower and scrubbed himself with near-scolding hot water. He took no chances with the dangerous chemicals. They had killed at least sixty Korean scientists and handlers since their creation on Marcus Island in Japan. Nevertheless, Operation Cocktail was a success. The combined Materials—X, Y, and Z—were ready for implementation of the Brilliant Comrade's master plan, Operation Water Snake.

Salmusa turned off the water, grabbed a towel, and dried himself. The next procedure was to pass through the radiation detector to see if any remnant of the Materials was left on his body. After he passed the scan, he quickly dressed and then went to the office at Lawrence Livermore National Laboratory in Livermore, California, where he'd spent much of the last three months. As the overseer of Operation Water Snake, Salmusa took this particular assignment far more seriously than anything he'd thus undertaken for Kim Jong-un and the Greater Korean Republic.

He sat and studied the scientists' reports. It was determined that to maintain the high levels of the three combined Source Materials, mixing and depositing the Cocktail worked best underwater. Unfortunately, team members who physically performed the below surface task of mixing and depositing the Cocktail would die from the exposure. The Brilliant Comrade already decreed that these volunteers would be designated as martyrs for the GKR.

Salmusa was pleased. It had been a long, complicated process to reach this point. Transporting the Source Materials from Marcus Island in Japan to Los Angeles, and then delivering them to Livermore, had taken months. Now it was time for the Korean People's Army Light Infantry Division to carry the

Materials to the five designated Deposit Locations on the western banks of the Mississippi River. By the beginning of February, Operation Water Snake would commence.

The Light Infantry was charged with staging and deployment of the Cocktail at Deposit Locations 2, 4, and 5. Two groups of American collaborators from Montana and Texas, code-named Red Eagle and Red Bison, respectively, were responsible for staging and deployment at Locations 1 and 3.

A knock at the door interrupted Salmusa's thoughts. "Yes?"

One of his assistants, a young man named Byun Jin-Sang, opened the door and stood at attention. "Sir! The radio broadcast you've been anticipating is on."

Salmusa stood quickly and followed Byun into another room where new electronic equipment, including a high-powered radio receiver, lined the walls and shelves.

The American was already speaking over the air-waves. Salmusa stood and listened, his eyes narrowing with hatred.

"—wish we could all, and I mean everyone in the world—and that means *you*, Koreans!—could remember John Lennon's words "give peace a chance." We're going to play some more of John Lennon's music—but first, I have this report from our correspondent Max in Texas.

"Apparently a misplaced airdrop of Korean Special Forces led to a hasty march through downtown Galveston, Texas, where the idiots were met with a nasty surprise. Elements of the Texas National Guard and an estimated ten thousand-plus citizens attacked the invading forces along Interstate-45 with a mixture of light infantry firearms and deer rifles. I regret to report that losses were tremendous on the American side, especially when the Norks called in air support. Attack helicopters showed up and made short work of the Texans' defensive positions. However, a minor victory occurred when several tugboat operators launched their explosive-laden ships against the Galveston Causeway, bringing it down. Score one for America! This distracted those dog-eating Koreans long enough for two dozen privately owned pleasure yachts packed with women and children to make it out of the Port of Galveston before those Korean Nazis managed to secure it. Our people slipped out under their very noses and sailed to Mexico."

Salmusa bristled at the announcer's depiction of his people.

"You know, folks, that just goes to show you that Americans are not going to just lie down and let those cowardly, slimy, emotionless, cold-hearted *bugs* that crawled out from under a rock run over us. Those Norks may think they're winning, but I'm hearing more and more accounts of the opposite.

"Say, I hear they call Kim Jong-un the 'Brilliant Comrade.' Well, from now on, on this radio station, he's going to be known as the Idiot Comrade. Did you know he comes from a long line of mutant baboons? His father was a baboon, his grandfather was a baboon, his entire family . . . baboons! Oh, I'm sorry, maybe that's an insult to the rest of the baboons. Heh heh, I got that one from Groucho Marx. I tell you what, faithful listeners. Let's have a contest. Whoever sends me the worst insult—or maybe I should say the *best* insult—for Kim *Dung*-un, I'll deliver it on the air and we can all have a good laugh at the Idiot Comrade's expense."

Fuming, Salmusa felt the blood rushing to his head. He had to stop this disrespect and dishonor. Now.

"I'm sorry, folks, I tend to get a little emotional. And here I am about to play music that's all about peace and love. Maybe that'll calm me down. Up next is John Lennon's solo masterpiece, his album from 1971, *Imagine*."

The music began and Salmusa glanced at Byun. The young assistant shook his head and made a "tsk tsk" sound. Salmusa turned to one of the operators. "Do you know where that signal is coming from?"

"Yes, sir," the technician replied. "We've used signal interceptors and triangulating signal positions to pinpoint where it is. Las Vegas, Nevada."

Salmusa nodded. He pushed past Byun and went back to his office to make a call to Kim Jong-un. He had known for months that the GKR's work at Hoover Dam provided Las Vegas with luxuries other occupied cities did not enjoy. As there was never any reason for the Koreans to waste time and resources with that useless community in the desert, they had reluctantly and carelessly left the city alone.

It was now apparent that Sin City had to go.

EIGHTEEN

JANUARY 24, 2026

The anniversary of the Korean invasion gave people cause to reflect. On the evening of January 16, hundreds of Las Vegas citizens gathered on the Strip, lining the blocks from the old Mandalay Bay Resort to downtown. Several ministers, a priest, and a rabbi from various congregations in the city conducted a candlelight vigil just after sunset. Walker and Wilcox attended; in fact, Walker was asked to say a few words, as he'd become something of a celebrity in town. He politely declined.

Ever since that somber occasion, Walker began having nightmares. He'd wake in the middle of the night in a cold sweat, alarming Kelsie, but unable to remember the dreams. All he knew was that they were premonitions of something bad about to happen. He didn't know what was coming, but he suggested to Wilcox that they stay prepared. They packed backpacks with emergency supplies—water, food, first aid—and fashioned a carrying case for their jury-rigged radio transmitter/receiver. The antenna was designed to collapse, umbrella-style, to the size of a ruler. Unfortunately, the generator was too heavy and cumbersome to consider taking in haste.

But the days passed without incident and life in Sin City went on as before. Walker continued his DJ Ben broadcasts, and he and Wilcox carried on as if they were married.

Then, just after midnight, on the twenty-fourth, Walker's forewarnings came true.

The couple was asleep in their room. The cool January breeze blew through the open windows and made their home in Caesars Palace quite comfortable. Street noise was nonexistent. All was quiet and peaceful, until the low hum of airplanes woke Wilcox. She opened her eyes and listened. The community was used to a Korean-controlled U.S. military aircraft flying overhead every now and then, usually headed east or west. This sounded more ominous. There were *many* planes.

"Ben, wake up," she nudged.

"Hmm?"

"Wake up. Listen."

"What?"

"Planes." She got up and looked out the window. At first she couldn't see anything, but then the blinking lights in the sky caught her attention. "Ben, there's a bunch of planes coming this way."

Then a massive explosion rocked their world. Wilcox screamed. Walker jumped out of bed and joined her at the window.

Another detonation, this one much closer.

"My God, what's going on?" she cried.

"We're being bombed!"

They scrambled to get on their clothes. Wilcox rushed into the bathroom and gathered a few necessities while Walker grabbed the M4 and ammunition.

Another explosion. This time, they felt the hotel lurch.

"Kelsie, we gotta run! Grab your backpack. We have to get outta here!"

They saw flashes of bright light through the window. Fires burned in the distance. Walker paused long enough to see an American F-35 drop its payload right on top of Harrah's, right across the street. He felt the impact's sonic boom as a fireball engulfed the huge hotel. Glass and steel flew out from the impact.

"Go!" he shouted.

They scrambled out the door with their backpacks and other things. Dozens of residents were already in the hallway, panicked and confused.

"Everyone get out of the building!" Walker shouted. They headed for the stairwell with the rest of the crowd, but there were too many people. The exit became bottlenecked, forcing the desperate ones to push and shove.

Amidst the screams were shouts of "Take it easy!" "Keep calm! "Stop pushing!" "Get out of the way!" Walker and Wilcox felt crushed as they squeezed through the stairwell door. The stampede carried them to the stairs, where things grew more precarious.

Another explosion jolted everyone off balance. Dozens fell down the stairs to the next landing. The ones who got to their feet first trampled on the people who couldn't get up in time.

Mass hysteria.

Walker and Wilcox were aware they were stepping on human beings but there was nothing they could do. The swarm had a life of its own and there was no fighting it. If they could simply remain upright, the mad charge would do the rest.

When the throng reached the second-floor landing, chunks of plaster rained from above. Several residents were hit on the head and collapsed, causing those behind them to trip and fall. Another wave of bodies crashed down the next set of stairs as the pandemonium increased in intensity. Wilcox was almost sucked with them but Walker quickly grabbed her by the waist to keep her from plummeting. At the same time, however, the mass behind them kept pushing forward, which created an avalanche of people. There was nothing to do but ride the surge, locked between arms and legs and torsos. Walker gripped the M4 as tightly as possible with one hand while holding on to Wilcox with the other. A foot slammed into his face, busting his lip, just as the rolling accumulation of humans smashed into the wall at the bottom of the stairwell.

At least the descent was over. Those that were able stood and ran into the lobby, leaving the injured piled on top of one another, struggling to break free.

Another explosion. The stairwell actually *shifted,* causing larger concrete pieces to drop on the helpless heap. Walker saw that Wilcox was dazed—she must have been hit by something or someone. He squirmed out of the stack of writhing bodies, managed to stand,

and pulled on her arms. She slipped out just as the entire stairwell caved in, burying the stragglers.

They ran into the casino, which was ablaze in several spots. The couple zigzagged through the maze of flames as portions of the ceiling collapsed around them.

Yet another explosion. And another.

A wall of heat and flames erupted from the building's core and rushed at the crowd of civilians, racing them to the exits. But just as Walker and Wilcox reached the main lobby, the floor buckled and swept dozens off their feet. The couple collided into a glass display case, shattering it to bits and lacerating Wilcox's arms and legs. It saved their lives, for the lobby ceiling completely collapsed behind them, killing everyone else.

"Can you get up?" Walker whispered.

She was in tears and frightened out of her wits, but she nodded. As he helped her out of the mound of broken glass, Walker saw that he, too, was cut badly in several places. They were both covered in blood.

Outside, the city was another Dresden. Frantic citizens filled the street, running for their lives. The swarm headed south, the closest way out of the city. Walker looked up in horror as he saw the F-35s make way for a squadron of B-2s that began circling and dropping their deadly consignment. He knew it wasn't going to stop until the entire city was rubble.

"Can you run?"

She nodded.

They followed the exodus, which from the sky likely resembled frenzied insects fleeing exterminators. Buildings all around them were partially or fully demolished and burning. The boulevard itself was an obstacle course of flaming chunks of debris. Charred and broken corpses littered the road. Every few seconds Walker saw someone on fire, screaming in agony, running blindly toward a private hell.

Miraculously the couple made it to the intersection of Las Vegas and Tropicana Boulevards. Sheriff Mack stood in the middle, waving the evacuation southward. Half of his uniform was blackened; his left side and face were badly burned, yet he continued to do his duty.

"Mack!" Walker shouted. "Come on, don't stand here! They can find their way, there's no other place to go!"

The man shook his head and yelled back. It was difficult to hear over the screams, the bomb blasts, and the crashing of buildings. "I'm the captain! I go down with the ship!"

"Don't be daft! There's nothing you can do!"

"Go on, Walker! If I see you again, great. If not, it's been real nice knowing you!" He leaned over and kissed Wilcox's bloody cheek. "Kelsie, take care of him." He looked at Walker. "And *you* take care of *her*! Go! Go!" He pushed them on; the couple couldn't afford to stand there and argue. They left him in the intersection and continued south.

More explosions behind them. Walker didn't dare look back. He knew the bombers were now targeting the fleeing civilians. Up ahead, the fiery remains of the Excalibur and Tropicana Hotels spilled onto the Strip.

Black, debris-filled smoke blanketed the streets, making it extremely difficult to see and breathe. Getting around the ruins was a challenge; too often people blindly ran into pieces of buildings. Fireballs and stone fragments continued to soar through the air, hitting the ground haphazardly. Repeatedly a human was in the way.

Eventually they made it to McCarran Airport, which was also in ruins. Another mile or two to go and they'd be out of the city limits. Despite the lack of oxygen, their wounds, and exhaustion, the couple didn't stop running. But just as they reached the I-215 overpass, another bomb struck the road in front of them. Walker tackled Wilcox and covered her body with his own as a gale of combustion and wreckage shot toward them. Hard, hot fragments of pavement pelted their backs, but the worst of the blast gushed over them. The unfortunate ones who hadn't hit the dirt were killed instantly.

They laid there for a minute until the rumble diminished a bit. Walker looked up and squinted through the smoke. The overpass was destroyed and there was no way they could get through to continue south.

"We have to take another way. Come on."

Wilcox went to stand, but as she got up she grimaced in pain. "Ow! Fuck, my ankle. I must have sprained it."

He helped her move toward a golf course on the left. Some of the greens were ablaze, but there seemed to be a safe passage leading east. A few people followed their lead and trailed behind as the couple half ran, half limped across the ground. Walker and Wilcox ducked reflexively at the roar overhead as the bombers turned for another pass. It was at this point that he laid eyes on the annihilation that spread to the north. He had never seen anything like it. Even the aftermath of the EMP in Los Angeles was nothing remotely similar to the tragic display in front of him. Las Vegas was gone. In its place was a burning, smoking mass of devastation that most likely had buried thousands of human beings. He knew then that he and Kelsie were among the lucky ones. They weren't out of danger yet, but areas farther south that led to the edge of the city limits were untouched.

"Come on, Kelsie, you can make it." She moaned in pain as he helped her along. "We have to keep moving."

Putting weight on her injured ankle, she nodded. "I'm okay." Only then did she get a good look at him. "You're covered in blood."

"So are you, sweetheart." He kissed her. "Come on."

They maneuvered out of the golf course and ended up on Sunset Road. This led them to the intersection of Gilespie Street, from which there appeared to be a clear thoroughfare under I-215 going south. They moved toward it as quickly as possible, deathly afraid the bombers would return to finish them off. Once they got to Warm Springs Road, they turned west toward Las Vegas Boulevard to follow it out of town. After what seemed to be an eon of running, Wilcox had to stop at Pebble Road. She sat on a curb and nursed her leg.

"You were lying about your ankle," Walker said. "It *is* bothering you."

"Shut up. I can make it. Just give me a sec."

"We don't have much farther to go. A couple of miles maybe."

"Great. Then we'll be in the desert in the middle of the night. Oh, Ben, how could this happen? Why did they do this? Why leave us alone for a year and suddenly decide to kick the shit out of us? What *good* does it do them?"

"It's so they can show us who's boss. They did it because they *can*."

After a couple of minutes, she let him help her up. She tried her ankle again and said, "It's better. It really is. It's probably just bruised, not sprained. Let's go."

Exhausted and demoralized, they walked the rest of the way toward the southern end of the city where civilization faded into wilderness. There, they joined a group of a hundred people or more that stood in terrified silence, watching the once majestic, controversial, and historic city they loved burn to the ground. No more casinos, showgirls, circus acts, comedy teams, high-rollers, gangsters, or tourists. No more jackpots, royal flushes, or dreams of fortune.

Game over.

NINETEEN

The sun beat down on the ragtag group of Las Vegas survivors as they marched wearily and painfully northeast along Interstate-15.

After the heartbreak of the firebombing, pockets of refugees surrounded the destroyed city and set off toward destinations unknown. At least Walker had a plan. He told Wilcox about the National Guard's objective to reach a hardened complex near Bryce Canyon in Utah. Lacking a better place to go, they decided to try that. The group of perhaps a hundred, with which the couple found themselves aligned the night of the bombing, camped out on the city's outskirts and set off after sunup on the twenty-fourth. Many of them didn't make it after two hours. Nearly half the group turned back, unable to take the heat. They figured it was better to pick through the Vegas ruins and perhaps find shelter in one of the undamaged homes on the outer edges.

Walker made no attempt to act as leader. When others asked him where he was headed, he simply said, "Utah," and gave no explanation as to why. He was well aware he and Kelsie had just enough supplies for two to last a few days. Most of the survivors had nothing, not having planned or prepared for an emergency evacuation. Eventually, though, both Walker and Wilcox broke down and donated three of their precious water bottles for the group to share. It wouldn't go far in the desert.

By sundown on the first day, a group of approximately thirty had managed to travel fifteen miles. At one point, Walker and Wilcox wanted to keep walking while others insisted on stopping to rest. After repeated occurrences, Walker finally said, "We're sorry, but Kelsie and I can't be responsible for all of you. I've already had one bad experience trying to survive in the desert before coming to Las Vegas. I'm afraid it's every man for himself out here. Either you came prepared or you didn't. If you're up for it, if you've got supplies of your own, you're welcome to join us. But we're moving at our own pace from here on."

One man tried to pick a fight. "But you've got water and food. How are we supposed to make it anywhere? You can't just leave us here!"

"I suggest you go back to Vegas. A lot of people did that last night. You'd probably have a better chance of finding food and water on the outskirts of town. There are still people there."

Wilcox spoke up. "Look, you have to understand if we broke out our food and water and shared it with everyone here, there would be none left in ten minutes. Ben and I have a plan and we're moving forward. Some of you do have food and water with you. It's up to you if you want to come with us. Like Ben said, you're welcome, but you have to keep up with our pace. We don't mean to be heartless, but we're in the desert. It's a harsh environment. It calls for harsh action."

The same man sneered as he indicated Walker's M4. "Says you with the big *gun*. If we tried to take your backpacks, you gonna shoot us?"

Wilcox answered, "No, we're not gonna—"

"Yes," Walker interrupted. "I'll shoot you." Even Wilcox looked at him with surprise. "Kelsie's right. The desert is no place for charity. There are *too many* of you. Now, Kelsie and I are moving on. If you've got your own water and food and you want to come, I'm not going to stop you. The rest of you, go back to Vegas. We wish you the best of luck." He turned to Wilcox and said, "Come on, Kelsie." He took her arm and they continued walking along the highway. Eight people with backpacks rushed to catch up with them. The nearly twenty that were left stood in shock and anger. The man who had challenged Walker attempted to garner support for a coup and attack the couple before they got out of sight. He wasn't successful. In the end, they all turned around and walked back to the pile of rubble that was Las Vegas.

Up ahead, no one but Wilcox could see that Walker had tears in his eyes.

JANUARY 25, 2026

After breaking away from the larger group, the ten individuals bonded pretty quickly. Besides Walker and Wilcox, there was a young Japanese couple named Makoto and Reiko; two middle-aged African-American ex-Army men, Prescott and Washington; a man in his fifties known only as Jim; and a single mother named Carla Janssen and her teenage twins, Will and Christine. The small band of refugees spent the night under the open sky, huddled together under a tarp belonging to Prescott. The next morning, each person contributed something from their packs for a communal breakfast. In most cases, it was fruit from the Vegas mess hall.

Wilcox already knew everyone, as she'd been a Vegas resident for a while. Walker had met Prescott and Washington, and knew Jim from his dealings with Sheriff Mack. Jim was a male nurse at one of the Vegas hospitals that remained open after the EMP, so at least there was some medical experience in the group. When asked why he never became a doctor, Jim replied that the profession had become too corrupt in the years of the economic crisis. The black market had reached out and ensnared a vast number of physicians who took payoffs to prescribe illegally obtained drugs and accepted kickbacks from insurance companies. Walker knew it to be true—he had done an exposé on the health care industry back in 2018 for a whistle-blowing news website.

Since it was blazingly hot during the day, they traveled only at night, and early morning. During the high temperatures of the day they fashioned a lean-to shelter with Prescott's tarp and two long branches cut from mesquite trees, and slept.

At one point during the next nocturnal hike, the two former soldiers got to talking to Walker.

"Those were F-Thirty-Fives and B-Twos that hit us," Washington said. "*Our* F-Thirty-Fives and B-Twos. The Air Force, I mean."

"That's what I thought, too," Walker agreed. "I couldn't think of any other type of plane that did what they did."

"I'll bet you anything the Norks got them from Whiteman Air Force Base in Missouri," Prescott offered. "It was probably one of their military targets."

"When were you fellas in the army?"

"Iraq, '04 to '07," Washington answered. "That seems like a long time ago now."

"That's when things started to go wrong in this country," Prescott said. "After September eleventh the whole world went screwy. Things just went downhill from there."

"I was ten years old when it happened," Walker said. "I was at school and the teacher started crying. I'll never forget that. I guess there's an event like that for every generation. My grandmother once said she'd never forget the day John F. Kennedy was shot. My mother said she'd never forget the day John Lennon was assassinated. Why is it that we only remember events of violence? The Alamo, Pearl Harbor, the bombing of Hiroshima, the assassinations of Martin Luther King and the Kennedys . . . ?"

Wilcox spoke up. "Come on, we remember lots of good things."

"Like what, Kelsie? Other than national holidays like Christmas and Easter and Thanksgiving, what nonviolent major events do we as a people collectively remember where we were and what we were doing when we heard about them?"

She thought for a minute and finally said, "Touché."

They marched on in silence.

FEBRUARY 2, 2026

After spending four days in the deserted community of Littlefield, Arizona, the "Ragtags," as Walker jokingly referred to the group, continued northeast along I-15 toward St. George, Utah, on bicycles.

Littlefield was a ghost town. Wilcox commented upon arrival that she expected to find corpses in every house, but it appeared that every single soul had just picked up and left. It was decided that the Ragtags split up in parties of two or three and search the place for food and supplies. An old Motel 6 was selected as a rendezvous. It was Makoto and Reiko who found the bicycle shop in the dilapidated downtown area. Walker hated to break in and loot the store, but it wasn't as if there was a line of customers standing outside the door. Each member of the Ragtags picked out a bike that was suitable and kept it with them in their motel rooms—which they also broke into. Most of the convenience stores and grocery stores had been picked over long ago, but Prescott and Washington knocked down a door to a bar tucked away in an alley near the court house. Surprisingly, there was plenty of bottled water and canned sodas, as well as liquor. They also found bags of salted nuts, which became the steady diet for the next few days. On the second night in Littlefield, they threw a party and got wasted. The next day, each person used a bottle of water for a sponge bath to clean off the grime and sweat . . . and blood.

They cycled out of Arizona and across the state line into Utah. Before reaching St. George, however, a small caravan of Korean Humvees and an Abrams tank—all decorated with the despicable Korean American flag—drove past the bicyclers in the same direction. The Ragtags stopped to watch them. The Korean soldiers stared expressionlessly at the Ragtags as they went by. They didn't see Walker's M4, which was safely stashed in a bag strapped to the back of his bike; otherwise there could have been trouble.

"Why didn't they stop and ask us for identity cards?" Wilcox asked.

"They must be in a hurry to get somewhere," Walker said. "You know, I don't have an identity card."

"Neither do I."

The others didn't either.

"What'll they do if you don't have one?" Reiko asked.

"I can't imagine they expect every single person in America to have one," Jim answered. "That's probably only in the occupied cities. There are too many towns and cities and villages in this country. The Koreans can't be everywhere."

It made sense. Walker felt better hearing that.

They reached St. George the same day they left Littlefield. There was still something of a population there. No running water or electricity, as expected, but the inhabitants had organized and developed farming procedures to produce food and they brought in water from the Dixie National Forest, located a short distance north of the city. The citizens immediately knew the Ragtags were newcomers and welcomed them to their humble community. Like in other towns, motels were used for lodging the homeless, but families with extra rooms were happy to put up visitors for a night or two. It was another example of America at its best.

As Walker and Wilcox sat down in an open diner for a dinner of mashed potatoes, broccoli, and beans, the appointed leader of St. George sat down and introduced himself.

"I'm Terrence Marshall, the mayor here. I guess you could say I'm in charge, for what that's worth. Welcome to our town."

"Thank you, sir," Walker said. "I'm Ben Walker and this is Kelsie Wilcox. It's very nice to have a warm meal. We've been on the road several days. A lot of that time we were on foot, walking through the desert."

"Jesus, where from?"

"Las Vegas."

The mayor's face turned grim.

"You know about it, huh?"

"We barely made it out alive," Wilcox said.

The mayor shook his head. "Terrible what those bastards did."

"We saw a tank and some Humvees headed your way earlier today."

Marshall nodded. "They drove right on through. I'm not sure where they were going. Just went straight on up I-15. We've seen quite a bit of that, to tell the truth. Every once in a while they stop and hand out propaganda. Back in November they paid a visit to me at city hall. Questioned me for several hours about resistance activity in the area."

Walker perked his ears. "And?"

"I told them I didn't know anything. Even after they did this." He showed them his left hand. Marshall's pinky finger was missing and in its place was a red, crusty stump. "Hasn't totally healed yet."

"Oh, you poor man," Wilcox said.

Walker clinched his teeth. "Sons of bitches. And is there resistance activity in the area?"

"Not here, but there is to the north and northeast. The Koreans occupy Salt Lake City and are intent on stealing shale oil and ores from our state. I hear Colorado has even more problems in that regard." The mayor gestured outside. "We don't have anything here they'd want."

Walker nodded. "I don't know about the others in our little group, but Kelsie here and I are going to move on in a day or two. If we could take advantage of your generous hospitality, it would be much appreciated."

"Stay as long as you like. You've been through a lot, I can tell. In fact, my wife and I have a spare room in our house. You can stay with us."

"Thank you."

After they finished their meal and stepped outside the diner, a bill pasted on a lamp post caught Walker's attention. He went closer to it and then turned away, repulsed.

"What?" Wilcox asked.

"Horace Danziger. They killed him."

She gasped and moved past him to see the leaflet for herself. It was a picture of the famous TV news pundit and Internet blogger, tied to a chair and hanged by the neck. Beneath the photo was printed: horace danziger died for these words: "fight the bastards in our streets and neighborhoods. pick up any weapon you can find and kill the first korean you see. organize into resistance groups and give them hell. i wish you luck."

Mayor Marshall joined them. "You haven't seen that?"

"No."

"The Norks distributed that flyer all over the country. I'm pretty sure they did it thinking it was gonna scare people. If you ask me, it backfired. It just made everyone more determined to fight back. That handbill did a lot for recruitment to the Resistance."

"I can see why," Walker said.

FEBRUARY 5, 2026

Walker, Wilcox, Prescott, Washington, and Jim moved on after a couple days of rest. The other Ragtags elected to stay in St. George, as it was relatively stable and safe. Both Prescott and Washington were as interested as Walker in finding the resistance cell near Bryce Canyon. They were, as they put it, "ready to get back into the fight." What had happened in Las Vegas convinced them they had never emotionally retired from the army.

The quintet bicycled north on I-15, passing Zion National Park, until they reached Cedar City, which took most of one day. Now armed with camping gear picked up in St. George, sleeping outdoors was more comfortable. The weather was much cooler than it had been in the deserts of Nevada and Arizona. While the landscape was still arid and rocky, the altitude was higher. The roads were also surrounded by the Dixie National Forest, which cooled things down considerably. Thus, the team was forced to dress more warmly, especially at night.

The cyclers turned east on Highway 14, which wound through a thicker section of the forest. By this time, a year after the EMP, less abandoned automobiles dotted the roads, allowing a clear, obstructionless passage. Walker considered this was possibly because they were in open country rather than near big cities. And it was beautiful country—Walker had never been in Utah before; it was stunning.

After another night in the forest, the Ragtags turned north on Highway 89 toward Bryce Canyon National Park. Here in the rocky wilderness, Walker could imagine that America had never been invaded, that there was no such thing as electricity for the EMP to snuff out, and that all was well with the world. But his idyllic daydreams were interrupted when they passed through a small deserted town by the name of Hatch. On the road ahead, just outside the village, were a couple of military Humvees and several men carrying weapons. Prescott didn't like the way the outfit was moving slowly in their direction, as if they were looking for someone or something.

The Ragtags quietly moved their bicycles off the highway and hid in the trees.

"I can't tell if they're Korean or not," Jim whispered.

"We'll know when they get closer," Walker replied.

The Humvees drove at ten or fifteen miles per hour. The men kept moving on and off the road, their weapons pointed into the trees. It wasn't long, though, before the Ragtags could see that they weren't Korean. The men were dressed in a patchwork collection of military uniforms—some from the Army, some from the National Guard, some from the Marines. Others wore police uniforms. A few were in civilian clothes. They all carried guns of various types.

"This is a resistance cell, folks," Walker announced. "I believe these boys are on our side!"

He stood and waved, making his presence known, and the others quickly joined him. The soldiers swung their rifles toward the Ragtags, but Walker called out, "Hey, we're Americans!" The men lowered their guns, waved, and moved forward. The two parties met in the middle of the road and shook hands. Walker and his team introduced themselves.

A tall and beefy blond soldier dressed in a Marine outfit appeared to be the man in charge. "I'm Weimar," he said, pronouncing the "W" as a "V."

"Where are you folks headed?"

"We're looking for you, I think," Walker answered. "We heard there was a resistance cell operating near Bryce Canyon. Would that be you?"

Weimar smiled. "We're part of it. We're on a routine patrol. We had intel that the enemy was close by, placing surveillance equipment along the roads. They're looking for us, too. So we've spent the last two days hunting for it, hoping to take it out before they figure out where our base is located."

A man coughed loudly from inside one of the Humvees. Walker couldn't help but look over Weimar's shoulder. "I know that cough," he said. "Is that—?"

The Humvee door opened and out stepped—

"Wally!" Walker rushed to him and gave Sergeant Kopple a big bear hug.

"Walker, you son-of-a-gun! You mean you haven't gotten yourself killed yet?"

"Not on your life, mister! Everything you taught me has paid off so far."

"I was worried about you when I heard about Vegas."

"I was there, man." He turned to his mates. "But we got out okay. We were a few of the lucky ones. Let me introduce you. You remember Kelsie?"

Kopple gave Wilcox a bigger hug and a sloppy kiss. Introductions were made all around, and the other men in the cell came forward to shake hands.

"Weimar," Kopple said, "let's take these folks back to the Dome and let them meet Nguyen. I think we're about done on this road, right?"

The blond nodded.

"We have bikes," Walker said. "Give us a sec and we'll go get 'em."

The Ragtags retrieved their bicycles and joined the unit as they headed up Highway 89 and turned right on Highway 12.

Kopple walked alongside Walker and Wilcox as they cycled slowly. "The Dome is that hardened complex we were talking about back when we met up with you in California," he said. "We were right. It was a great little resistance cell. A Vietnamese fellow's in charge. Do you know about the Vietnamese coming over to help us?"

Walker shook his head. "What? No."

"It's true. Isn't that a piece of irony? When Vietnam joined the Korean alliance, a lot of resistance fighters came over here to help the American effort. They arrived last fall and spread out all over the country to join existing cells or organize new ones. Our guy is Nguyen Huu Giap. His great uncle was the famous Viet Cong general, Vo Nguyen Giap, who gave our American boys a whole lotta shit over there during the Vietnam War."

"Really?"

"Nguyen is a brilliant tactics guy." He coughed and spat red and brown phlegm.

"Jesus, Wally, that looks awful."

"It's the big C. But I'm still standing."

Walker noted the sergeant's QBZ-03. "I see you still have that Chinese gun."

"It's done pretty good by me so far."

"How many guys do you have in the cell?"

Kopple shook his head. "Now only about twelve. Well, seventeen with you guys joining up. We did have thirty! We got into a big firefight with the Koreans last week on this very road. They know we're around here, but the Dome is well hidden and camouflaged. The bastards won that fight, wiped out more than half our guys, including Captain Hennings. But we've been contacted by another cell operating in Montrose, Colorado. We're about to head out and join up with them."

When they reached the edge of the forest, before the trees thinned out to rocky, barren land near the national park entrance, the team stopped while two men removed what appeared to be a natural barrier in the trees on the north side of the road. It was a gate fashioned out of branches and foliage that was cleverly tied together. Walker would never have known it was there. Once the way was clear, the Humvees and men turned into the forest and the men replaced the barrier. They traveled another mile on a man-made path and came to the Dome, which was a concrete and steel "bubble" built into the ground and painted with camouflage. A bomb shelter iron door gained entrance to the facility, which was all belowground. As soon as the team arrived, the door swung open and out climbed a Vietnamese soldier dressed in the fatigues of his home country. Nguyen Huu Giap was in his thirties, was wiry and fit, and displayed a fierce, no-nonsense expression.

"Nguyen, this is my good buddy Ben Walker,"

Kopple said. He continued to introduce the rest of the newcomers. Nguyen shook Walker's hand.

"Thank you for your efforts, sir."

"You very welcome," the Vietnamese soldier said without smiling. "We use you. You hungry? Inside is food."

He gestured to the iron door and started to move toward it when the shriek of an incoming missile pulled everyone's attention to the tops of the trees. It exploded with significant force on top of the hardened Dome, but did no damage. Nevertheless, the impact knocked everyone to the ground. This was immediately followed by machine gun fire coming from the path through the forest on which the Humvees had just come.

"Fuck!" Kopple shouted. "They found us!"

TWENTY

"Stay down, stay down!" Weimar yelled as a barrage of bullets whipped laterally a couple of feet over their bodies.

Walker squinted at the trees and saw dozens of red and yellow flashes, indicating the resistance cell was outnumbered by a long shot. He reached over and grasped Wilcox's arm and whispered, "You hit?"

"No!"

But three of Weimar's men were. Riddled with rounds, the soldiers died instantly and collapsed where they'd been standing. Kopple crawled over to check on one, but shook his head.

One of the Humvees was equipped with an M134 six-barreled machine gun. The soldier inside had the presence of mind to immediately swerve the gun to the trees and fire indiscriminately at the indistinct, but human, shapes. This bought time for Giap to leap to his feet and run to a covered position behind the vehicle. He possessed a superior weapon known as an FN SCAR, an assault rifle used by U.S. Army Rangers. Giap exposed enough of himself to aim across the Humvee's hood and blast away targets with precision.

As other members of the team moved forward and assumed spots behind trees or the other Humvee,

Walker told Wilcox, "Stay down!" He removed his rifle, quickly shoved in a magazine, and crawled to the enclave's iron door. He lifted it open and found the hinges were made so that the door remained perpendicular to the ground. Walker used it for cover after climbing in and standing on the top steps that led into the bunker. He fired his weapon at the enemy, who advanced with fortitude into the Americans' gunfire. The Koreans were brave, Walker had to hand them that.

Three more resistance fighters climbed up the steps from the conclave beneath him—two men and a woman. The top guy said, "Whoever the hell you are, cover us!" Walker nodded and spray-fired in bursts as the three subterraneans emerged from the entrance and ran toward another Humvee that just appeared on the forest path. Crouching behind it when the vehicle halted, they commenced shooting at the Koreans. Walker recognized the new Humvee as the one with the M2 heavy machine gun from the California National Guard unit. None other than Johnson was at the wheel. Someone operated the CROWS within to fire the M2 at the approaching enemy.

"Crawl inside the compound!" Walker shouted at Wilcox and Jim, since they were unarmed.

"Give us some weapons!" cried Prescott. Kopple heard him and gave him a thumbs-up sign. He squat-ran to the nearest Humvee, opened the door, reached inside, and came out with two assault rifles—an M16 and an M4. He tossed them to the two army men, and then stuck his head back inside. He emerged with two extra magazines for each gun and threw them to Prescott and Washington. But as soon as the two men locked and loaded, Washington was hit. Walker winced as the man jolted violently and fell backward, a line of red, bloody holes dotting his chest cavity.

Weimar waved to the two men and one woman that had come out of the hole. They dashed to the other Humvee as the Koreans' onslaught intensified. Suddenly, a new and unexpected volley of gunfire erupted from the right side of the forest. Before anyone had realized it, the Koreans had spread out and approached the site from the flank. Weimar and his three companions were down. Giap flung himself to the ground and rolled beneath the Humvee to avoid being hit. From there he lay on his stomach and continued to fire the SCAR at the second enemy offensive. Walker, now without cover, ducked into the entrance as bullets ricocheted off the iron door. Pinned inside, he was unable to help his new compatriots.

"What's going on?" Wilcox asked. She stood on the steps below him, her eyes wide with fear.

"Doesn't look good," Walker spat. "They've got us on two sides."

Then he heard a new sound—a whirr of a machine passed over his head, followed by four bursts of rocket fire and screams in the forest.

What the hell was that?

A shout of "Hooray!" echoed from above, so he dared to raise his head. Walker's jaw dropped when he saw what was making mincemeat of the advancing Koreans. He knew such things existed, but to him it was right out of a science fiction movie.

My God, it's a robot!

It was a vehicle a little larger than a dune buggy, smaller than a tank, but had the DNA of both. Rolling back and forth on six wheels, the machine seemed to have a mind of its own as a high-powered machine gun on top swatted the KPA away as if they were flies. A four-barreled rocket launcher, which was the arsenal Walker had just heard, *reloaded itself,* and fired again. The explosions off in the trees were dead-on, obliterating groups of the enemy with uncanny accuracy.

The machine's internal mechanisms whirred again as if it were listening to new commands—and then it took off and traversed the perimeter of the complex, rolling over the bodies of dead Koreans. The machine gun, similar to an M240G/B, continued to whip out its payload at the remaining enemy force. This allowed the surviving resistance fighters to break cover and take a more offensive role in the fight.

Walker climbed out of the hole to join them and recalled Kopple's instructions to move with the M4's scope to his eye. Zeroing in on a group of three Koreans headed his way, he released two bursts of rounds and annihilated the threat. He then swung around and targeted six more men who were closing in on Kopple and others crouching behind a Humvee. Walker eradicated four of them, but the other two veered toward him and fired. He felt the searing hot stream of two bullets—one passing between his legs, dangerously close to his crotch, and the other just over his left shoulder. Walker leapt forward, flattening himself on the ground as Kopple obliterated the two men with his QBZ-03.

Walker's heart beat furiously and he could barely catch his breath. The excitement of the battle was like nothing he'd ever felt. He felt *exhilarated*. Jumping up for more, eager to exterminate the enemy, he was almost disappointed to find it was all over. His fellow soldiers had already stepped into the forest to mop up. Every now and then a man delivered a blast into a wounded Korean to finish him off; otherwise, there was none of the enemy left alive. Whatever that six-wheeled monster was, it had saved the day.

The bad news was the Resistance had lost eight members, including Washington.

Giap rolled out from under the Humvee and announced, "They know we here. We move on soon as possible."

Walker approached the robot-vehicle and turned to Kopple. "What is this thing?"

"That's Goliath," the sergeant answered after a coughing spell. "Unmanned Ground Combat Vehicle, invented and built by DARPA a few years ago back when the Department of Defense had money to spend on stuff."

"How does it know what to do?"

"You'll meet his master in—"

But as Kopple spoke, Walker caught movement out the corner of his eye and spun around to witness an Asian man materialize from the trees.

Another Korean!

Walker shouted, "Hey!" and raised the M4, ready to blow the guy away; but Kopple yelled, "Don't shoot!" The sergeant swiftly grabbed Walker's rifle and thrust it into the air. "No! He's one of us!" Walker's gun discharged, causing every resistance member to swing guns at him.

"Sorry!" he cried. "Didn't mean it! Mistake! Sorry!"

Everyone relaxed. The Korean newcomer stood frozen in his tracks, ready to fire his own M16. Kopple said, "Hopper, come here. Let me introduce you to my buddy."

"He's your *buddy*? Are you sure about that?" the man spoke perfect English with no accent. The guy was obviously an American.

"Sorry, I thought you were Korean," Walker said, holding out his hand.

The man shook it. "I *am* Korean, by birth. But I was born and raised in San Francisco. Hopper Lee."

"Ben Walker." He introduced Kelsie to him and then pointed at Goliath. "This is yours?"

"It belongs to all of us, but yeah, I'm the one who teaches it tricks. So far I haven't got it to shake hands, roll over, or speak on command, but it does just about every thing else I tell it to do." He held up a stainless-steel box the size of a DVD player. Knobs, buttons, a view screen, and a small antenna adorned the top. "The magic is all here in this device. I rebuilt it myself."

"That's awesome, man."

"I was out with Goliath on a reconnaissance mission when you guys were attacked. I guess I got here just in time."

"I'll say."

Walker noticed the other soldiers tending to their dead comrades. Giap instructed his men to bury their dead and leave the Koreans to rot. Besides, there were too many of them. By his count, the resistance cell had wiped out forty men. Next they were to grab necessary supplies from the Dome and be ready to move out before sundown. It wouldn't be long before the enemy knew their unit had been vanquished and reinforcements would arrive. The longer the resistance cell lingered there, the greater the danger.

"Where're their tanks and other vehicles? We saw a tank the other day near St. George. I assume it was on its way here," Walker said to Kopple.

The sergeant coughed, spat, and replied, "A tank won't fit in the path. We don't own a tank so it didn't matter to us. That's one reason why we're going to Colorado to join up with that other cell. They have a *lot* more stuff. Who knows where that tank you saw was going? Could be Salt Lake City. "

"I recognize two of these Humvees. Didn't you have three before? And what happened to your horses?"

"We lost one Humvee in a battle we fought between Vegas and here. Giap here had one. The horses, well, they didn't make it across the desert, sorry to say." He handed Walker a shovel. "If you're volunteering, I guess you better start digging."

The motley crew of Ragtags and the Bryce Canyon resistance cell, which in total comprised seven men and two women, evacuated the Dome quickly, headed northeast of the national park, and had their dinner deep in the forest. A couple of men doled out sandwiches made of peanut butter and bananas, and another broke out water bottles. While Giap and Kopple planned the route they would take across Utah and into Colorado, Walker and Wilcox had a chance to sit with Hopper Lee and hear the story of the invasion from a Korean American's perspective.

Lee was in his early thirties and had a small frame, but he had an energetic, wiry temperament; he spoke and gestured a mile-a-minute. What was most distinctive about the man, however, was the facial disfigurement. Two long recent scars ran from his right eyebrow, over an eye, across his cheek, and down to the bottom of his chin.

"I know you're wondering about my face," he said intuitively. "Happened in San Francisco. I'm a casualty of the race riots. You heard about them?"

"Yeah," Walker replied. "Damned ridiculous, if you ask me."

"It was a gang of redneck sons of bitches who had nothing better to do than terrorize Korean families in our neighborhoods. The creeps were in the process of raping a fifteen-year-old girl when I stepped in to try and stop it. Left-handed asshole with a knife did this to my face. That knocked the fight out of me, I'm afraid. Couldn't save the girl. I still hear her screams to this day. I never found out what became of her. When I came to, another Korean-American family had taken me into their house to patch me up. Turned out I didn't lose my eye and I could still see. Fucking miracle, if you ask me. But the riots continued. It was chaos outside. Our goddamned fellow Americans wanted to kill us. But hey, that's all in the past. Once the North Koreans started instituting martial law in the city and cracking down on violence, the riots eased off."

Like Walker, Lee was a civilian who hadn't had real military training. He explained that he was a third generation Korean American who had earned his living as an electrical engineer and mechanic. Once Wilcox heard that, she and Lee engaged in a techno-babble conversation that went over Walker's head, but he was pleased she had found a kindred spirit. The couple learned that Lee was an all-around fix-it man in San Francisco before the EMP and had won several awards at events like the DARPA Grand Challenge. After the occupation, he was recruited by the North Koreans to repair military and essential equipment for their needs.

"I had no choice. It was either perform their slave work, under the auspices of 'employment,' or be executed. I kind of like being alive, even if it's under enemy occupation, so I did what I had to do. That didn't make things better in my community. I was branded a collaborator in some circles. But last summer, I joined a resistance cell in the city. I was able to provide intel on what the Norks were doing. Then, one day, I discovered Goliath.

"Its systems have some shielding that protected it from the EMP, so it still worked. I just had to restart it, so to speak. The remote control box, however, didn't.

I had to get it up and running on the sly. Took me two months. Then, one day, I liberated Goliath, stole him from the Koreans right out from under their snotty noses. I never went back to work. I guess I'll be fired. I won't be able to get a letter of recommendation from 'em." He snorted at his own joke.

"Anyway, I eventually heard through the grapevine about this cell in Montrose, Colorado, where we're going. There's a big operation there to prevent the Koreans from taking over the shale oil mining that's outside of town. Last word I got was they needed people to help steal some jet fuel from the mine. I didn't ask permission, I just left San Francisco with Goliath. I met up with Nguyen along the way and I got sidetracked. So here I am."

Walker and Wilcox related their own stories as the sun began to set. Giap announced they would continue their journey at two a.m., so they should all get a little rest for a few hours. Before retiring, Walker and Lee got to discussing race and nationalism and the conflicts of being a Korean American.

"Look, Ben," said Hopper, "despite what happened in the race riots, no one is more patriotic than me. I'm not anti-Korean, but you better believe I'm anti-Korean *government*. What Kim Jong-un has done is despicable. He's no better than Hitler. He has shamed our people and my heritage. I would like nothing more than to go over to Pyongyang and kick his little butt. Well, I'd let Goliath do it. I'm afraid I'm not much of a combat guy. Are you?"

"Not really, but I've learned a lot in the past year.

Wally taught me a bunch of stuff a while back. I'm a pretty good shot. I just don't have much combat experience. Today was my second firefight. I don't count what happened in Vegas."

Lee chuckled wryly. "Yeah, well, what happens in Vegas . . . " Then he realized it wasn't funny and shut up.

They all settled on the ground with sleeping bags and blankets. While some of the men smoked cigarettes made from tobacco they'd grown themselves, Lee pulled a shortwave radio and a generator from one of the Humvees and showed them to Walker and Wilcox. Giap appeared and explained, "We listen every day. Sometimes we hear news from the Resistance."

Walker looked at Wilcox. "Kelsie, do you think we could hook up our transistor board to this thing? I haven't made a broadcast since before the Vegas bombing."

Lee frowned at Walker. "You make broadcasts?"

"Ever hear of DJ Ben?"

Lee's eyes widened. "*You're* DJ Ben? Holy shit! We love you! Nguyen, this is DJ Ben!"

Giap smiled for the first time in Walker's presence. He delivered a slight bow of his head and remarked, "Glad you with us."

Kopple came over to the group and asked, "What's going on? I thought we were going to bed."

"Kopple, Ben here is DJ Ben!"

The sergeant eyed Walker up and down and nodded. "I knew that."

"No you didn't!" Lee turned on the radio and

twisted the tuner until the static cleared. The airwaves were silent.

"Do you hear much chatter?" Walker asked.

"Not much. But it's increased over the last two or three months. Especially after you started playing your music," Lee said. "Every now and then we'll hear something from resistance cells around the country. There's a guy in Washington State that broadcasts a lot."

"Do you mean Yankee Doodle?"

"Yeah, that's him! And there's a guy in Texas—"

"Max?"

"Uh huh. Do you know Cecilia, up in North Dakota?"

"Uhm, no, I haven't heard of her." Walker addressed both Giap and Lee. "Mind if we try to bring DJ Ben back on the air?"

No one objected, so Wilcox spent the next half hour working with Lee to make the two units compatible. Giap commented in his inimitable broken English that the couple's combined expertise would be a valuable asset to the cell.

Finally, Wilcox opened the antenna and set it on top of one of the Humvees.

"I'm not sure what kind of signal we'll be able to send since we're so deep in the forest. We may not get anything out at all," she warned.

Lee marveled at the transmitter she had created. "This is incredible. Very clever. I think with the added *umpf* from my receiver, we should be able to get something over the air. Look, see that indicator?

It jumps when I tap your microphone. There's definitely a signal. Let's just hope it gets past the tops of these trees."

Wilcox handed the mike to Walker. "You're live, sweetheart. Knock yourself out."

Walker suddenly felt self-conscious with everyone watching him. Nevertheless, he cleared his throat and spoke. "Good evening, my fellow Americans, this is DJ Ben coming to you from an undisclosed location in our beloved United States. I'm sorry to have been out of touch the last couple of weeks, but we've had some serious setbacks. I don't know if you've heard, but Las Vegas was carpet bombed by the Norks on January twenty-fourth. That's right, the city of Las Vegas was completely destroyed. Thousands of people died at the hands of those Korean monsters. They used F-Thirty-Fives and B-Twos stolen from our own military bases. Up to that day, the enemy left Las Vegas alone. Why did they decide to suddenly bomb the shit out of a city that was no threat to them? I can't answer that, my friends. It was an act of pure evil. Who can explain evil? How can anyone justify the slaughter of innocent civilians? This *will not stand*!"

The sudden intensity in Walker's voice startled those around him.

"The time has come, more than ever, for you to resist these fuckers who have hijacked our country. It's time to say, 'that is enough!' Some of you are already fighting back. Resistance cells are popping up all over the country. And guess what. The Koreans *don't like it*! The more we keep 'em busy chasing resistance cells, the less they'll be stealing our natural resources and imprisoning and killing civilians. So let's give 'em a taste of old-fashioned American spirit and start kicking their asses!"

He paused a moment to calm down. Then he looked up at the night sky peeking through the tops of the trees. "Unfortunately, I have no way to play music tonight, folks. You're going to need to imagine it. But if I could play something tonight, I would probably go with that old Jefferson Airplane tune, 'Volunteers.' Any of you remember that?" He winked at Wilcox. "My girlfriend's grandma used to play it back in the day. 'Volunteers of America, volunteers of America.' I know you've heard it. Well, it's time to volunteer, my friends. If you can do it, join up. The Resistance needs you. This is DJ Ben signing off, for now. Good night."

As soon as Wilcox switched off the transmitter, everyone applauded. Walker shrugged and held up his hands with modesty.

"Thanks, everybody," he said. "Let's get some shut-eye now, what do you say?"

Lee put away the equipment as Walker and Wilcox prepared their sleeping bags. Kopple squatted beside them and whispered, "Walker, that was great."

"Thanks, man."

"Listen, I think you could go even further with that stuff."

"What do you mean?"

"I don't know." He coughed and spat away from them. "Damn, that hurt."

"You all right?"

"Yeah. I mean that kind of cheerleading you do. You could become the 'voice of the Resistance.'"

"I just tell the truth. What more can I do?"

Wilcox answered, "Ben, that's what *I've* been telling you to do! The truth is exactly what needs to be told. You could be the Keeper of the Truth."

Kopple agreed. "Yeah, forget DJ Ben and this music stuff. Focus your efforts on creating a different persona. DJ Ben served his purpose, but things are more serious now. You've got the gift of gab, man. Use it."

Walker wasn't sure what to make of that. "Okay."

"Okay. Good night, you two."

"'Night, Wally," Wilcox said.

In fifteen minutes, the entire cell was asleep.

WALKER'S JOURNAL

After the location of the Dome was compromised, the Ragtags and Nguyen Giap's resistance cell traveled on back roads from Bryce Canyon over to Capitol Reef National Park. Then we had to go out of our way southeast simply because the terrain was too impassable to go straight east. We went down to Orange Cliffs Canyon and White Canyon, and then ended up in a ghost town called Blanding. From there we marched north again and hooked up with Route 666—I kid you not—and took that east into Colorado. Oh, and there are a lot of mountains.

During the trek from Utah, Kelsie and I trained with Wally. He instructed Kelsie how to handle a gun and some basics on defending herself. Mostly he taught us plain old soldier chutzpah. Nguyen got into the act, too. During time off when we weren't traveling, he gave us tips on guerilla tactics and ran drills in which we practiced stealth. That guy is sharp. Kelsie now carries a handgun. In fact, we both do. Wally gave us each M9s, so now I have that and my trusty M4.

We reached Montrose, Colorado, on March 8th.

Through radio communications, we met up with a resistance cell located there at an abandoned machine parts warehouse in town. At first, both sides were

*wary of each other, because Hopper had picked up
some warning transmissions that the Norks were
sometimes posing as Americans over the airwaves—or
forcing Americans to make the transmissions, which
seems more likely—and setting up ambushes. This
happened to a cell in Texas. My friend Max reported
that a group from Austin consisting of Texas Rangers
and former Highway Patrolmen was completely
wiped out after they thought they were getting reinforcements from an Arkansas cell. Very disturbing.*

Anyway, our rendezvous turned out okay.

*The Montrose cell is led by a black guy named
Boone Karlson, who was formerly a policeman in the
city. It was the first resistance cell in Montrose; apparently there are more popping up in different sections.
Boone's is a group of about 40 people that live in a
camouflaged compound called Home, and it's a really
cool place. It's located in the abandoned southeastern
suburbs of the town, hidden right in a normal neighborhood of houses. Home takes up several houses and
backyards bordered by tall thick trees, between which
is suspended a camo mesh to conceal it from aerial
surveillance. They've got an underground tunnel
through which they enter and exit when performing
military missions, so as not to draw attention to the
compound. There are entire families living there—
women and children—and a small army of men.
They've set up a nice little communal system where
they grow their own food, catch rainwater, use power
generators for essential tasks, and repair electronics as
needed. There's even a school for the kids and swing*

sets in the yards. Areas have their own functions; for example, there's a spot where a guy does nothing but repair circuit boards and electronics. Another fellow raises goats in a pen for the milk. They've even got a guy who blows glass! I saw him making bowls and drinking glasses for everyone to use. The military aspect is well organized. I'm really impressed.

There are some interesting characters in the cell, too. The guy you can't miss is Connor Morgan, a true legend of the Resistance. I think he's a little older than me, from North Carolina. Connor's a one-man army, but I think he's a bit off. I don't know if he's just plain crazy or if he's just overly intense, but I find him intimidating. He may be a loose cannon, but he's a gung-ho fighter and everyone respects him. I don't think he's afraid of a damn thing.

As for Boone, he's pushing 40, I'd guess, and he's pretty down to earth. Smart man. Seems a little world-weary, but I guess that comes with the territory when you're the leader. He and Connor are sometimes at loggerheads, but you can tell they really admire each other. So far, Boone and Nguyen get along and there's been no vying for the leadership role. Nguyen understands Boone is in charge of the Montrose cell. The Ragtags and the Utah folks instinctively tend to follow Nguyen's orders, but Boone could supersede those if he wanted.

Then there's Rianna, an attractive woman in her late 20s who I think is part Hispanic. She's a tough cookie, having grown up in the backwoods of Colorado. She's apparently very skilled at guerilla tactics. She's kind of quiet, but I can tell she doesn't miss a thing. I get the feeling she could be pretty dangerous, but Kelsie and I like her a lot.

There's a light Korean presence in Montrose, but the word on the street is a massive force is coming to exploit the nearby oil shale mining industry. The cell captured a KPA infantry man last week and Connor had no qualms about torturing the guy for information (Connor tends to enjoy doing that). The soldier said the Koreans plan to build labor camps and draft the civilian population into working the mines. The KPA also intend to build a fucking wall around the city to keep people inside. I have a feeling it's going to get pretty bad here soon.

Kelsie and I carry fake ID cards now. Everyone in Montrose has to do so. When we're not at Home, we do go into town and act like normal citizens. A KPA soldier could appear at any time on the street and ask anyone for his or her identity card. If you're caught without one, you're taken to KPA headquarters in downtown Montrose for an interrogation. They figure you're either new to town, in which case you might be a member of the growing Resistance, or you're bucking the system by not carrying a card, in which case you might be a member of the growing Resistance! No matter what, they give you a hard time.

Boone told Kelsie and me about an abandoned radio station in Montrose. It was a local one that back in the day broadcasted country and western music. Kelsie and I took a look at it and decided we could use it. There's a big antenna on the roof that's busted, but *there's still a lot of equipment inside. Kelsie thinks she can repair it; at the very least, she hopes we can plug in our transistor board to the station's control console and broadcast a message that'll reach the entire U.S. from West Coast to East Coast and from Canada to Mexico. We have to sneak into town by way of the tunnel, but we started the job two days ago. Kelsie figures it might take a month to get it up and running. In the meantime, I've been using Hopper's radio to make DJ Ben transmissions with no music. Hopper's afraid the Koreans might be able to trace the signal to Home, so Kelsie and I have been moving around town in the evenings and broadcasting from different secluded spots. One night we got inside an old, closed Wal-Mart. Another time it was at the top of a water tower! That was a little hairy, climbing up there and trying to do a transmission without being seen by Korean sentries. So far, though, we haven't been caught. On a clear night we've heard back from several other resistance cells. There really is an entire network of underground radio folks out there. Besides my buddies Yankee Doodle and Max, I made contact with Cecilia up in North Dakota and a fellow named Derby in, I think, Kansas City. But the radio station is our best bet for a long-range broadcast.*

Rianna just rang the bell for chow time. All this resistance work makes me hungry, so I'm signing off for now.

Writing this in haste . . . Some good news and some really bad news.

Last night, Connor and a reconnaissance team took out a Korean supply unit west of town. I wasn't there, but I wish I had been just to see Connor in action. He's a madman. He risked revealing his association with the Resistance by attacking the Koreans, but he knew they probably had some good intel. Turned out they did. Well, in typical Connor fashion, he and his men killed all of the Koreans except for one, and they brought him back for a little interrogation of our own. The good news is Connor's team also brought back a lot of the Koreans' stuff, like meat *in a refrigerated truck. That's going to be nice to hold on to, but we have to keep it hidden.*

Anyway, the bad news—Hopper translated some of the Korean orders and determined the supply unit was only stopping temporarily in Montrose. They were actually on their way to Muscatine, Iowa. Everyone was puzzled by that. Why the hell are Koreans stationed in Muscatine, Iowa? So Connor tortured the Korean prisoner, and that's how we found out what's happened to the Mississippi River.

Christ Almighty. It's bad. It's really bad.

TWENTY-ONE

APRIL 4, 2026

As the MH-10 Scout helicopter flew over Muscatine, Iowa, Salmusa had a bird's-eye view of the mission's progress. Even at a height of four thousand feet, Salmusa took care to wear an Iron Fish suit. The air above the deserted city and the polluted river next to it was seriously dangerous. He didn't care about the weak Americans contracting radiation poisoning, but he certainly didn't want to experience that horrible death himself.

It had been a busy four months to reach this point. When he finished his preliminary work on Operation Water Snake at the Lawrence Livermore National Laboratory, the Korean agent continued to oversee the next and most important stage of the Brilliant Comrade's most ingenious attack on the United States of America. It was the culmination of years of thought, effort, and sacrifice.

It was known from the very beginning that in the pursuit of its many noble and glorious goals around the globe to confirm the Greater Korean Republic at its rightful place at the top of the new world order, the Occupational Forces in America faced a unique dilemma. As detailed by the Brilliant Comrade himself in Executive Order 434, the objective in America was to not only deliver a quick strike to expunge the land and its people of any remaining natural and technological resources, but also to exact revenge for enduring decades of the country's arrogant "superiority." However, even after the successful deployment of the EMP blast and the crippling effect it had on the American population and infrastructure, the Occupational Forces, which consisted of army and naval troops, weapons, food, medical supplies, vehicles, and contraband, would no doubt find themselves stretched to capacity. The Brilliant Comrade was wise to acknowledge the Korean forces did not have the necessary resources needed to invade, occupy—even temporarily—and systematically exploit the entire region of the continental United States to the fullest extent.

The enemy's western territory contained the lion's share of American natural and technological resources. On the other hand, although eastern America held little value for the Occupational Forces, it was still home to over eighty million residents. Since the EMP blast, the East still posed a threat and had a clear motivation to fight.

Kim Jong-un wisely decided to create an impenetrable barrier to ensure that eastern Americans would not be able to provide significant assistance to their western counterparts or additional resistance to the Occupational Forces. Years ago, when the Brilliant Comrade began planning the occupation of America, he immediately latched on to the lucky fluke that the

Mississippi River was a natural dividing line between everything the Koreans wanted and the more problematic East Coast territories. How could the GKR keep the hordes of Americans residing east of the river to stay put, and at the same time subjugate the population west of the river?

After consulting with the genius Dr. Mae Chin Ho from the People's Military Science Institute in Pyongyang, Kim came up with Operation Water Snake, a revolutionary plan fitting only for the enduring legacy of the Brilliant Comrade. It was an inspired, albeit nefarious, scheme that would turn the Mississippi River into an impassable barrier.

Operation Water Snake's goal was the systematic irradiating of the Mississippi River with highly radioactive solvents—a deadly cocktail. A radio-active Mississippi River would create the desired noxious barricade spanning from the Great Lakes to the Gulf of Mexico, dividing the country. All cities within a hundred mile radius of the river would become contaminated and uninhabitable, forcing evacuations from north to south.

Not only would the operation create the deadly "fence" and redesign world maps forever in the Brilliant Comrade's vision, it was also the most cost-effective strategy. This conviction included the deaths of over four thousand martyrs—many scientists, soldiers, and American collaborators.

The final phase finally executed in February 2026, Operation Water Snake was an extremely dangerous undertaking, but it was an unqualified success.

There were five Deposit Locations on the western banks of the river—Lake Itasca and Winona in Minnesota; Muscatine, Iowa; Cape Girardeau, Missouri; and St. Joseph, Louisiana. The five strategic Deposit Locations up and down the river played the role of planting a radioactive seed in the river; however, it was the river itself that was responsible for spreading its effect far beyond. The sheer size of the river, north to south, insured nearly three thousand miles of radioactive cover along the valley alone. The speed of the river's flow constantly cultivated the materials in the water, creating volatility between the hazardous elements and thus increasing the radioactive potency. The connected tributaries, rivers, creeks, and streams pushed the contamination east and west almost three hundred miles in each direction in select areas. The powerful discharge into the Gulf of Mexico stretched the effects of the radioactivity around the tip of Florida all the way to the Atlantic Ocean. In the end, Operation Water Snake contributed to the contamination of almost 210,000 square miles of land, river, and sea within the continental United States.

Even Salmusa, a man with a steely fortitude, shuddered to think of the physical effects of the Cocktail on human beings. Most of the exposure to the uranium fission fragments was through water and food. Ten hours after exposure, spontaneous symptoms would set in. After fatigue and severe nausea, victims would experience a phase of several weeks of relative normalcy called a "dormant phase" or "walking ghost." After this, cells were killed in the intestinal tissue, resulting in substantial diarrhea, intestinal bleeding, and water loss. Death followed delirium and coma after a collapse of the circulation and nervous system. The only treatment available was palliative management.

The consequences of Operation Water Snake would remain relevant for years to come. Possible long-term effects included chromosomal abnormality, leukemia, anemia, and Down syndrome effects on offspring.

In addition, Operation Water Snake would force more than half of the four hundred different wildlife species to evacuate to more livable habitats. Those that were too damaged or sick to leave would produce additional health hazards to humans as the radioactive carcasses spread disease and further contamination.

Salmusa had no doubt the success of the operation would also produce psychological effects on the American population. The people, once they learned of what happened to their beloved river, would likely develop depression and anxiety, paranoia, and fear and distrust of all outside influences. Large parts of the populace would be brought to a halt, unable to function and operate normally under the constant fear of another attack.

It was a brilliant plan.

Salmusa was proud to have offered an addendum to Executive Order 434, which Kim Jong-un implemented. While no one actually made "suggestions" to the Brilliant Comrade, it was possible to phrase one so that it seemed as if the idea was a natural extension of the leader's wishes. Salmusa was better at that ploy than most of Kim's advisors and yes-men. His suggestion was that in order to maintain the integrity of the new Mississippi Border for the length of the Occupation and through completion of the Greater Korean Republic's plans, the Light Infantry Division would redeposit additional Source Term supplies of the Cocktail every seventeen to twenty-four months.

A subdivision of the Occupational Police would be responsible for regular patrol of the border through the use of armed drones at bridges and other points of crossing. Additionally, every three to six months, a special division would set grass and forest fires in strategic areas within a ten-mile radius surrounding the river. Fires could mobilize the radioactivity material again, converting the elements to an airborne form that would enter the atmosphere in a different structure and redistribute itself across the landscape and population.

Now, two months after Operation Water Snake was accomplished, Salmusa watched as fires raged on the ground below. It didn't matter that Muscatine, Iowa, would be destroyed. There was no longer anyone living there.

Human beings could not be within five miles of the river without wearing an Iron Fish or comparable radioactivity-resistant suit. Even then, five hours was the maximum amount of exposure a person could take. No one knew exactly how high the airborne contamination reached; needless to say, simply walking or driving across a bridge without a suit was impossible.

The Brilliant Comrade would be pleased. Salmusa had finished touring all five Deposit Locations and confirmed that everything was in order. It was time to return to GKR headquarters in San Francisco, for his work with Operation Water Snake was completed. He thought wryly that from north to south the Mighty Mississippi was no longer Old Man River.

It was now Dead Man River.

TWENTY-TWO

APRIL 6, 2026

Walker stepped into the space at Home that the leaders facetiously called the "War Room." Situated in one of the first-floor bedrooms in one of the houses, it was where Boone Karlson, Nguyen Giap, Hopper Lee, Wally Kopple, and Connor Morgan met to discuss resistance strategy.

"You guys wanted to see me?"

"Come in, Ben," Karlson said. "Have a seat."

They were situated around a table. A large map of Montrose adorned one wall, while a map of the United States decorated the other. Various colored pins dotted each map in key locations.

Walker took a chair. "So are we going to save the world today? What's up?"

"Ben, we've been discussing your plans to broadcast from that old radio station. How soon will you and Kelsie be ready to do so?"

"Five or six days, I should think. Why?"

"You think you can be ready in four?"

Walker rubbed his chin. "I don't know. Maybe. I'd have to ask Kelsie. She's really the brains of the team. I just complain. Why?"

Morgan answered for Karlson. "Because the Norks will probably be here by the tenth. They'll be crawling over this town like cockroaches."

Karlson added, "We received intel that a heavy Korean force is headed this way. The information we got out of our prisoner is true. Montrose is a key target because of the shale oil mining outside of town. They're bringing tanks and a battalion of an estimated five hundred light infantry soldiers. We think there are already fifty to a hundred men in Montrose already, so a liberal estimate makes it a total of six hundred. There are roughly thirty fighting men and women here at Home. The odds are comparable to that of the Alamo."

"Jesus," Walker said.

"Let 'em come!" Morgan growled. "I ain't gettin' any action sittin' here on my ass!"

Karlson ignored him. "There are other resistance cells besides us, of course, but I have no idea how big they are. Eventually we've got to establish communications with them and coordinate our efforts. But until then, with the added Korean troops, it means it's going to be even more difficult for us to accomplish tasks in town. We're not sure how much access you're going to have to the radio station once they're here."

Kopple started to speak but went into a coughing spasm instead. Everyone looked at him with concern and shared worried glances with the others around the table. The sergeant gasped for breath and Giap handed him a bottle of water. Kopple took a few sips and eventually relaxed. "Sorry about that," he said. "I was about to say we all think what you and Kelsie are doing is important. You and I have talked about how the resistance can use your natural ability to fire up people. We want you to make a broadcast before the Koreans get here and make sure everyone knows about the Mississippi River. And you need to tell anyone listening to join the Resistance. No more complacency. No more submission."

Karlson continued. "We know the Koreans can pinpoint where a radio signal is coming from. Unless you can get the station up and running before they get here, you're not going to have a chance to make the broadcast."

Walker said, "We could continue to use Hopper's equipment. So far Kelsie and I have managed to get away with making broadcasts from different areas of town. I haven't made any transmissions in the last few days because we've been so busy repairing the station, but we could try and slip in some quickies at night. We haven't gotten caught yet. If the Koreans are listening, they're probably confused as to where we really are because we keep moving."

"But the whole point of using the radio station is for its long-range capacity," Karlson said. "We need you to get the word out to all of America."

"I understand that." Walker rubbed his chin. "You do know there's an elementary school on the same street as the radio station? And it's in service. There are children there."

"So maybe that'll help with your cover. A lot of parents are seen in the mornings and in the afternoons picking up their kids. It's one of the few elementary schools still active in Montrose."

Walker nodded. "Okay. So you're saying we have until the tenth."

"Right."

Walker sighed. "Then I guess we better get to work."

APRIL 9, 2026

Over the next three days, Walker and Wilcox worked like madmen to finish repairing the station.

Located on Rose Lane, the building hadn't been used in perhaps a decade. Much of the electrical equipment was fried by the EMP. The antenna on the roof was useless, so Wilcox had to build a new Yagi-Uda-style device from scratch. Although she was able to plunder parts from the old aerial, the trick was going to be attaching the new antenna to the roof without any Korean sentries in town noticing. One advantage was that Rose Lane was somewhat isolated in the northeast area of town, with the station on the far end of a dead-end street. The elementary school, built during the previous decade, was located in the middle of the block.

The Korean presence was mostly concentrated downtown, with occasional visits by patrols to the suburban regions. Walker and Wilcox thought it prudent to enlist Jim's help and the services of the cell's baker, a woman named Naomi.

In order for Walker and Wilcox to work longer hours at the station, they needed someone to stand

guard and warn them if a KPA soldier came sniff-
ing. The cell's electronics team had already repaired
a number of walkie-talkies. Karlson, Morgan, Lee,
and Giap used them to communicate with each other
when they were away from Home. Walker asked if
two more instruments could be quickly repaired and
allocated to him. Thus, Jim would position himself
with one at the entrance of Rose Lane and man a cart
containing samples of Naomi's homemade bread to
"sell." His walkie-talkie was hidden in a bread loaf,
to be used only in case of an emergency. To prevent
someone wanting to buy the crucial loaf, it was "decorated" with coloring that resembled mold. Karlson
approved the plan because it would also generate
some income for the cell.

On the day before the expected influx of Korean
troops, the couple was ready to mount the antenna
on the roof. They had cut a hole in the studio ceiling and placed a step ladder under it so Wilcox
could access the roof quickly without having to go
outdoors. Inside the building, the studio's console
was almost repaired and functioning. Wilcox had
built new input jacks so they could plug in their
homemade transistor board and microphone. Even
though it was LPAM—low-powered AM broadcasting—which wasn't as strong as Wilcox would have
liked, by pushing their signal through the studio's
more powerful transmitter and out the Yagi-Uda,
allegedly it would reach both coasts. The only thing
remaining to be done was rewiring a mess of cords
beneath the console. Since it reminded Walker of

spaghetti, he left that intimidating job for last.

Wilcox stood on the roof and surveyed the dark sky. "Looks like a storm is coming," she called down through the hole.

Walker stood inside the studio at the base of the ladder. "We gotta remember to put the cover on when we leave tonight. You ready to plug in the drill?"

"Sure." She knelt with a power drill in hand, the cord strung down into the room. Walker plugged it into a hand-cart-mounted engine-generator they had brought from Home. Although portable, the machine was heavy enough that two people were required to carry it.

"Okay!"

"Fire that baby up!"

Karlson allotted only so much gas for the generator. They had to use it sparingly, but drilling holes in the roof for the antenna base was necessary. Wilcox fit the stand where she'd made marks and proceeded to work.

Two blocks away, at the other end of Rose Lane, Jim sat in a lawn chair under a beach umbrella. So far he'd sold six loaves of bread since setting up shop that morning. There were only four left. Poor Naomi couldn't churn out enough product, for which there seemed to be a demand, especially with all the parents dropping off their kids at the school in the mornings. What would he do when there were no more loaves to sell? How could he justify remaining on the sidewalk if the KPA came around? It wasn't going to take long for word to get back to the Koreans that he was selling bread on the street. They were sure to check him out sooner or later.

A woman with a baby stroller appeared along Main Street/Highway 50, saw the stand, and approached him. "How much for the bread?" she asked.

"A dollar a loaf."

"That's very reasonable. I'll take two."

"Money's not worth a lot these days, you know," Jim said. "Just trying to help out our neighbors."

He considered raising the prices in the future to discourage customers.

Two loaves left and it was only mid-afternoon.

School let out. Most parents didn't want their kids walking home, so they came to pick them up. Jim's anxiety increased as several moms and dads strolled past with their sons and daughters, but luckily no one stopped to shop.

Back at the radio station, Wilcox finished drilling. Walker shut off the generator, climbed the ladder, and helped her with the antenna. After telescoping it, the thing was twelve feet long. With the added height of the building, it would stick up over thirty feet in the air. Given that Montrose's elevation was approximately 5,800 feet above sea level, the broadcast quality should be pretty good.

"Okay, I'll need you to hold it steady while I attach it to the base," she told him. Together they raised the antenna upright and positioned it over the holes she'd drilled in the base. The wind had risen, so Walker had to struggle with the aerial to keep it still.

"I see what you mean about a storm coming." The

bottom slipped out of place, knocking a bolt out of Wilcox's hand. It rolled off the roof. "Damn!"

"Ben, hold it!"

"I'm trying!"

Jim looked back at the end of the lane. The station building was visible from where he sat, but it was far enough away that activity on the inside wasn't easily discernable. However, with Walker and Wilcox on the roof erecting the antenna, they weren't hard to spot.

He turned back to see another woman and a teenage girl approach the stand. Jim stood and smiled. "May I help you, ma'am?"

Then his spine turned to ice. A man wearing the unmistakable dark olive green Korean People's Army uniform appeared on his rounds at the intersection of Rose Lane and Main Street. He saw the bread cart and started walking toward it.

"Let's see," the woman said. "You have three loaves left?"

"Uhm, just two, ma'am. See, that one there is a little moldy."

"Oh. Eww." She laughed a little. "Well, I can't say I haven't eaten a little moldy bread in the past year."

Hurry up, lady! Jim thought. He had to warn Walker.

"I'll take all three. That's a dollar each, right?"

"Uhm, I'm sorry, ma'am, but I can't in good conscience sell you that moldy loaf. I'm a doctor, you see. Well, not technically, I was a male nurse before all the trouble began, but I know a lot about this stuff. You'd get pretty sick if you ate that loaf."

The Korean was twenty yards away.

The woman frowned and said, "Well, all right. I'll take those other two, then. Next time you need to come out here with a lot more."

"Er, my wife can make only so many at a time. You know how scarce flour is." He packaged the two loaves just as the Korean approached the stand and stood a few feet behind the woman. He stared at Jim with interest.

The woman felt the soldier's presence and turned. "Oh," she said. Returning her focus to Jim, she made a face. "I guess I'll take my bread and go."

"Yes, ma'am." She gave him two dollars and departed quickly with her daughter, leaving the vendor alone with the Korean.

"Hello," Jim said. "I'm sorry, I just sold my last loaf. You'll have to come back tomorrow."

The soldier took three steps closer and barked, "Identity card!"

Shit, shit, shit! He willed the Korean, *Don't look over my shoulder! Don't look down the block!*

Jim dug into his pocket and pulled out the proper identification. "Here you go."

The officer took it and examined its details. He looked at Jim's face and the photo on the card, back and forth, three times. "This your address?" the man asked, referring to what was printed on the ID.

"Yes."

"Where is?"

"The street?" Jim didn't know. All of their IDs at Home were fake. He pointed west to redirect the

Korean's attention from the length of street behind him. "That way, about three blocks."

The Korean whipped out a hand-held portable electronic device and punched in the address.

Oh, shit . . .

The officer frowned and asked again, "*Where* is?"

Jim shook his head. "I'm sorry, I may be turned around here. What does that say?"

Obviously, the Korean's English wasn't very good. "Where is!" he demanded again.

Flustered, Jim allowed his desperation to show. "I said I'm turned around! I'm not sure. Isn't it that way?" He pointed west again.

The soldier didn't like the American's tone. It sounded uncooperative. He pointed to the pavement. "On knees!"

Jim's heart pounded in his chest. "What?" He glanced nervously at the moldy loaf of bread in the cart.

"On knees!"

He did as he was told. The Korean moved behind him and ordered, "Hands behind!"

Oh my God . . . !

Handcuffs snapped around Jim's wrists. The Korean frisked him; once satisfied the American wasn't carrying any weapons, he turned his attention to the bread cart.

Meanwhile, Walker and Wilcox were unaware of what was happening within sight of the building. Walker grappled with the antenna as the wind threatened to blow it right out of his hands. Wilcox had managed to screw in half the bolts. "Ben, I swear if you don't hold that thing steady, I'm going to drill *you* to the roof!"

"I'm doing my best, damn it!"

She screwed in two more bolts. Two more to go.

The Korean opened the bread cart and made sure there were no hidden compartments where the American might keep a weapon. Then he picked up the loaf of bread and grimaced when he saw the mold. He sniffed it and turned to his prisoner. "Bad food!" he snarled.

Jim nodded. "I know. It's moldy. I was going to throw it away."

The Korean made a sound of disgust and dropped the bread on the sidewalk. It split in two, revealing the walkie-talkie. The instrument spurted static.

The officer glared at it and then shifted his dark eyes to Jim.

The American had only one thought: *I have to pull his attention away from Ben and Kelsie!* Before the guard could touch him, Jim impulsively bolted to his feet and ran west on Main Street.

"Halt!" the officer shouted. He drew a Baek-Du-San, the North Korean copy of the Czech CZ-75 pistol. "Halt!" he called again as he took a bead on the running man.

Jim didn't stop.

The Korean had to squeeze the trigger only once. Struck in the back, the resistance fighter fell forward on his face, pushed himself forward a few inches with his feet, and then lost consciousness. The soldier calmly walked to the dying man and emptied another round in the back of the escapee's head.

Back on the roof, Wilcox had just finished bolting the antenna to the stand, when they both heard the gunshots.

"What the hell was that?" Walker asked. Wilcox stood beside him and they squinted down Rose Lane.

"I don't see Jim at his stand," she said.

"Neither do I." The Korean walked back into view. "Fuck! Get inside!"

Wilcox clambered into the hole and down the ladder. Walker followed and replaced the cover. Once he was on the floor, she asked, "What do we do? Stay here and be quiet?"

Walker had stupidly left the walkie-talkie on the console. He picked it up and started to call Jim—and hesitated. "Jim's dead."

"How do you know?"

"Just a feeling. I think we should get out of here. Let's leave our shit here and go out the back door. We'll walk up to the highway like we're an ordinary couple. If the KPA stops us, we'll say we're out for an afternoon stroll. There's no law against that. It's the middle of the day."

"Why don't we just stay here?"

"'Cause we need to see what happened to Jim. We owe him that. We're done here for today, right?" He pointed to the mess of wiring under the console. "All we have left to do is rewire that mess and plug in our transistor board?"

"Yeah."

"Then we're all set for tomorrow, right on schedule.

So let's get out of here."

She nodded. "All right."

He had left his automatic assault rifle back at Home, but they both packed their M9 pistols.

"If we get frisked, we're screwed," she said.

"There's no reason for them to do that. Just keep cool, okay? But just in case, I'm disengaging the safety on mine."

She did the same, returned the weapon to her concealed holster at the base of her spine, took a deep breath, and said, "Let's go."

Once outside, they pulled their jackets around them not only to disguise their guns but also because the temperature had dropped. The wind had picked up considerably. They walked arm in arm, pretending to be embroiled in a conversation and laughing at a joke when they reached the bread cart. From there they saw Jim's body in the middle of the road and the Korean standing over him, speaking into a communication device. Otherwise, the street was deserted.

"Oh God," Wilcox whispered.

"Just keep moving."

The soldier spotted them and shouted, "Halt!" He quickly strutted toward them, his handgun in hand. "Identity cards!"

Walker and Wilcox looked at each other and nodded. They dug into their pockets and produced the items. The Korean snatched them and, for a few tense moments, the couple wondered why the man was taking so long in examining them. Eventually, though, he handed the cards back and holstered his pistol. Then he said, "Recite oath!"

The couple didn't know what he meant. "Excuse me?" Walker asked.

"Oath of Loyalty! Recite!"

Walker swallowed. He didn't know it. He felt a rush of terror and the onset of a cold sweat.

Then Wilcox spoke with a slight shake in her voice, "I hereby affirm on oath a loyalty to the New Juche Revolution and the righteous creation of the New Democratic People's Republic of America. To dedicate myself to the struggle of the sum in pursuit of the new revolutionary thought of the Great Chairman, Comrade Kim Jong-un, and offer my highest loyalty to the authority of the Great Chairman, Comrade Kim Jong-un."

She paused, struggling to remember the rest. The Korean watched her with cruel anticipation.

"Further, I denounce and reject any devotion to the State of which I have heretofore been subject." Her voice broke unintentionally when Wilcox ended the recitation with, "I make this oath freely and by my own burden and not in submission to any outside influence."

The soldier smiled sadistically. He enjoyed her discomfort. Apparently, that satisfied him; without turning to Walker for a repeat performance, the Korean jerked his head and snapped, "Go!"

An overwhelming sense of relief flooded over Walker. He smiled at the man and nodded. "Good day," he said, and then he took Wilcox's arm. But his partner jerked away from him, reached behind her back, and drew the M9. Before the Korean could

react, Wilcox aimed and discharged a bullet in the soldier's face. Blood and gray matter burst out the back
of his head, and then the officer toppled over in front
of her. As soon as he was down, Wilcox kicked him
several times and the spat on the corpse.

"Fuck you! You dirty bastard, I didn't mean a word
of it!" she cried. The tears flowed.

Walker took hold of her and squeezed her tightly.
"Whoa, Kelsie, whoa. It's okay." She broke down in
a catharsis of emotion. He let her sob against his chest
as he stroked her hair. He gave her some time for the
release and then had the presence of mind to say, "We
need to get rid of his body, or this street will be swarming with Norks tomorrow." He looked around. The
road was still empty. "No one can see us. Let's put him
in the cart and take him back to the radio station."

Wilcox pulled away from him, holstered her gun,
sniffed, and wiped her face with her hands. "What
about Jim?"

Walker shook his head. "I hate to say it, but we
have to leave him."

Together, they picked up and stuffed the soldier's
body in the cart, closed the door, and wheeled it up
the block.

APRIL 10, 2026

Walker and Wilcox put the finishing touches on the
radio station console and antenna just as the Korean
force appeared on Highway 50 and civilians stampeded
back toward the elementary school. The resistance cell

hunkered down at the intersection with Rose Lane, aiming to hold off the onslaught until Walker made his broadcast. Under the pressure of strong winds, the advancing army, and jury-rigged equipment, the couple hit the air waves as the battle outside commenced. The old radio station building, not quite a hundred yards away from the melee, rattled with every detonation.

Giap blurted the new orders over the walkie-talkie. "Walker! Two minutes! You copy, my friend? Over."

Walker grabbed the radio and answered. "All right!"

"We blow horn, yes? You move! Out!"

Wilcox looked at him with anticipation.

He unfolded a scrap of paper upon which he had scribbled, tapped the microphone again, and froze. Walker had rehearsed his speech a dozen times and suddenly he couldn't open his mouth. It was too important to mess up.

"Ben?"

He didn't move.

"Ben! Snap out of it!"

Walker waved her off. "I'm okay."

Then he spoke into the mic.

"People of America! If you are hearing this, then you are not alone! All over this great country of ours is a movement. A movement of resistance. We cannot allow our land to be occupied any longer.

"We all know our Korean occupiers have committed appalling atrocities in various cities across our nation, but I must impart to you this terrible news. Some of you listening may already know this, but for

those of you who don't—the Koreans have *destroyed*
the Mississippi River from top to bottom! They have
somehow managed to pollute this lifeline of our
country with radioactive chemicals, killing everything
along its banks and causing the evacuation of every
town and city on its shores. There is no telling how
this monstrous deed will affect generations to come.
In short, our country is *divided*! The people east of
the river are cut off from those of us in the west. This
is the most heinous act ever committed on American
soil, my friends, and one of the worst corruptions of
nature ever caused by human hands. She cannot be
crossed! I repeat—*any attempt means certain death!*

"If invading our country wasn't enough, this sick,
inhuman crime is the last straw. We *must* stand up
and fight back. No more complacency! No more submission! Two-hundred-and-fifty years ago, in 1776,
a small band of revolutionaries stood against the
mighty British Empire in a bid for independence and
freedom. We can do it again. George Washington,
the founder of our country, once said these words to
the Continental Army: 'The time is now near at hand
which must probably determine whether Americans
are to be freemen or slaves; whether they are to have
any property they can call their own; whether their
houses and farms are to be pillaged and destroyed,
and themselves consigned to a state of wretchedness
from which no human efforts will deliver them. The
fate of unborn millions will now depend, under God,
on the courage and conduct of this army. Our cruel
and unrelenting enemy leaves us only the choice of

brave resistance, or the most abject submission. We have, therefore, to resolve to conquer or die.'

"My friends, let Washington's words ring true again today. The Second American Revolution is here. Resistance cells are scattered everywhere. Find them. Join them. Do not give up hope. If you have access to radio equipment, I urge you to use it to transmit the *truth*. We can forge a network of communication once again, my friends. We *must*!"

The gunfire grew louder. They heard shouts outside the building. And then—the dreaded bugle call. Time to go.

"This is all I have to say at the moment, but I will be back. Keep your radios on."

A massive explosion rocked the building. A section of the control room wall collapsed inward, filling the space with smoke and debris.

"Ben, we gotta go!" Kelsie shouted.

Walker continued, "This is Be—" He hesitated, thinking it unwise to relay his real name. "This is the Voice of Freedom, broadcasting to you from America!"

He pulled his circuit board out of the console and thrust it into his backpack. Kelsie shut off the generator, and together they carried it out the front door of the old radio station. Members of the cell ran past them, some turning backward to fire at the advancing enemy. They spotted dozens of parents with children rushing toward the school building up ahead.

"Kelsie, run!" Walker shouted.

"Ben, we have to leave the generator. We can't run with it."

But before Walker dropped his end, Goliath rumbled up next to them.

"Kelsie, our ride's here. Quick!"

They lifted the thirty-pound generator, placed it in a compartment on top of the vehicle, and climbed aboard. Lee must have been watching them, for the ingeniously-designed contraption bolted forward just as they were settled.

"Hold on!"

Goliath's speed increased to fifty miles-per-hour as it shot ahead of the running resistance members. It was now a race to reach Cedar Cemetery, where the entire group could scatter like flies. It was possible a few fighters might be caught—but most would make it to Home unseen and alive.

Walker's walkie-talkie crackled. It was Kopple.

"Nice job, Walker. For a city boy." Even through the static Ben could hear the resilient sergeant huffing as he ran.

"You heard it?"

"I had my transistor radio in my shirt pocket. Heard every word. 'Voice of Freedom,' huh? I like it."

"Thanks."

"Now pardon me while I run my ass off and you enjoy your taxi ride. See you at Home."

By the time the Koreans had swarmed into the battered radio station and spread westward into the town, the combined Utah and Colorado cells were already dispersed in dozens of different directions through Montrose's southeast suburbs.

They had lived another day.

WALKER'S JOURNAL

APRIL 10, 2026

We made it back Home in one piece. Well, not all of us. We lost eight. Six from Boone's cell and two from Nguyen's. It pains me to say we had to leave them, lying in the streets of suburbia, bleeding to death or blown to pieces. Even worse than that was the number of civilian casualties. I don't know how many there were, but a lot of adults and children were killed in the melee. Tragically bad timing for that school to let out just when the battle started. It will haunt me to my dying day.

But on a happier note, I made my best broadcast today, the first of its kind!

No more music or half-assed news reports. That was all well and good, and it probably did a lot for morale, but it was time to get serious. I sure hope to God that someone heard me. And I hope they spread the word. At any rate, DJ Ben is dead. I dubbed myself the Voice of Freedom. It has a nice ring to it.

Despite the horror of what happened today, I think we turned a corner. Sure, we're all on the run and the Koreans have Montrose. But Kelsie and I accomplished something I hope will end up being *important. I never thought I'd be a "real" journalist again. I don't recognize myself when I look in the cloudy, dirty mirrors we have at Home. I'm a very different person than I was eighteen months ago, back when I was a disillusioned, cynical celebrity/pop news reporter in Hollywood. Back then, I didn't give a shit who I hurt or walked on to get a stupid story.*

Life and death meant nothing to me then. But now? I feel more alive than I ever have . . .

APRIL 12, 2026

We know the Norks are in town doing exactly what was foretold. They've set up checkpoints in more areas and there's a massive presence on the streets. I guess when the guy Kelsie killed didn't show up after his rounds, the shit hit the fan. Maybe they'll find his body in the rubble of the radio station. Who knows . . .

MAY 1, 2026

They've started building the wall. It's going to enclose the city and turn Montrose into one big concentration camp. Over the last couple of weeks, the Koreans have been busy constructing all kinds of crap. They turned City Hall into an "employment center" for shale oil mining operations. If you ask me, it's slave labor. I have no idea if they're actually paying people to work for them, but I'm not eager to find out.

The cell made a couple of raids on the bastards since April 10th. Connor took a team and knocked out

one of the construction sites where part of the wall
was being built. Just blew it all to smithereens. Wish
I could've seen it. I went on the other mission, which
was last week. Connor and Wally led a group of us
to one of the checkpoints not far from Home. Boone
didn't like its close proximity, so we took it out. Wasn't
a big operation—just had to engage fifteen soldiers in
battle and blow up their makeshift building. None of
our guys got hurt. Took the bastards by surprise, so it
was all over in five minutes. I know I shot at least one
guy, but it's hard to know for sure. I never knew how
confusing and chaotic battle really is. You've seen war
movies and all that, but you never get a sense of just
how much of a mind-fuck it is. You go in thinking your
team and your plans are organized, but when the shit
hits the fan, all that goes out the window. When bullets
are flying every which way, explosions are going off all
around you, people are shouting orders, the enemy is
yelling, and you're running through smoke and flames
and debris—it's just crazy. It's entirely possible to "run
around like an idiot."

Anyway, Boone and Wally think Kelsie and I
should stay out of the fight and concentrate on being
the Voice of Freedom. The name stuck. We made two
more broadcasts with Hopper's portable radio and
our transistor board. The first one we made from the
old golf course and the second one we made from
the west side of town in an abandoned McDonald's.
I reported how more Koreans had moved in to
Montrose, and I also heard from two of my followers.
They're calling themselves "the Voice of Freedom,"

too. Yankee Doodle in Washington State and Cecilia up in North Dakota said they're part of the Voice of Freedom "Network." That made me feel good. I think I really have started something.

MAY 8, 2026

Nguyen was killed yesterday. I can't believe it. I'm really broken up about it, too.

He led a team to confront a large contingent of the enemy at the intersection of Highways 50 and 550. Well, it turned out the enemy force was larger than they'd thought. We lost three people, including Nguyen, before the team realized they were committing suicide. They had to turn back and run away. I don't blame them one bit.

Nguyen Huu Giap was a hero. I paid tribute to him in a broadcast about him last night. Derby, in Kansas City, acknowledged the report and forwarded it through the Voice of Freedom Network.

There are about ten of us now that I know of. More and more people have repaired radios that work. The Voice of Freedom Network is spreading like wildfire. I'm really proud, but I'm going to miss Nguyen . . .

MAY 9, 2026

I've decided to leave Montrose. I think my usefulness with Boone's cell has run its course. I had a long talk with Kelsie about it, and she agrees and wants to get the hell out of Dodge, too.

Last night we presented our decision to Boone, Wally, and Connor. They're sorry to see us go, of course, but they totally understand our intentions.

The thing is, I want to see the Mississippi River. I have to. I want to see for myself the horror the Norks inflicted upon our country. I need to report it through the VoF Network.

And most of all . . . I want to cross it. I have to see what's going on east of the river. No one has heard anything from Washington. Nobody knows if our president is alive or dead, although the VoF Network reports rumors that he's in the UK. We have no idea if the Koreans are present in New York or D.C. or Boston or Philadelphia.

I have to know . . .

So tomorrow morning, Kelsie and I are heading out. The cell has donated a repaired 1999 Jeep Cherokee SUV for us to use, as well as a decent supply of gas. Hopper gave us his portable radio. The cell has two more, so he didn't need it. We're taking the hand-cart generator, too, so we can make broadcasts on the road.

We're going to head east toward Kansas City. Derby already said he'd meet up with us. From there I guess we'll go to St. Louis and see about getting on the other side of the river. I don't know how we'll do it, but as the saying goes, we'll cross that bridge when we come to it.

JUNE 18, 2026

It's been Road Trip Heaven and Hell.

Kelsie and I are in Salina, Kansas. I can't believe it's taken this long to get only this far.

First, the good stuff. Interstate-70 is surprisingly uncluttered with derelict cars. The highway infrastructure is not a junkyard like it was a year ago when I was first traveling cross-country. Either people have moved them off the roads, stolen and repaired them, or whatever. We still see a few rotting hulks on the side of the highway, but not as many as before. There are also many more repaired vehicles actually driving. I was afraid our SUV would be too conspicuous, but so far we've blended right in with the light traffic—VERY light traffic. It still isn't the kind of thing that was normal ten years ago, or even two years ago before the EMP. But I reckon a car passes us in either direction every five or ten minutes. We usually wave and they wave back. I've also seen some black market gas stations every now and then. I'd say that's progress.

More good stuff. The people we've come into contact with have all been nice and helpful. There's not a lot of Korean presence on the road, but we do see a convoy of troops every now and then. They don't bother stopping the cars on the highway. They act like they're on a mission to get somewhere. We don't bother them, they don't bother us. I guess that's good.

Now the bad stuff.

You'd think we were in the Great Depression again, only ten times worse. Kansas is deserted. Yes, there are pockets of people, and they've all been nice and helpful like I said above. But finding a pocket of people takes some doing. Maybe they're all living

*away from I-70, or maybe they've just plain evacu-
ated the state and moved to a big city somewhere.
Apparently the Koreans have taken over a lot of the
farms. They're sucking our agricultural industry dry.
And rather than being forced to help them do it, the
farmers and townspeople just left.*

*I also found out through the Voice of Freedom
Network there was major trouble in Salt Lake City,
Utah. Apparently there was a large uprising by
the civilian population against the Korean military
occupation, and it worked—at first. They took back
control of the greater Salt Lake City area, commandeered Korean vehicles, and imprisoned occupational
leaders! But on May 16th, the bastards responded
by firebombing downtown with a series of Massive
Ordnance Air Blast bombs—or MOABs, as they're
called (the "Mother of All Bombs"). I can only imagine how terrible it was. There were more civilians in
the city than there were in Vegas when it got whacked.
Then I received an even uglier report, and I sincerely
hope it's a rumor. In the ensuing couple of weeks of
clean-up operations, the Koreans supposedly executed
any man they found who was over the age of sixteen.*

*Last night I broadcasted this news over the VoF
Network. If that doesn't raise the level of outrage in
this country, I don't know what will.*

*The last bit of bad news was that the SUV broke
down near the Colorado-Kansas border and we were
stuck there for three weeks before someone came
along that happened to have a badly needed gas filter.
It was a worrisome three weeks, too. The closest town*

was a ten-mile walk to Burlington, Colorado, and there was nothing there. No one around. So after trying that, Kelsie and I went back and stayed with the SUV. We lived off of crackers and apples and water. And love. I guess you could say that's what really kept us going.

In the end, a couple of guys in a tow truck (!) happened to come by. I couldn't believe it. It was almost as if we were suddenly back in the good old days when motor clubs would send out guys to fix your car if it broke down on the road. Anyway, Benny and Charlie—that was their names—they had a bunch of automobile parts for emergencies, and they happened to have spark plugs that fit. They wouldn't take anything for payment.

America. You gotta love it.

TWENTY-THREE

JULY 5, 2026

Salmusa never took a holiday.

The Americans' former Independence Day proved to be a challenge for the KPA all over the nation. Protests occurred all over the country. Fortunately, Salmusa had received intelligence that such displays of disloyalty were going to occur. Where possible, KPA Light Infantry divisions dispersed the protests with tear gas, beatings, and arrests. In addition, resis-tance movements made it a point to celebrate the so-called "Fourth of July" by attacking various Korean out-posts. Some were successful. Korean units in Dallas, San Diego, Montrose, and Oklahoma City were hit hard. The KPA simply couldn't be everywhere at once.

Thus, the week leading up to the Fourth was a busy one. While minions under his command felt the need for a day off, Salmusa allowed no such thing. The GKR never rested, not until all goals and objectives were met.

Always setting an example to others, it was the crack of dawn when Salmusa stepped into his office at the Greater Korean Republic's military headquarters in San Francisco's old city hall. Other than the security guards who manned the building 24/7, he was always the first one there. The first hour he spent exercising in the gym, for it was important to keep in shape. Salmusa believed the second most essential requirement for any member of the Korean People's Party, after loyalty and allegiance to the Brilliant Comrade, was discipline over one's body.

Following his workout, Salmusa spent a couple of hours analyzing intelligence reports from around America. Kim Jong-un had expressly dictated that resistance cells be squashed like bugs, so the operative was determined to locate every rebel hideout and destroy it. The task was proving to be more difficult than he had imagined. These simpleminded Americans had more fortitude than anyone in North Korea had predicted. Salmusa thought the military analysts in Pyongyang were fools. They had not lived in the United States as citizens, as he had done. Had he been the one to set military policy and goals in the New Democratic People's Republic of America, Salmusa would have been much harsher in dealing with the population from the first day of the invasion. In his opinion, the approach was too soft. There was no need to build shelters for the homeless, provide food and clothing, or allow them to keep owned property. If he'd been in charge, Salmusa would have slaughtered all the men and male children. Best to keep the vermin from reproducing.

Of course, he knew that would have been an impossible undertaking, but he enjoyed the fantasy.

Salmusa checked the clock. It was time for a

scheduled video call with the Brilliant Comrade. How privileged he was that he had direct access to Kim Jong-un! Only three other KPA men stationed in America could now claim such an honor.

After the usual satellite linkups and security checks, Salmusa was connected to Kim's office in Pyongyang. When his handsome face appeared on the monitor, Salmusa was reminded of the man's godlike charisma. He had watched the leader grow and mature from the days when they were both toddlers. Even then, Salmusa knew that one day Jong-un would be a great ruler. One of the most meaningful moments of Salmusa's life was when Kim Jong-un commented that he considered the two of them brothers.

Salmusa bowed slightly and said, "Good day to you, Brilliant Comrade."

"And to you, Salmusa."

"I hope you are well."

"I am fine. I understand you've had a difficult week."

Salmusa shook his head. "It's never too difficult to serve the Greater Korean Republic and the New Juche Revolution."

"You are a loyal servant, Dae-Hyun. Still, there were several uprisings and protests yesterday."

"Yes. We took care of every situation. The Americans will think twice before staging demonstrations in the future."

"But we lost some units?"

"Unfortunately, yes. But not many. Compared to the damage we inflicted on the Resistance and the general population, it was a worthwhile sacrifice."

"Very well. However, while I agree with your sentiments regarding the American people, the Greater Korean Republic must take care with regard to the international community and its perception of our treatment of the population. Our propaganda campaign is powerful and reaches every country in the world, but these resistance cells are managing to spread stories of our . . . work. We cannot allow it."

"No, sir."

"The so-called Voice of Freedom is a thorn in my foot, Salmusa. We have discussed him before."

"Yes, Brilliant Comrade. I am focusing all my energy in attempting to locate this infidel, the instigator of the radio network."

"Recordings of his broadcasts were delivered to me. We conducted an analysis of his voice and determined the Voice of Freedom is the same man who once went by the name 'DJ Ben.'"

Salmusa stiffened. "I was under the impression that DJ Ben was dead. After Las Vegas—"

"He continued to make broadcasts as DJ Ben following the strike on Las Vegas, so obviously he escaped prior to the bombing. Then—he was silent for a while. But he returned as the Voice of Freedom. And now he has a nationwide network of followers and collaborators. He is single-handedly the best recruitment vehicle for the American Resistance. He must be stopped."

"I understand, my Brilliant Comrade."

"I place you in charge, Salmusa. I trust no one else

to find him and eliminate this threat."

"I will see to it that he is hung by the neck in public, my Brilliant Comrade."

"You are to suspend your other activities and concentrate solely on this task. I have the utmost faith in your abilities."

"Thank you, sir. It is my duty and pleasure to serve."

Salmusa spent the rest of the afternoon with his communications analysts and technicians. While they didn't possess recordings of every transmission the Voice of Freedom had made, there were enough to establish a pattern of physical movement across the American landscape. The first broadcast, as they all knew, was made on April 10 in Montrose, Colorado, the same day a battalion of troops arrived in the town to begin the shale oil mining operations. KPA security forces confirmed that the radio speech was made in an abandoned radio station—now de-stroyed. Subsequent transmissions occurred in a variety of locations around Montrose.

Salmusa trembled with anger. *Why did the security forces not find him then? How difficult could it be? Idiots!*

Other broadcasts were made along Interstate-70 in Colorado, moving in an easterly direction. The most recent was in Kansas. Where was the man headed? Surely not the Mississippi River. Did he not know it was certain death to get near it?

Salmusa studied the U.S. map on the wall in front

of him. It was possible the Voice of Freedom might head south toward Oklahoma City or Dallas, Texas. There were reports of strong resistance cells in those cities. However, Kansas City was also a hub to various points. From there, the insurgent could travel to Arkansas or eastern Texas, or perhaps to Des Moines, Iowa. He could disrupt GKR activities in those areas with his despicable, radical commentaries. The man was obviously moving with some purpose in mind.

The operative made a decision. Salmusa returned to his office and began assembling a small team. They would fly as soon as possible to Kansas City. If that was where the Voice of Freedom was going, then Salmusa would be there to snare him in a trap.

TWENTY-FOUR

JULY 21, 2026

Walker and Wilcox sat with the man known only as "Derby" in a coffee shop located near Blue Valley Park, not far from the Truman Sports Complex in Kansas City. After having arrived in the city a week earlier, the couple found the Korean presence in town to be more frightening than what they'd seen so far. Kansas City was a large, sprawling city, and it took a great number of troops to regulate it. An entire brigade of an estimated four thousand men policed the metropolis, although Walker wasn't entirely clear why. Kansas was known for its agricultural resources, for which the Koreans demonstrated a desire—but the city itself held no strategic value. Or did it?

"It's the gateway into Missouri," Derby explained. "And because Missouri butts up against the Mississippi River, it's important."

Connecting with a member of the Voice of Freedom Network proved to be a challenging prospect. Walker and Wilcox were well aware the Koreans listened to the VoF broadcasts. Other resistance cells also made transmissions; it was the only way Americans could communicate with each other. Cellphone service was still nonexistent and landlines had never been repaired. Therefore, a code was established that had to be intuitive to American listeners and bewildering to the enemy. Walker figured most people knew the works of the Beatles so he tried preceding any meet-up information with a reference to a Beatles song, which he hoped would make no sense to the North Koreans. A little later in the broadcast, Walker cited a different Beatles allusion and another piece of the rendezvous information. For example, he might say, "Good evening, my fellow Americans. This is Mean Mr. Mustard looking for a Ticket to Ride with Derby. In today's news . . . " Then, after his report, he'd say, "They got a crazy way of loving there, and I'm gonna get me some. Coffee at Blue Valley Park." The first part was a lyric from the Wilbert Harrison tune called "Kansas City," which the Beatles covered on an early album. This meant the meeting would take place in Kansas City. Later in the broadcast, Walker would say, "Goo-goo-ka-choo, Tuesday at three," which quoted the nonsensical lyric in "I Am the Walrus," followed by the day and time of the rendezvous. It took awhile for resistance members to catch on; but like a lightbulb snapping on in one's head, once the connection was made there didn't seem to be a problem.

Derby was a thin and diminutive middle-aged man who appeared extremely nervous to be meeting in public with the Voice of Freedom himself. Walker knew him at once because Derby wore a faded Beatles T-shirt. The shop, a former Starbucks, specialized in coffee made with homegrown coffee beans and boiled rainwater. They did a brisk business.

The threesome sat at a table on the sidewalk in plain view of Korean soldiers who stood across the street eyeing every pedestrian. Walker figured the less suspiciously one behaved, the better the chances of the guards not noticing.

"What's your real name?" Derby asked. "Mine is—"

Walker held up his hand. "Best not to reveal our real names. If one of us were to be caught and tortured, well . . . you know."

"Oh, right. I hadn't thought of that. By the way, that was very clever of you to come up with the Beatles code. At first I didn't know what the hell you were saying, but I finally figured it out. I was a huge fan when I was younger. It was like—*duh!*—when it hit me. Very cool."

"Thanks."

"So how can I be of help?"

"We want to start broadcasting while we're here. Do you know of any old radio stations we could use? Our portable unit is fine, but we'd prefer more power so we can reach more people. On our way here we passed one in Topeka that had a huge antenna, so we went back the other night and broke in. It's still operational. I think it's still being used as a religious-talk station."

Derby laughed. "I know which one you mean. That Family Radio station's been around forever, it seems. Yeah, they're still broadcasting. They must have a huge generator and a lot of gas. I guess the Lord provides when His message is being told."

"They did have a big mother of a generator. And the place was easy to break into. I hate doing that, but as you know, the Voice of Freedom messages need to get out. They're as important as God's."

"You said it. Well, I'm not sure about radio stations in Kansas City, but I know a college with its own station. The school is in session, too. The Koreans allow most people to live their lives as best they can, even without cars or electricity or running water. However, the kids at the college repaired the equipment and use a generator to play music in the afternoons after classes."

Wilcox nodded. "Sure, lots of colleges had radio stations. My high school had a radio club, too. I think a lot did, at least the ones that had money for one. I'm surprised the Koreans let them use it."

"Oh, the Norks checked it out, all right. As long as the students just broadcast music and school news, they don't care. However, all radio transmissions are closely monitored these days. I guess you know that. It's become very dangerous for the Resistance."

"That's why we move around and never broadcast from the same place," Walker said. "So how would we do it? Get into the school at night, that is."

"I know one of the janitors. He's in the cell I'm in. Should be no problem. Can you be on the air tonight at ten o'clock?"

"We can try."

"I'll send you a message regarding the day and time."
He wrote down the university's name and address

on his napkin. "It's over the state line in Parkville, Missouri, but it's really still part of the Kansas City metropolis. There's a loading dock in the back of the main building. I'll meet you there at the appointed time. We'll do it after dark, because it's pitch black there without outdoor lighting."

"That sounds good."

"So what do you think of those garbled transmissions that have been coming through lately?"

Walker looked at Wilcox and she shrugged. "I don't know what you mean," he answered.

"You haven't heard them? They come on every night at midnight. Someone's speaking, but the signal is really bad. Goes in and out, full of static, and difficult to make out."

"No, I haven't heard them. When did this start?"

"Eight days ago."

"Oh, well we've been on the air only once in that time. It took us a while to get settled here."

"Where are you staying? Did you hook up with a resistance cell?"

"We're in a trailer park with a lot of other transient folks. I'm thinking we need to move, though, 'cause the Koreans were there yesterday searching the vehicles and checking everyone's IDs. We were out when it happened, but I'm sure they'll be back. They're looking for someone or something. Probably me."

Derby nodded. "You may be right. They're cracking down on the Resistance, big time. I'm sorry, I don't think I heard your broadcast. What night was it?"

"Three nights ago. We found a six-floor apartment

building where squatters lived. We used the top floor. So tell me more about these garbled messages."

"Here, I wrote some of them down, at least what I could make out." He dug into his pocket and removed scraps of paper. "This was part of the first one. 'Something something something . . . persons attempting to find a moral in it will be banished . . . something something . . . ' and that's all I got." Derby slid it over to Walker for him to study. It made no sense to him. "Here's another. 'After supper she got out her book and learned me about Moses . . . something something something . . . ' and then the transmission died."

Walker frowned. "Now *that* sounds familiar." He rubbed his chin. "Keep going."

"'Something something . . . he got stuck up on account of having seen the devil and been rode by witches.'"

Wilcox made a face. "*What?*" She shook her head. "It's nonsense."

"I'm not so sure," Walker said. "You have more?"

"One more, this was last night's. 'Something something . . . and cussed everything and everybody he could think of, and then cussed them all over again . . . something something . . . polished off with a kind of general cuss all around . . . something something.'"

"Can I take these?"

"Sure. I hope you can figure 'em out. Either it's some kind of code or someone's just plain nuts and using up valuable air space."

"It could be Korean probing," Wilcox ventured. "Maybe they're trying to get one of us to respond."

"I thought of that, too," Walker said. "I'm gonna listen tonight, like we agreed."

"The thing is," Derby whispered, "we're pretty sure these transmissions are coming from somewhere *east* of the Mississippi River!"

Salmusa, flanked by ten Light Infantry men, stormed into the Family Radio station on 10th Street in Topeka, Kansas, where three nights earlier, Walker and Wilcox made a Voice of Freedom transmission. It was true, the facility possessed a tower over five hundred feet tall, providing it with a strong signal throughout the state and beyond.

The place was manned with a skeleton crew—just a DJ in the booth and an engineer at the mixing board. When the soldiers burst into the control room, the announcer was in the middle of quoting scripture and urging his listeners to pray several times a day for "deliverance from evil."

"Turn off the radio!" Salmusa snapped. "Now!"

The engineer stood. "Wait a minute. We're not doing anything wrong."

Salmusa drew his Daewoo, grasped it by the barrel, and pistol-whipped the man across the face. The DJ rushed into the control room, knelt by his companion, and shouted, "Why did you do that? What's wrong? What do you want?"

The engineer was able to sit up, but there was a nasty, bleeding gash across his right cheek.

"The Voice of Freedom made a broadcast from this station three nights ago. Where is he?"

The announcer wrinkled his brow. "Who?"

"You can't tell me you don't know who the Voice of Freedom is."

The two men shook their heads. "No, we don't know. But you're right, someone broke in here the other night. We found the back door jimmied open. Someone was in the control room. But nothing was stolen."

"Show me."

The DJ left the engineer sitting on the floor, nursing his wound. He took Salmusa and two other men to the back of the station and pointed at the broken door jamb. The Korean considered that the men might be telling the truth. However, he needed to send a deterrent to the Voice of Freedom.

"Go back to your microphone," he ordered. "I want you to broadcast something for me."

Knowing better than to argue, the DJ returned to the studio booth and sat behind the console. Salmusa gestured with his pistol for the engineer to return to his seat and do his job. The Korean then entered the booth and stood behind the announcer. When the red light came on, the engineer said, "We're live."

"Repeat after me," Salmusa commanded. "This message is to the Voice of Freedom and his network of rebels and dissidents."

The man did as he was told.

"You will no longer use radio stations to make your disloyal and treasonous commentaries." After the DJ replicated the words, Salmusa said, "Now identify yourself and this station." The man obeyed. "Now continue repeating what I say. To show you that your traitorous words will do you and the Resistance no good, the Korean People's Army will hereby execute me and my engineer."

The DJ's eyes widened. He turned to Salmusa. "What?"

"*Say it!*" He lifted the Daewoo's and touched the barrel to the man's temple.

The announcer met the eyes of his colleague through the window separating the booth from the control room. One of the other soldiers also held a gun to the engineer's head.

"To show you that your . . . what?"

"Traitorous words will do you and the Resistance no good . . . "

"Traitorous . . . words will do you . . . and the Resistance no good . . . oh God, please help us! Jesus Christ!"

Salmusa cruelly jammed the barrel into the side of the DJ's head. " . . . the Korean People's Army will hereby execute me and my engineer! Say it!"

"Please, don't do this . . . "

Salmusa nodded at his man through the window. The soldier squeezed the trigger of his weapon and blew the engineer's brains out. The DJ screamed.

"If you do not say the rest, I will torture you for hours and *then* execute you," Salmusa said.

With tears running down his face, the DJ stammered, but he managed to get the rest out.

"Very good," Salmusa said. Then he pulled the trigger, making sure the noisy discharge went out over the airwaves for all to hear.

* * *

Walker and Wilcox set up their portable generator and radio in the seclusion of an abandoned gas station three miles from the trailer park. At eight o'clock, they went on the air. The frequency on their board was still set to that of the religious radio station where they'd last made a transmission. As soon as Wilcox fine-tuned the signal, they heard a broadcast—the voice of a very frightened announcer reciting words that another man in the control booth was dictating.

"This message is to the Voice of Freedom and his network of rebels and dissidents." Pause. "You will no longer use radio stations to make your disloyal and treasonous commentaries." There was mumbling and then the DJ identified himself and the station's call numbers. There was no doubt it was the same place where the couple had been.

There were more unintelligible words between the two men, and then the DJ asked, "What?"

"Say it!"

Pause. "To show you that your . . . what? . . . traitorous . . . words will do you . . . and the Resistance no good . . . oh God, please help us! Jesus Christ!"

The sound of a distorted thud made Walker and Wilcox jump. They shared a glance, instinctively identifying the cause. After a moment, the DJ continued through sobs. "Please, don't do this . . . " Another pause, and then the announcer screamed bloody murder. After a further moment of inarticulate words between the men in the control booth, the DJ stammered and said, " . . . the Korean People's Army will hereby execute me and my engineer!"

This was followed by the sharp, jolting sound of a gunshot.

The recording repeated after a short silence. It was obviously on a loop so it could be heard continuously.

"Oh, my God, Ben, we got those poor people killed," Wilcox said.

Walker stood and walked away. He kicked a chair across the room. He picked up a screwdriver someone had left on the floor long ago and threw it hard at the wall.

"There's something else, Kelsie," he said. "I think I'm responsible for Las Vegas, too."

"What do you mean?"

"The Koreans track our signals, right? They must have heard DJ Ben's broadcasts, didn't like them, and figured out they were coming from Vegas. I bet they bombed the city because of me."

"You don't know that, Ben. The Norks did it to exert their dominance over us. Come on, don't go thinking that."

Walker shook his head, leaned against a workbench, and breathed heavily until he came to a decision. With purpose, he strode back to the radio, picked up the microphone, and spoke.

"My fellow Americans, this is the Voice of Freedom. This message is for our Korean occupiers. I know you're out there. How *dare* you murder innocent human beings. How dare *you* use *me* as a reason to slaughter people. Every one of you bastards is a *coward*. You have no honor. You have no decency. You are the scum of the earth, the lowest of the low. And you know what? Your Idiot Comrade Kim *Dung*-un is the biggest coward of you all. He sits over there on his puny ass, preaching to the world what a peace-loving dickhead he is, and all the while he gives the orders to do *this* to innocent people. Let me tell you something, you uninvited sons of bitches who are in our country. The Resistance is gonna kick your asses out. Mark my words! It may not be tomorrow and it may not be next month. It may not even be next year. But one day it's going to happen, and you're going to regret stepping foot on our beloved soil. You are no better than slimy dung beetles, and we don't want you here! The Resistance will *bury* you! Americans, are you with me? Are we going to *bury* these cowardly bastards? Are we going to kick our boots so far up their butts that our feet'll bust out their noses? *Hell yeah!* Repeat after me! *Hell yeah!* Come on, louder—*Hell yeah!* Louder, louder! *Hell yeah! Hell yeah! Hell yeah!*"

He chanted for a full minute, screaming his lungs out, using the emotional outburst as a cathartic release for his pain. And when he stopped, Wilcox grabbed his arm.

"Ben," she whispered. "Listen."

At first he didn't know what she was talking about. Then he heard it. Voices. Outside.

Walker stood, went out the back door, and put his ears to the wind.

It was distant and it was faint, but it was in unison.

Hell yeah! Hell yeah! Hell yeah!

Thousands of voices across America had answered his call.

Salmusa made it a point to monitor radio traffic at night. The Voice of Freedom usually made his transmissions between eight and midnight. He had heard the eight o'clock broadcast and the ensuing cry of protest that echoed in the sky. He was so angry that he walked out on a pedestrian-filled Kansas City street and shot the first person he saw.

When the chatter began later that evening, Salmusa recognized the Voice of Freedom and another network operative known only as "Derby."

"It's been a Hard Day's Night, my friends," the VoF said. "And I'm looking for a place of higher learning."

"Tomorrow Never Knows," Derby answered. "Not until ten o'clock, anyway."

"I copy that, sir. This is the Voice of Freedom signing off."

Salmusa stared at the radio speakers. *What was that all about?* Obviously it was code for something. However, there was something about the phraseology that rang a bell. He clapped his hands for Byun, his assistant, who obediently jumped into the superior's office.

"Get me the transcripts of the Voice of Freedom's last ten broadcasts."

The underling fetched them quickly. Salmusa laid them on the table and studied the texts.

Then he smiled.

His former wife Kianna had been a Beatles fan. She had played the disgusting Western rock music until he was forced to wear earplugs. But some of the words, song titles, and lyrics sank in.

He thought he understood the code.

Salmusa stood and entered the room where his team was working.

"Find me a school—a college or a high school—that has a working radio station!" he commanded.

JULY 22, 2026

Derby and his janitor friend, Eric, quietly rode their bicycles toward the university's loading dock. They stopped at the entrance of the long expanse of road that led to the campus. It bordered a lush park. They could barely see where they were going in the dim light.

"What time is it?" Eric asked.

"I don't know. It's almost ten. I hope we're not late."

"This makes me nervous."

"Relax. It'll be all right. The Voice of Freedom will make his broadcast in five minutes and we'll be gone before the Koreans can figure out we were here."

The sky was black. There was no moon and the stars were hiding. Even though it was the middle of summer, Derby felt a chill in the air. "Come on, let's get going."

They rode on, pushing through the final mile to the campus. There were no cars in the parking lot in front; the building was dark and silent. They pedaled the bikes around to the back and stopped at the loading dock.

As soon as they dismounted, a floodlight cracked on, bathing the dock—and them—in bright light.

"Hands up! Do not move!"

The Korean officer barked the command through a megaphone. The voice was so loud and strident that the two men yelped in fright. The light blinded him, but Derby made out several uniformed soldiers pointing rifles at them. The man with the megaphone approached, now backlit so that his silhouette stood ominously before them.

"Which one of you is the Voice of Freedom?" he asked.

The men were too scared to speak.

"Or are you meeting the Voice of Freedom here and he hasn't arrived yet?"

Salmusa moved closer so he could examine the fear in the captives' faces. His eyes went from one to the other and back again. "You better speak, or I will kill one of you in three seconds. Are either of you the Voice of Freedom or his colleague Derby? I am counting to three. One."

Derby swallowed.

"Two."

"Wait! I am the Voice of Freedom!"

Salmusa wasn't sure. The timbre and inflection in the man's speech was familiar, but it wasn't what he'd expected. He addressed Eric. "And who are you?"

"I'm just a janitor here at the college."

"And you were going to let the rebels into the radio station?"

Eric hesitated.

"Tell him the truth, Eric," Derby said.

The man nodded. Salmusa smiled. He was pleased. He turned and clapped his hands. Four solders trotted to the threesome. Indicating the janitor, Salmusa said, "Take this man and hang him from one of the light poles in front of the college."

"No!" Derby cried. "No!" There was nothing he could do. The troops dragged Eric away and around the building to the other side.

Salmusa eyed Derby again. "So you are the Voice of Freedom?"

"Yeah."

"Prove it."

"What?"

"Prove it. I want to hear you speak. Tell me what you were going to broadcast tonight. I want to hear you *in action.*"

Derby knew that wasn't going to work. But could he warn the real Voice of Freedom not to show up? The man was probably on his way to the college at that very moment.

"May I use your megaphone?" Derby asked.

Salmusa was surprised by the request. "Why?"

"If this is my last broadcast, don't you want me to share it with anyone who can hear?"

Salmusa thought, *Why not?* He handed over the device.

Derby fiddled with it for a second, making sure it was on and at full volume. He raised it to his mouth . . . and started singing at the top of his voice.

"You better run for your life if you can, little girl, hide your head in the sand, little girl, catch you with another man, that's the end, little girl!"

Derby's delivery resounded through the parking lot and beyond. He started to walk toward the floodlight, continuing to sing.

"You better run for your life if you can, little girl, hide your head in the sand, little girl, catch you with another man, that's the—"

A gunshot interrupted the performance. Salmusa lowered the Daewoo and watched the dissident drop to the pavement and bleed to death.

Walker and Wilcox heard it all.

They had left the SUV in a secluded spot in the park across from the college. They were walking along the road near the campus with their radio equipment in backpacks when the megaphone singing filled the air.

"That's Derby!" Walker whispered.

The gun blast abruptly ended the song.

"Christ. That was the Beatles song, 'Run For Your Life.' He was trying to warn us. Let's get out of here!"

Keeping to the shadows, the couple quickly moved back to a densely wooded area in the park and watched in horror as the Koreans hung a man from a light pole in front of the main building.

"Is that him?" Wilcox asked.

"I don't think so. That must be his friend."

They waited in the dark for an hour. Finally, the Koreans left in a Humvee that was parked in the blackness behind the school. When they felt it was safe, the couple returned to the SUV and escaped.

They stopped at an old, rundown drive-in theater. After parking the SUV, Walker started to set up the portable radio.

"What are you doing?"

"It's almost midnight. I want to hear something."

He was very shaken by what had occurred. Because of him, now at least four men had given their lives for the Voice of Freedom Network's cause. Walker had not anticipated the bloodshed.

"I've been naïve, Kelsie," he said. "Why didn't I think people might die for this?"

"Ben, it's not your fault. Come on, we all know what we're doing is dangerous. It's a risk and we signed on for it. Don't beat yourself up."

He shook his head as he plugged in the transistor board. "If I had known folks would die—for *me*—I wouldn't have done it. Why did I let Wally talk me into this Voice of Freedom bullshit?"

"It's not bullshit, Ben, and you know it! Stop it! And Wally wasn't the only one who talked you into it, remember? You're upset, I know. I am, too. What, are you going to just lay down and let the Koreans take away everything? Are we giving up?"

As the radio kicked on, Walker sighed. "No. You're right. Still . . . "

"I know." She nodded toward the radio. "What are you looking for?"

"Those messages Derby told us about. See if you can find them."

She fiddled with the tuner but uncovered nothing

but static. "I wish he'd told us the frequency."

They caught a little music, surprisingly, and then kept looking. A minute passed. Nothing.

"Keep trying."

She turned the knob backwards, going over frequencies she'd already tried. And then—

A burst of noise. A human voice, terribly garbled.

"There!"

They listened hard, attempting to make sense of the words.

" . . . *We catched fish and talked, and we took a swim now and then to keep off sleepiness. It was kind of solemn, drifting down the big, still river, laying on our backs looking up at the stars* . . . " And then more static. " . . . *nothing ever happened to us at all—that night, nor the next, nor the next* . . . "

Walker's mouth dropped. "I know this! By God, I know this!"

"What? What is it?"

"Kelsie! It's *Huckleberry Finn*!"

"What?"

"He's reading *The Adventures of Huckleberry Finn*! Kelsie, that whole book is about the Mississippi River. Don't you realize what this means?"

"That the broadcast is coming from the other side? From the east, like Derby said?"

"Yes, but not only that! It's a coded message, Kelsie. Someone is trying to tell us—we *need to cross the river*!"

TWENTY-FIVE

SEPTEMBER 25, 2026

Salmusa gave the signal to drop tear gas into the air vents. Without precious oxygen, the resistance traitors would be forced to flee their underground bomb shelter and grovel at the feet of their masters.

The KPA team had tracked the Voice of Freedom eastward, but Salmusa was frustrated with the lack of success. Just when he thought he had located the man and prepared to ensnare him, the rebel slipped away undetected. Following the locations of the insurgent's treasonous broadcasts, Salmusa's team traveled a zigzagging route between Kansas City and Columbia, Missouri, where they were at present. The Voice of Freedom apparently knew he was being pursued, so he cleverly avoided moving in a straight line across the state. After a transmission in Springfield, in southern Missouri, the next one was in Kirksville, in the north. Salmusa was certain the man was intentionally leading them on a wildly unpredictable chase.

KPA intelligence reported the discovery of a Columbia resistance cell hideout after a recent VoF broadcast in the area. Salmusa and his men immediately joined the Light Infantry there and were now in the process of exterminating the vermin. But first, he had some questions to ask.

The tear gas did its job. In pairs, sixteen men and women burst out of the bomb shelter door with guns blazing. The KPA opened fire and mowed them down as they came into sight. The scene reminded Salmusa of when he and Kim Jong-un were teenagers, home on holiday from their school in Switzerland; they amused themselves by hunting and shooting rats that congregated in some of Pyongyang's poverty-stricken neighborhoods.

The Infantry had strict orders to aim for the rebels' legs to disable them, not kill them. Each American now writhed in agony on the ground, helpless and frightened. It was exactly the way Salmusa liked them. He approached one fighter and pressed his boot on the insurgent's wounded thigh, causing the man to scream from the torture.

"Who is your leader?" Salmusa asked.

A woman, also wounded and on the ground a few feet away, spoke up. "I am! Talk to me!"

Salmusa released the first rebel and approached her. "I am looking for the Voice of Freedom. Where is he?"

The revolutionary smiled through her pain. "You just missed him. He's gone."

"But he was here."

"Yeah. He was here."

"Where is he going?"

"To the east. He's crossing the river. And you can't stop him."

Salmusa frowned. *Was the Voice of Freedom an*

imbecile? How did he expect to cross the Mississippi? It was impossible!

"He's headed for St. Louis, isn't he?" the Korean asked.

"No. That's what he wants you to think. He's going south into Arkansas. He plans to cross the river somewhere down there."

Salmusa knew the woman was lying, but it was obvious she would do anything to protect the Voice of Freedom.

The Korean turned to his men and ordered, "Finish them off. Then we'll move on to St. Louis. That's where our prey is headed."

The Light Infantry spent the next sixty seconds emptying their weapons into the Columbia resistance cell members and the next half hour stringing up the corpses from trees in the town square.

OCTOBER 12, 2026

Walker and Wilcox were exhausted. They had been on the run for nearly three months, attempting to stay one step ahead of the KPA outfit that was pursuing them. There had been too many close calls. Just to confuse the enemy, they backtracked several times—even gone all the way back to Kansas City for a broadcast—and back to the proximity of St. Louis, where they were now. Walker knew full well he was a marked man. Too many people with whom he had come in contact were murdered simply for having been in his presence. But he had continued the Voice of Freedom transmissions, gathering information from his various network associates, and delivering the truth to America. It was all he lived for now—that, and Kelsie. He could see, though, that she was tiring of the life on the road. Never staying in one place very long was hard on both of them, but lately it seemed to bother her more.

Despite the devastating contamination of the Mississippi River, pockets of humanity still lived in the far western sections of the St. Louis urban sprawl. People who had no way of leaving simply migrated away from the certain death of the eastern sections of town, leaving behind a ghostly shell of a once thriving metropolis of life, music, and culture. Now it was a graveyard, covered by a layer of dense, toxic, gray fog emanating from the river. The Missouri River, which ran north and south between the suburbs of St. Charles on the west and Bridgeton and Maryland Heights on the east, was as close to the city proper as one could safely venture. It was still relatively unpolluted, but it wouldn't be for long. The deadly chemicals in the Mississippi were spreading and had already tainted Missouri's leg north of St. Louis, which ran from Pelican Island to the Mississippi. Instances of radioactive poisoning ran rampant. Thousands were sick and dying.

With the help of several underground resistance members with radios, Walker and Wilcox hooked up with a small cell in St. Peters, a northwestern suburb of St. Louis, approximately fifteen miles from the Missouri River. The group was run by a former history professor at St. Louis University by the name of Thomas Bendix. Consisting of only nine members, the cell was terribly understaffed and poorly armed. They got around on bicycles and lived in an abandoned motel on the I-70 feeder road. The group did possess a repaired radio, which was how Walker first discovered their existence.

After a dinner of fried eggs cooked over a generator-run hotplate, the small cell gathered in the motel's lobby with the couple. Bendix left fourteen-year-old Sammy, an orphan, in charge of monitoring the radio in the motel office while the adults met. Only five men in the cell had weapons. One of them, Darrell Julian, was a Connor Morgan–type who had military experience and was gung-ho for the cause. A tattoo-decorated, heavyset, middle-aged biker chick named Martha Malloy also packed a 9mm Browning she claimed once belonged to her husband, a casualty of the initial Korean invasion. Before the meeting, Malloy took Wilcox into her room to show off a restored 1978 Kawasaki Z-1.

"I'm keeping this fueled up and ready to go in case I have to skedaddle," Malloy explained.

The woman also supplied the cell with never-ending liquor from a source she wouldn't reveal.

Professor Bendix passed around one of Malloy's bottles of vodka for everyone to sample and then began the meeting. "We welcome our friend the Voice of Freedom and his colleague. We're all big supporters of your work and what you're trying to do."

"Thanks," Walker said. "It's really people like you

who are keeping the Resistance alive."

Malloy snorted. "Are you kidding? We're one step away from being on life support. There ain't much resistance going on in St. Louis, believe me."

Julian scoffed, "That's 'cause you're usually drunk on your ass and not out on patrol with me and the boys. We see *plenty* of action."

Bendix held up his hands, "Boys and girls, play nice. We have guests."

The woman narrowed her eyes at Walker and Wilcox. "Besides, most of the resistance fighters are buried in Busch Stadium."

Bendix nodded and explained. "The Koreans used Busch Stadium as a mass grave for executed 'dissidents' before the river was irradiated." Before Walker could react to that news, the leader addressed the group. "Our friend has asked me about something for which he could use some opinions." He turned to Walker. "Would you like to explain what it is you want to do?"

Walker nodded and said, "I want to cross the Mississippi and get on the other side. It's been too long not knowing what's going on over there. I've received some radio transmissions from persons unknown over there, but they don't tell us a lot. I've never engaged in an actual conversation with anyone in the East. Every broadcast I've heard seems to be a recorded message. I've piddled around over here far too long. It's time to do something about it."

"How are you going to get across?" Julian asked.

"That's why I want your opinions. How would you

do it if you had no choice? What are the dangers?"

Bendix answered that one. "You can't get within five miles of the river without wearing a protective suit. By that I mean a full-body rubber suit that's iron-lined. Even then, it's dangerous to be in close proximity to the water. I reckon that even with a suit a person couldn't take more than four or five hours of exposure. Everything is toxic the closer you get. The air, the ground you walk on, the objects you touch. And the true horror of it is that it's the same the entire length of the river, from Canada to Mexico. I would say the only way to get across is to fly, and the only folks who have planes are the Norks."

"What *about* the KPA? Where are they located? They can't be in the city, can they?"

"No. They're all stationed in ad-hoc camps along the Missouri River. There's a checkpoint at every crossing. They keep anyone from going farther east. They shoot first, ask questions later. And they're well-protected. I think you'd have to have a tank to get past one."

"I wonder where I could get one of those protective suits," Walker said.

Julian replied, "They have 'em at most of those checkpoints."

"Do the soldiers use them?"

"Sure. I imagine they don't like going into the city any more than we would. But they'll put 'em on if they have to."

Malloy spoke up. "They also set fires on the city outskirts every now and then. That drives even more people out of the only livable areas around here."

"Man, I'm all for you getting across the river," Julian said, "but pardon me for saying so—it's a suicide mission."

"That's what I've been telling him," Wilcox said suddenly. Walker looked at her with disappointment. She met his reaction with, "Well, it's true. Do you want to die of radiation poisoning? You saw those people we passed on the road. Their exposure was minimal, too."

Walker wasn't happy that Wilcox had made their bone of contention public.

Sammy interrupted the meeting by popping his head out of the office. "Professor, there's a transmission coming in. I think it's stuff we've been waiting for!"

Bendix rose, saying, "Excuse me." He disappeared into the office, leaving Julian to outline his plans for an attack on a Korean supply truck when it made its monthly deliveries. "It comes around once a month," he explained to Walker. "Brings food and water and more to the various checkpoints."

The professor returned and said, "Our shipment will be here in an hour. We need to get to the rendezvous." For Walker's benefit, he elucidated, "Every three months we get a supply of stuff from resistance cells in Kansas City. They've managed to find all kinds of ways to get them to us. Last time someone drove an old ice-cream truck—without the ice cream, unfortunately."

"I hope for God's sake they sent more weapons this time," Julian said. "How can we fight the enemy if

only six of us have guns? Oh, wait a minute, Martha
don't count. Make that five guns."

"Shut up, Julian," Malloy snapped. "You know as
well as I do I'm a lousy shot and would probably end
up killing one of our own."

"Then why don't you let someone else have your
gun?"

"Because it's all I have left of Boogle." She leaned
over to Wilcox. "Boogle was my husband."

Bendix, Julian, and two other men donned empty
backpacks.

"May I join you?" Walker asked.

"I don't see why not."

"Why don't I drive? Might be able to carry more
stuff in the SUV."

Julian looked at Bendix for a say-so. The professor
shrugged and nodded. "Bring your M4."

Wilcox elected to stay at the motel. She gave Walker
a quick kiss on the cheek and asked him to not get
killed, and then disappeared into Malloy's room.
He was well aware that things were tense between
them, so he was glad to get away and go on the
supply run. The rendezvous point was a two-level
parking garage in a tiny deserted community called
All Saints Village, located three miles from I-70 at
the southern end of St. Peters. The building still had
cars sitting in it from the EMP blast, but Bendix
assured Walker that no one ever ventured into it.
Walker parked the SUV on the first floor and they
all poured out to wait outside. Julian held binocu-

lars to his eyes and scanned the roads in all directions. It was so quiet and desolate that they may as well have been the only people on the planet.

Time passed. Eventually, Julian asked Bendix, "You sure about the meet-up? Where are they?"

"I guess they're late."

"Hope they didn't run into trouble," another man said.

Walker paced the ground outside the parking garage, also using his own pair of binoculars to study the converging streets. At first there was nothing to see but fog, but then he noticed something moving in the distance. He called Bendix over and handed him the field glasses. "What do you make of this? It's a vehicle."

Bendix took the binoculars, studied the view, and nodded. "Yeah. The air's too hazy to get a clear view, but you're right. It's some kind of vehicle. It's coming our way."

"Is it the supply unit?" Julian asked. He also focused on the street in question.

"Don't know."

The seconds ticked by. The vehicle finally reached a range in which its shape was discernable.

"It's a goddamned tank," Julian said.

Bendix gasped. "Did the Koreans intercept our messages?"

"They must have!"

Walker took back his binoculars and looked again. Sure enough, he made out the dreaded flag of the New Democratic People's Republic of America—the heretical red-washed United States flag dominated by the Korean coat of arms. The tank was covered with the profane emblems.

"We better hide," he said. "Can't risk driving the SUV out of the garage. They'll see us."

Bendix issued the orders. "Everyone take cover. Don't fire a shot unless I give the signal."

The five men dispersed. Walker ran into the parking garage and knelt behind a concrete wall. He thrust a magazine in his M4 and pulled back the charging handle. Locked and loaded.

The tank rumbled louder as it grew closer. It moved slowly and ominously down the stretch of road. Walker dared to take a peek, studied its shape, and determined it was an American Abrams, most likely one that was confiscated by the KPA.

No one moved. The group wouldn't give itself away unless infantry jumped out of the tank to search the garage. They had neither the personnel nor firepower to take down an Abrams.

The roar of the tank's engines growled to peak volume as the vehicle rolled onto the drive in front of the garage. Then it stopped. Obviously, the site was indeed the tank's destination. Now there was no doubt—the resistance cell's secret supply rendezvous was blown.

The men held their breath.

Then, music piped out of the Abrams' loudspeaker system, the volume cranked to a deafening level—the Beatles' recording of "Revolution." The searing fuzz-distorted guitar and John Lennon's passionate singing pierced the street's deadly silence.

What the fuck? Walker thought. *Was this a trap? Was the KPA playing us at our own game?*

He held up his palm and shook his head at Bendix—*wait*.

After another nerve-biting minute of nothing but music, the tank's top hatch opened. A man appeared and he wasn't Korean.

After a long and hoarse coughing spasm followed by a spit of phlegm over the side of the tank, the American turned down the music and called out, "Are you guys here, or what?"

Walker didn't know whether to laugh or cry. He jumped up and went outside to the tank.

"Wally Kopple, you old son of a bitch!"

The sergeant's eyes widened when he saw the Voice of Freedom.

"Holy Mother of God!" Kopple yelped. "I had a feeling I might find you here. Could you or your friends use some assistance?"

WALKER'S JOURNAL

NOVEMBER 2, 2026

A lot has happened since I last wrote.

First of all, I've reunited with my good friend Wally Kopple. About a month ago he broke off from Boone's resistance cell in Montrose and started heading east in search of me, or so he says. Wally told me he believes in what I'm doing and wants to offer some assistance. He met up with another cell in the Denver area and helped them take down a Korean weapons storage facility. They captured a bunch of tanks and weapons, which is great for the Resistance. Anyway, they let Wally have one of the tanks and he took off east again. Then he worked with a Kansas City cell for a while and that's how he got wind of where I was. This cell was making supply deliveries to the St. Peters outfit every three months, so Wally volunteered to bring the supplies in the tank this time. And here we are. Besides the much-needed food and water and gasoline, Wally brought a bunch of explosives. No guns, unfortunately, but maybe the C-4 will come in handy. The cell might use it to blow up some Korean checkpoints or supply centers. The stuff even comes with a couple of remote control devices to set off the firecrackers. *Just push a button and* kaboom! *Wally told me Hopper Lee himself repaired the remotes and got them to work.*

His cough is terrible. He's lost a lot of weight and his skin is pale. The poor guy doesn't have the strength he once had, and he can stay active only a few hours a day. The rest of the time he has to lie down. Wally's dying. I don't know how long he's got, but it's bad. If I had to make an honest guess—and I'm no doctor— then I fear he won't make it to the New Year.

Still, it's good to have him around. At least he hasn't lost his sense of humor.

Kelsie's another thing altogether. Something has happened and I'm damned if I know what it is. She's changed. It started around the end of September or beginning of October. She became moody and quiet, which is totally unlike her. I asked her what was wrong and she kept putting me off. Said it was nothing. Then, finally, during one of my endless sessions of thinking out loud about how we were going to cross the Mississippi River, she came out with it. She didn't want to do it. She has an aversion to getting near the river but won't tell me why. She said if I'm going to cross the river, I have to do it without her. I don't understand it. I know it's dangerous and it's a big risk, but haven't we been doing dangerous stuff and taking big risks for months? She knows how much it means to me to see what's on the other side. It's important.

So things have been kind of weird between us. She still loves me—she says so, every day. And I still love her. But I think something else is bothering her and she won't open up about it. Like a typical stupid male, I don't know what I can do. At least she has Martha to keep her company. In the month we've been in St. Peters, Kelsie and Martha have become good friends. Martha's funny. She was once married to a Hell's Angels type of guy, but he died a year or so ago. Martha must be in her 50s. She owns a fucking beautiful motorcycle that I'd love to get my hands on. She acts tough but she's really a softie with a lot of heart. So she's taken Kelsie under her wing and I think it's done some good. I wonder if I should ask Martha what I can do about Kelsie. Maybe Kelsie's confided in her.

Nevertheless, I'm still determined to cross the river. Against Kelsie's wishes, I've been discussing a plan of action with Wally, the professor, and Julian. I think we've come up with something that just might work.

All we need is a tank—which we have; a bicycle—there are plenty around here; and some of those protective suits. That's the hard part.

TWENTY-SIX

NOVEMBER 10, 2026

It was the night before Walker's attempt to cross the Mississippi River.

As he went over what he needed to take, Wilcox sat on the motel room bed and watched.

He knew he needed two or three changes of clothes, the M4 and M9, ammunition, a working flashlight, water, food, a jacket, and what camping gear he could carry. Kopple had also given him some bricks of C-4 explosives, a portion of the supplies he had brought to the cell. The sergeant had shown Walker how to place the explosives, set the detonator, and use the remote control to trigger the big bang. Walker stuffed his backpack and went over everything one more time. Then he picked up the portable transistor board that Wilcox had made and sat beside her.

"Kelsie, you need to hold on to this."

"Why? You need it. You're the Voice of Freedom."

"Darling, unless you're coming with me, then you need to keep it and use it yourself. You might . . . you might need to carry on my work."

"Don't say that."

"Come on, Kelsie, we both know it's possible. First

of all, this plan of ours may not work. I could die tomorrow. Secondly, if it succeeds and I do get across, there's no telling what I'm going to find. I could die over there, too. But hopefully there will be people with radios in the East. I will find them and I will continue my broadcasts. But I want you to promise me something. If you don't hear me make a broadcast within two weeks, you're to continue as the new Voice of Freedom. You can do it. You have the gift of gab, too, you just haven't used it. Will you promise me that, Kelsie?"

She looked away, but a tear ran down her cheek. "I can't imagine losing you."

"You're not going to lose me. We'll be together again, I swear. I'll either be back or I'll find a way to get you across. Now will you promise me?"

After a moment's hesitation, she nodded and took the circuit board. She got up and placed it in her backpack, already full of emergency equipment for a quick getaway if necessary. Then she returned to the bed and he put his arms around her.

"Last chance, Kelsie. Will you come with me?"

Wilcox shook her head. "You need to do this alone, Ben. I'll wait for you here. It's all right. Professor Bendix and his crew are good people. Martha will take care of me. If anything bad happens, she's already said there's room for me on the back of her motorcycle."

Walker nodded. "Stick with her. That's a good idea."

The couple looked at each other in silence for a few moments.

"Why won't you tell me what's wrong?" he asked.

"There's nothing wrong."

"The hell there isn't. You haven't been yourself the last couple of months. I even asked Martha about it. She told me it was a 'female thing' and I should be smart enough to figure it out. Well, I guess I'm pretty dumb about female things. I always have been. That's one reason why my wife left me all those years ago. So help me out. What is it I'm missing?"

Wilcox smiled and placed a hand on Walker's face. "Oh, Ben, you're not dumb. You're the smartest and bravest and most wonderful man I've ever known. Don't worry about me. It's something personal I have to work out."

"Does it have anything to do with us?"

She made a face, thinking about the answer. "Hmm. Maybe. But not right now. The important thing is for you to concentrate on the job tomorrow and getting across the river." He shook his head, bewildered and frustrated. She laughed. "Stop. It's okay. Really. Chalk it up to the never-ending mysteries of the opposite sex."

"I guess I'll have to." He leaned over and kissed her.

"Are you done packing?"

"I think so."

"Is it bedtime?"

"I guess so."

"Wanna fool around?"

"You don't have to ask me twice."

She laughed as she took off her top. "At least that's one thing regarding women you don't have a problem with."

NOVEMBER 11, 2026

The weather turned miserable. Cold rain blanketed St. Louis, eastern Missouri, and southwestern Illinois. Added to the thick gray fog that seeped from the polluted river, the showers reduced visibility to a new low. Bendix and the others attempted to talk Walker out of his plan and wait until the weather cleared—but the Voice of Freedom insisted the bad climate would improve his chances of succeeding. There was less likelihood that surveillance helicopters would fly in the present conditions. In fact, Walker asserted, the circumstances couldn't be better.

Wilcox had already said her goodbyes the night before after an intense session of lovemaking Walker would never forget. She didn't want to see him in the morning when he took off. Instead, she hid in Malloy's room and spent the rest of the night there. Walker was upset about it, but he understood. A tearful farewell in front of the rest of the cell would have been uncomfortable for everyone.

Bendix and the others wished him well, saying they hoped to see him again soon. Then, he and Kopple strapped a Schwinn Sporterra bicycle on the back of the Abrams tank, climbed inside, and drove away, leaving the motel, the resistance cell, and Kelsie Wilcox behind them.

As they traveled along Interstate-70 through St. Charles, Walker asked if Kopple could see well enough to drive. The sergeant looked terrible. He had spent most of the week in bed, coughing up blood and maybe half his lungs. What antibiotics the cell managed to obtain for him did no good. They both knew the inevitable was soon.

"I'm fine," Kopple answered. "I've always been almost blind anyway. A little rain and fog ain't gonna make much difference. As long as I don't run into an old truck or something that's in the middle of the highway, we'll be okay."

Even with the headlights on, they could barely see ten feet in front of them. The fog grew thicker as they moved farther east and the rain never let up for a second. Kopple described it as driving through "gray soup."

At the intersection of I-70 and Highway 90, large signs written in Korean and English warned travelers to turn back. danger! radiation poisoning! korean people's army checkpoint ahead!

"I couldn't read those, could you, Wally?" Walker asked facetiously.

"Nah. I can't read or see nothin'."

The M1A3 Abrams tank was armed with the standard M256A1 120mm smoothbore gun that shot a variety of ammunition, including high explosives, multiple flechette, anti-personnel, advanced kinetic energy, and advanced multipurpose rounds. There were also three machine guns, one of which could be fired by the commander while the tank was buttoned up with all hatches closed to protect the crew.

The intel the St. Peters cell managed to obtain about the Korean checkpoint on I-70 indicated there were roughly thirty troops stationed there. While the enemy had no tanks at the location, the soldiers employed a stationary T8 anti-tank gun the U.S. Army once used as a towed field weapon. It was capable of firing 105mm caliber rounds up to a range of over a dozen miles. Kopple and Walker knew the gun could inflict serious damage on the Abrams, so it would have to be taken out first. Besides automatic assault rifles, the infantry most likely also had grenade launchers, bazookas, and flamethrowers.

It wasn't going to be easy.

The tank rolled over Arena Parkway Road. The Missouri River checkpoint was just ahead. More signs declared: trespassers subject to arrest.

Walker put the binoculars to his eyes, looked through the tank's viewport, and studied the checkpoint through the thick haze. "I can't see shit," he said. "Wait. The anti-tank gun is on top of the building. Do you see it?"

"Nah. We'll have to get closer."

"There are men coming out. Six, seven, eight . . . geez, there are twenty of 'em, at least. They've got their rifles aimed at us. You sure that Korean flag is displayed in the front?"

"Unless the rain blew it off. I made sure it was secure."

The Abrams displayed the Korean-made New Democratic People's Republic of America flags on all sides. It was a tremendous gamble, but Walker and Kopple hoped that would fool the KPA into allowing the tank to pull up close.

"I see the T-Eight now," Kopple said. "I've got to

raise the gun a bit. Think they'll notice?"

"Yeah, I do."

"Don't have a choice, do I?"

"No, you don't."

Kopple stopped the vehicle thirty yards from the checkpoint. Besides the portable building, a gate stretched across the road and was protected by piles of sandbags. Soldiers stood in front of it, guns ready.

Walker felt the familiar rush of adrenaline. The next few seconds would determine whether or not the Voice of Freedom lived or died. Flashes of the last twenty months flipped through the recesses of his brain. One image stood out—the lovely face of Kelsie Wilcox.

He felt a brief stab of guilt for leaving her behind, but he knew now why she hadn't come with him. Before she'd left their bed to spend the rest of the night in Martha Malloy's room, she'd revealed what had been troubling her.

The revelation hit him like a ton of bricks.

But Walker couldn't think about that now; he forced himself to concentrate on what was going on outside the Abrams. The KPA seemed confused by the tank's arrival. Five men marched forward. Walker figured they'd been trying to contact the tank by radio to confirm the identity of its occupants. He focused on the anti-tank gun and saw it move.

"Wally, they're aiming the gun at us. If you're gonna do something, do it *now*."

Kopple peered through the CROWS sight and lifted the rifled-gun's crosshairs to the checkpoint roof and the deadly T8 on top. The KPA officers noted the rising cannon and halted in their tracks. One man turned and shouted orders to the men on the roof. Three soldiers huddled over the T8, moved the gun into place, and aimed it directly at the Abrams.

"Wally! Now, for God's sake!"

Kopple fired the gun. A thunderous report rocked the bridge; Walker felt the tank lurch from the recoil. Looking out the viewport, he saw nothing but smoke and haze. He placed his hands on the 7.62mm M240 machine gun trigger in the loader's hatch, where he sat, and squeezed, blindly mowing down whatever was in front of the tank. Kopple did the same with the 12.7mm M2HB in the commander's hatch.

"Did you hit the anti-tank gun?" Walker shouted over the cacophony.

"I have no idea!"

"Hold your fire and let's see what damage we've done."

They released the triggers and heard enemy gunfire outside the tank. Walker peered through the viewport; the smoke had cleared some. Men had taken cover in the building, behind sandbags and other objects—but more than a dozen bodies littered the pavement. The top of the checkpoint was ablaze, even in the rain.

"Wally, you got it! Damn, it looks like the roof caved in. The place is on fire."

Kopple held out his hand. "Let me see." Walker gave him the binoculars. "Shit," he growled.

"What?"

"You're right, I must have hit the roof, but not the T-Eight. It fell through intact and undamaged, and now they're maneuvering it into the checkpoint doorway." He threw the field glasses at Walker and immediately began lowering the cannon to aim it at the building.

"We can't destroy the place, Wally, we need the suits inside."

He coughed twice and said, "Buddy, if that T-Eight hits us, you'll never get the suits. Shoot the bastards in the doorway!"

Walker gazed through the machine gun sights and fired. Because of the flames, the debris, the fog, and the rain, visibility was worse than before. He aimed for the door and hoped for the best. Kopple finally got the cannon in position.

"Here we go again!" He released the shell—and another powerful explosion jolted the tank. Walker kept his eyes on the building and waited for the black clouds to clear. The structure still stood but now there was a massive hole in the front. Several KPA still fired assault rifles from concealed positions.

"You got it, Wally! Now we just have to mop up."

They both manned the machine guns and spray-fired the gate and sandbags; but as long as the enemy stayed behind cover, the battle would remain a stalemate.

Kopple revved up the tank's engine and drove forward.

"What are you doing?" Walker yelled.

"There's only one way we're gonna finish this!"

The Abrams lunged forward and rammed the temporary structure's front. The walls collapsed around it and more men scattered on the road. Now there was nothing to hide behind. Walker swerved the machine gun around and caught the men retreating from the sandbags. Kopple cut down the infantry on the other side. Then, he grabbed his own QBZ-03 and climbed up to the hatch. "I'll cover you," he said. "You get out there and find one of them goddamned suits!"

He unlocked and swung open the hatch, thrust his upper torso through it, and fired his weapon like a maniac. Walker squeezed up behind him, slipped out, and jumped onto the tank's hull. With the M4 up and aimed at any object in his way, he leaped to the pavement and pushed into the burning debris that was once the checkpoint structure. There were no clear spaces to step without trampling on bloody, burned body parts or remains of the anti-tank gun. Kopple continued to fire at anything else that moved while Walker searched the rubble. He finally found a metal locker on its side, its door flung open but the contents intact.

Six rubber iron-lined suits.

He picked up two—they were much heavier than he'd expected—and made his way out of the ruins. Kopple stopped shooting.

"If there's anyone else alive, they've run off," he said.

Walker took that moment to survey the bridge. More than twenty Korean corpses lay in jumbled, misshapen arrangements. Many of them were missing limbs and other body parts. The gate, surprisingly, was still standing. There was nothing left of the checkpoint aside from the dregs of its destruction.

He climbed back atop the Abrams and handed one
of the suits to Kopple. "This is for you."

The sergeant grimaced. "You know I don't need
this." He tossed it on the ground below.

"I thought you might change your mind."

Kopple shook his head. "That ain't gonna happen.
Let's get out of here before the reinforcements come.
You know they will."

Once they were safely inside the tank, the sergeant
fired it up and slammed through the gate. Surrounded
by dense rain and fog, the tank continued along I-70
through Bridgeton and Maryland Heights, the western suburbs, and finally into dark, deserted, and dead
St. Louis.

The squad surrounded the motel on I-70 and the men
indicated they were ready. Salmusa gave the order
to fire an 81mm high explosive, white phosphorous
shell from a mortar aimed at the building's office.
The explosion brutally shook the structure and filled
the street with thick black smoke. The five armed
resistance cell members burst from their rooms, guns
blazing, but they were quickly wiped away by a KPA
Light Infantry assault weapon barrage. The remaining, unarmed rebels emerged from the motel with
arms up and white handkerchiefs in their hands. The
troops roughly herded them into a circle. Salmusa
calmly walked around them, his hands clasped behind
his back. He approached one of the men and asked,
"Which one is your leader?"

The insurgent pointed to the dead man on the

ground. "Professor Bendix. That's him."

"Where is the Voice of Freedom?"

The survivors all shared a glance. "Who?"

Salmusa cold-cocked the man with his Daewoo. Two KPA dragged his body away from the small group and emptied three bullets into his head. Salmusa addressed the rest. "I know the Voice of Freedom was here. I know he was here *this morning*. I want to know where he's gone and what his plan is."

Suddenly, one of the motel doors opened, following by the roar of a motorcycle engine. A Kawasaki practically flew out the room, skidded in front of the KPA and its captives, made a sharp turn, and sped off onto the feeder road. Two women sat astride it—a heavier one driving in front, and another in back, holding the driver's waist for dear life. The KPA quickly knelt, aimed their weapons, and fired at the fleeing bike. The driver gunned the engine and shot forward as bullets sprayed the road behind them.

"Let them go," Salmusa shouted. "It was just a couple of weak and cowardly American women." The soldiers obeyed, stood, and resumed positions around the captives.

"Now then," the Korean said. "Are you going to tell me what I want to know? No? Then who do I get to torture first?"

TWENTY-SEVEN

The turnoff to merge with I-170 North didn't exist anymore. The overpass was in ruins, the casualty of some earlier battle or act of vandalism. The plan had been to connect with I-270, but now they couldn't. Kopple dug into the recesses of his memory to recall St. Louis' street layout, for he'd been there a few times in his past. Eventually he took the Lucas–Hunt Road exit and headed north through a labyrinth of rotting vehicle hulls.

"Can't you go faster?" Walker asked. "Those reinforcements are surely on our tail by now."

Kopple coughed violently and spat. "You wanna drive, Walker? If you'd look in front of us, the road is an obstacle course and it's still raining and the fog is so thick only a chainsaw could get through it."

"Sorry."

It seemed to take forever for the tank to reach Halls Ferry Road, where they turned left and drove north to the Interstate. The going was no better, but Kopple increased the speed the best he could.

"What happened here, Wally? The road's all torn up, buildings are demolished . . . I know they had to evacuate, but it looks like bombs were dropped on St. Louis, too."

"I don't know anything about that, but Bendix told me he'd heard a rumor that the residents initiated a scorched-earth policy when they left. If they couldn't have St. Louis, then neither could the Koreans. Looks like the rumor is true. I can't imagine what good it did. Even if the river gets cleaned up, no one can live here for years and years, not even the Norks."

Walker shook his head. "I used to hate driving during road construction. Road destruction is no better."

The tank finally made it to I-270, sped up the ramp, and steered east toward the river.

Kopple said, "Ben, you better put on that suit now."

Malloy veered the Kawasaki off I-70 at Highway 61. She had pushed the motorcycle hard since their escape from St. Peters. Behind her, Wilcox panted, "Oh my God, oh my God . . . "

"You all right back there? You're squeezin' the shit out of me."

"Sorry. That was a, er, fast ride. And bumpy. Yeah, I'm okay. You think we made it?"

"They're not behind us. I guess they figured we weren't worth the chase."

Wilcox dug into her backpack and retrieved a bottle of water. She took a swig and handed it to Malloy. "So what now?"

"We've got enough gas to get a third across the state. I have some contacts in Jefferson City. Why don't we head there first and see if we can find gas. Then I say we move on to Kansas City."

"That's where I told Ben I'd be."

"I figured. Did you end up telling him about the other thing?"

"Yeah, I did."

Malloy turned to look at her. "And is it all good?"

"I don't know, Martha. I don't know. I really don't want to talk about it. Let's keep moving. I'll try not to squeeze the shit out of you."

"Okay, honey." After a long drink, she handed the water bottle back to Wilcox and revved the engine. "Let's burn rubber."

And she did.

Dressed in an Iron Fish protective suit, Salmusa rode in the front passenger seat of one of the squad's Humvees. He held the radio mike to his mouth and repeated his orders once again. "I want two Apache helicopters over the bridge on Interstate-270 connecting Missouri with Illinois. *Now*."

Reception in the bad weather was terrible, but a voice broke through the static. "But, sir, the pilots insist the inclement weather prevents them from flying. Visibility is—"

"I don't give a damn about visibility! You tell the pilots the first two men who get the choppers in the air and over the bridge will be promoted and the others will face a firing squad! Tell them!"

He threw down the mic and slammed his fist in the window next to him. Salmusa knew if the Voice of Freedom made it across the river he would disappear forever. This was the Korean's only chance to catch the vermin.

"Drive faster!" he barked to Byun, the driver. The underling did as he was told, but he and none of the other men in the squad were pleased with venturing into toxic St. Louis. Why did Salmusa get to wear a radioactivity-shielded suit while no one else had protection? The leader had seen fit to bring an Iron Fish for himself and neglected to mention it to his men.

Salmusa glanced in the side mirror and confirmed the two other KPA-controlled Humvees trailed closely behind his. Conditions on the road were terrible. Wrecked automobiles, sections of razed buildings, fallen telephone poles and street lights marred the streets—St. Louis was a wasteland. Salmusa was thankful he didn't have to spend much time in such a crypt.

"Sir, the turnoff to Interstate-One-Seventy appears to be destroyed."

Salmusa punched the dashboard in front of him. "Damn it! Find another way! We need to get to 270!" He picked up the mic. "Have you got me some helicopters yet?"

"Yes, sir. Two Apaches are on their way."

"They are to knock down the bridge by any means available. Hurry!"

The Abrams reached Riverview Drive, just a mile or two from the New Chain of Rocks Bridge on I-270 that connected Missouri to Illinois. Immediately south and parallel to this conduit was the original Chain of Rocks Bridge that dated from 1929. Its name came from a large shoal, which made that section of the

Mississippi River extremely hazardous to navigate by boat. The old bridge was once U.S. Highway Route 66, but it closed in 1968 when Interstate-270 was completed and the New Chain of Rocks Bridge became the official crossing for vehicular traffic. The original Chain of Rocks Bridge was instead relegated for bicycle and pedestrian passage only. Like its newer counterpart, the smaller, narrow two-lane bridge connected Missouri with Chouteau Island, part of Madison, Illinois.

The tank finally reached the head of the New Chain of Rocks Bridge and stopped. As the resistance cell's intel predicted, it was guarded by three small drones that resembled miniature tanks, the size of Labrador Retrievers. As soon as the Abrams got within thirty yards of the bridge, the unmanned ground vehicles perked up and aimed their weapons.

"See those little fuckers?" Kopple asked. "Those are Gomez-Miller TALON SWORDS units. The SWORDS stands for Special Weapons Observation Reconnaissance Detection System. Goddamned Norks stole 'em from the U.S. Army. Bendix told me they've got those pesky robots guarding all the bridges. Look, see how they activated as soon as we got near? If we get closer, they're gonna start firing."

"With what?" Inside the iron-lined protective suit, Walker's voice sounded like he was shouting from the bottom of a barrel.

"Oh, I imagine they've got a grenade launcher or two, a SAW M249, some machine guns of various calibers, a friggin' flamethrower. . . . The Koreans must've figured the drones wouldn't come up against anything but resistance fighters on foot or in cars or something. But you know what? They ain't no match for a genuine Abrams motherfuckin' *tank*. Watch *this!*"

Kopple coughed ferociously before he could do anything, and then he vomited all over his lap. "Aww, fuck," he said. "I guess I don't feel so good."

"Wally?"

The sergeant shook his head. "It's the radiation. I'm starting to feel it, man. But hey—maybe it'll fight off some of the cancer that's inside me."

"God, Wally. What can I do?"

"Nothing! Where was I? Shit, I'm losing it . . . Oh, yeah. I'm gonna blow the smithereens out of those automated cigarette lighters."

He pulled the M256A1 smoothbore gun down, peered through the targeting sight, and placed the crosshairs on the middle robot.

"Don't put a hole in the bridge!" Walker implored.

"Shut up, I know what I'm doing. It's just like bowling. Watch this strike."

He pulled the trigger; the anti-personnel round shot out the cannon with a satisfying *zzzip*. The ensuing explosion completely obliterated the targeted drone and knocked the one on its right off the bridge and into the water below. The drone on the left remained standing and began firing its ineffectual machine gun.

"Okay, so I'll get a spare," Kopple said. He swung the gun a few feet over and fired again. When the smoke cleared, there was nothing left of the robot.

"Nice shooting, cowboy," Walker said.

"Now for Part Two. Bendix said there's a control station somewhere around here. It directs any other drones within a couple of miles. Probably manages robots on the Illinois side of the bridge, too. Do you see it? It's probably a big metal box-like thing, looks like an electrical power generator or something."

"Uhhh, *no*," Walker answered. He couldn't see anything except what was straight in front of him due to the limited sight lines of the suit's viewport.

"Oh, right. Hold on." Kopple climbed up to the hatch and opened it. Rain showered inside the tank as he looked around. "Goddamn gray soup! I don't—wait, there it is!" He ducked back in and shut the hatch. "It's over to the right, in between the two bridges." Kopple manipulated the cannon's targeting controls and veered the gun in position. "I think a high explosive is called for here. Remember the Alamo!" He fired the weapon and the two men heard the blast in the distance. Gazing through the viewfinder, he confirmed the hit.

Kopple turned to Walker. "You need help with the bicycle?"

"No, I can get it. I hope it's still strapped on the back of the tank!"

"It's there."

For a moment they didn't know what to say.

"I'm not gonna hug you with that creepy suit on you," Kopple said. He held out his hand. "Good luck, Ben Walker. May the Voice of Freedom live on and lead our country back to the glory it once was."

"Damn it, Wally, you sure you want to do this? You could go on back to the motel."

"Shut up." He coughed and wheezed. "You hear that? It's over, man. I'm checking out. I can't take any more of the pain. Besides, I'm about to pass out. I expended every bit of energy I have left getting you here. Now go on, get out. Go do your hero thing."

They clasped hands tightly and then Walker climbed out of the tank.

The small KPA caravan rushed past Riverview Drive and approached the New Chain of Rocks Bridge.

"Where are my Apaches?" Salmusa shouted into the mic. He saw nothing through the Iron Fish's viewport. He punched Byun. "Do you see them?"

The driver swerved the Humvee and almost crashed into the guardrail, but he quickly pulled the vehicle back on the road.

"You fool! What's the matter with you?"

Byun felt nauseous and could barely keep his head up, much less drive. Already the toxic air had affected everyone on the team except Salmusa. The sound of a collision behind them drew the operative's attention to the side mirror. One of the Humvees had slammed into a light pole on the side of the highway. Its driver must have passed out from the exposure.

Salmusa faced forward again and saw the Abrams tank shoot forward across the bridge.

"Stop!" Salmusa shouted. "Let me out!"

Byun managed to put on the brakes and immediately vomited. Salmusa looked behind him. The other infantrymen were unconscious. The other Humvee rolled to a stop by ramming the back of the first vehicle. Everyone inside was too sick to move. Cursing, Salmusa opened the door and stormed outside. He moved as fast as he could in the bulky iron-lined suit to the edge of the bridge.

The tank's taillights disappeared into the thick rain and fog.

"Where are my helicopters!" he shouted to the sky.

And then he heard them. Scarcely visible through the dark haze, two Boeing AH-64 Apaches, confiscated from the United States Army, soared overhead. Salmusa raised a fist at them and ran back to the Humvee to grab his radio.

"Put me in contact with the pilots! Hello? Hello!" The receiver garbled with static. "Damn it, can you hear me?"

"Sir! Yes, sir, you're breaking up—"

"Put me in contact with the pilots! Now!"

More radio noise followed; Salmusa was tempted to smash the mic against the dash. Finally, he got an answer from the Apaches.

"Do you see the tank on the bridge?"

"Yes, sir!"

"Blow it to hell! Now!"

The two pilots fought the raging elements to remain airborne and managed to fly to advantageous positions from which to attack. The first chopper placed itself north of the bridge and then unleashed two AGM-114 Hellfire anti-tank missiles from its stubwing pylons. They were direct hits on the Abrams.

At the same time, the other Apache hovered on the southern side of the bridge and let loose two Stinger missiles. They struck the bridge itself, just in front of the speeding tank.

Colossal explosions shook the structure, producing so much black smoke that Salmusa couldn't see the results of the strike. Then, with the velocity of molasses, huge chunks of steel and concrete dropped into the radioactive water, causing mammoth tidal waves in north-south directions. An enormous section of the bridge collapsed, bringing with it the remains of a burning, annihilated Abrams tank.

"Yes!" Salmusa shouted. "I got him! The Voice of Freedom is no more!"

One of the pilots spoke. "Sir, we await further instructions."

"Go back to base. Mission accomplished."

"Yes, sir!"

The two choppers wavered unsteadily in the heavy rain, then turned toward the city and shot away.

Terribly pleased with himself, Salmusa couldn't wait to get back to base and contact the Brilliant Comrade. Kim Jong-un would be happy with the news. It had taken several frustrating months, but Salmusa had not let down his leader.

The operative opened the doors to the Humvee, grabbed hold of Byun and the unconscious soldiers, one by one, and tossed them out on the road. They would die anyway, he thought. They were useless to him now.

Just as he was ready to get in the driver's seat, a

glint of light pierced the haze to the south.

What the hell was that?

Salmusa rummaged through the front of the Humvee and found his pair of binoculars. He then got out, took several steps away from the vehicle, and focused the glasses on the old Chain of Rocks Bridge, the smaller one that zigzagged across the river. It wasn't very far away, maybe between two and three thousand feet.

There! That glint of light again. It was *moving east across the bridge!*

No!

A bicycle.

A man, wearing an Iron Fish, was riding a bicycle across the Mississippi River.

TWENTY-EIGHT

The original pavement of the narrow old Chain of Rocks Bridge was covered with a smooth, brownish concrete surfacing more conducive to bicycles and foot traffic. An ancient sign declared it was once a part of "historic" Route 66. It was open to the elements, but steel girders and latticework surrounded the sides and top. Walker pedaled the bike as fast as possible on the crossing, but the weight and bulkiness of the protective suit, plus the added load of his backpack and weapon, slowed him down considerably. Nevertheless, he made good progress until he saw the Apache helicopters hit the I-270 bridge and the Abrams tank. He felt as if he'd been stabbed in the chest. The force of the explosions nearly toppled the bicycle, so Walker stopped and watched the heartbreaking destruction with tears in his eyes. He said a silent goodbye to Sergeant Wally Kopple, and then pedaled on.

Salmusa jumped into the driver's seat of the Humvee, started the ignition, and turned the vehicle around. He gunned it westward, back over I-270 to the Riverview Drive exit, where he veered off and headed south to the old Chain of Rocks Bridge entrance. On the way he spotted the demolished drone control station and cursed the Americans' resilience. Reaching the turn-off, he plowed through the guardrail and plunged past the useless, deactivated drones. He increased his speed and pushed the Humvee forward onto the bridge, which was barely wide enough for the vehicle.

The rain and fog, together with the poor visibility of the Iron Fish's viewport, obscured the road more than twenty feet ahead. Salmusa drove on pure faith that he would catch up with the Voice of Freedom before the man reached the other side. After all, a Humvee was faster than a bicycle. Salmusa couldn't see the bike, but he knew it was just ahead of him . . . somewhere.

Walker approached the halfway mark across the bridge, where there was a slight jog to the left; on both sides of the crossing were old stone buildings jutting up from the water. Were they ancient lighthouses? He didn't know.

Then he heard the engine noise behind him. He stopped to look, but couldn't make out anything beyond a few dozen feet away. Walker knew what the sound was, though—a vehicle on the bridge. They had discovered his bait-and-switch ploy. It was most likely a Humvee or a jeep or something. The bridge was too narrow for a tank.

Could he make it across before the vehicle reached him?

Walker couldn't allow the Koreans to follow him to the other side. He had to stop them somehow. Thinking quickly, he got off the bicycle and stood it up next to the guardrail. He removed his backpack and dug inside for the C-4 bricks and remote control box that Kopple had given him.

The question was—did he have enough time?

The Humvee scraped the side of the guardrail, causing Salmusa to reflexively pull the steering wheel too far to the right. The vehicle slammed into the rail on the other side of the bridge, forcing him to stop. He cursed aloud again, threw the Humvee into reverse, pulled out of the tangled steel girder, and continued forward. That blunder had cost him a precious thirty seconds.

He floored the gas to compensate for lost time.

Walker hopped on the bicycle and pedaled like a demon from hell. It was impossible to determine how far behind him the KPA were and there was also no way of knowing how much distance he needed to put between him and the little surprise he'd left on the bridge. He figured another hundred feet or so would be enough, so he strained to cycle faster.

The noise of the vehicle grew louder. It wasn't far away.

It was now or never.

Walker stopped pedaling, rested the bike with one foot on the bridge, and held up the remote control device.

He now saw a pair of headlights cutting through the gray soup some forty yards behind him.

"So long, suckers," he said as he pushed the button.

Nothing happened.

Fuck!
What did he do wrong?
The headlights kept coming.
He frantically examined the remote control.
Christ—the on/off switch!
He flicked it on and then pressed the trigger button.

I have him!
Salmusa squinted as the man known as the Voice of Freedom came into view. The fool was standing in the middle of the bridge some thirty or forty yards away. It was going to be easy after all. The Humvee would plow into the dissident and drag his body all the way to the eastern side of the bridge. If the treacherous American wanted to reach the other side so badly, then Salmusa would help him!

Yi Dae-Hyun wanted to laugh, but instead he shouted, *"Die for the Brilliant Comrade, you piece of vermin!"*

He floored the gas pedal; but a flash of bright light blinded him before he heard the powerful detonation that engulfed the Humvee. An intense blanket of fire instantly smothered the Korean operative, disintegrating the Iron Fish and liquefying his skin.

Salmusa's final thought was not that he was dying, but that he had failed his friend and brother, the mighty Kim Jong-un. The Asian viper had lost every shred of honor he had managed to achieve during his glorious years of service to Korea. He was nothing now. He deserved this blazing, molten fate and a watery, radioactive grave for all time.

Forgive me, Jong-un! I love y—

* * *

The strength of the explosion knocked Walker down. He fell over with the bicycle and landed hard on the bridge surface. He feared he had punctured the protective suit and that radioactivity was pouring over his body—but the iron lining prevented a tear. He had merely bruised himself.

Walker managed to raise himself on one arm to watch the devastation behind him. A large chunk of the old bridge broke away and plummeted to the river below. A tremendous surge of smoke and debris masked the headlights. Pieces of girder and concrete flew at him, forcing Walker to duck his head to avoid injury. The bridge section upon which he lay creaked and lurched; for a moment he feared the entire thing would fall apart.

He counted to ten. To twenty.

The bridge *tilted down*. Walker started sliding toward the abyss created by the detonation. He frantically scissor-locked his legs around the Schwinn to keep from losing it and lunged wildly for the steel girders on the side of the railing. The suit gloves, wet from the rain, slipped against the metal. His body—and the bike—glided precariously farther along the incline. Walker tried again, blindly waving his hands at anything he could grasp.

He caught another girder and this time the grip held.

Walker dared to look down toward the demolished section. Smoke still covered it, but there were no more headlights. No sound of a vehicle. Keeping his legs tight around the bicycle, he pulled himself up to get a better clasp on the girder. Calling on every bit of strength he had left, he reached down, drew the bike to his waist, slipped his arm under the top tube, and heaved the entire thing up so he could carry it on his shoulder. Then, slowly and carefully, he climbed the latticework up the tilted bridge some thirty feet until he reached a level, flat surface.

It was all over.

Walker pushed himself off the concrete and stood. He moved to the guardrail and looked down at the bubbling, raging river. There it was. Walker saw the Humvee sinking in the toxic deathtrap. Was there a man desperately attempting to save himself? It was too murky to know for sure, but there was no question that whoever was in the vehicle would not survive.

Never having been a religious person in the past, Walker felt obliged to say a prayer of thanks. He then got on the bicycle and continued the rest of the way across to the east.

Malloy handed Wilcox a plate of cold beans and spooned some for herself. "It's not T.G.I. Friday's, but it's better than starving," she said. They sat on a picnic table located at an old roadside rest stop on the western side of Jefferson City, Missouri. The contacts Malloy counted on had come through—the Kawasaki's fuel tank was full and nothing would stop them from reaching Kansas City.

Wilcox ate her dinner in silence, but her mind was

buzzing a mile a minute. So many things to think about. So much to plan for.

Was Ben all right? What was happening back in St. Louis? Would she—

She suddenly stiffened.

"What?" Malloy asked. "What's wrong?"

Wilcox blinked and took a breath. "I don't know. Just a feeling."

"What?"

"I think he made it, Martha," she said. "Ben crossed the river. I know he did."

Kelsie Wilcox smiled and continued her meal.

WALKER'S JOURNAL

NOVEMBER 11, 2026

This date was once known as Armistice Day. I wonder if it means anything that it's also the date the Voice of Freedom crossed the Mississippi River from the west to the east. Who knows?

What's important is that I did it. I'm here in Illinois. Of course, I don't know what the hell I'm going to do next, but I'm sure I'll think of something. I was just so excited and goddamn proud of myself that I had to stop and write this down.

I don't know what I'm going to find here in the "great unknown" east of the river. In many ways, it's the opposite of what occurred those centuries ago when settlers crossed from the east to explore the mysterious territory west of the Mississippi. St. Louis, after all, was always called the "Gateway to the West." I guess now it's the Gateway to the East.

I keep thinking about that son of a bitch Wally and his ultimate sacrifice. He drew the Koreans' attention away from me so I could cross the river. I will remember him until the day I die. He is a true hero, worthy of the highest honor.

Kelsie is certainly on my mind. I have to find a way

to get a message to her as soon as possible. She needs to know I'm safe. I miss her terribly. After the BIG NEWS she told me last night, I can't wait to accomplish whatever it is I'm going to do over here and then get back to her. What a reunion it will be. I love her more than anything.

After all, she's carrying my child. Can you believe it? Later, man.